BREAK ME DADDY

Skyler Snow

Break Me Daddy © Copyrighted Skyler Snow 2022

This is a work of fiction and is for mature audiences only. Names, characters, businesses, places, events, and incidents are either the products of the author's imagination or used in a fictitious manner. Any resemblance to actual persons, living or dead, or actual events is purely coincidental.

No part of this publication may be reproduced, stored in a retrieval system, or transmitted in any form or by any means, including electronically or mechanical, without the prior written permission of the copyright holder.

All products and brand names mentioned are registered trademarks of their respective holder and or company. I do not own the rights to these, nor do I claim to."

Cover Artist: Charli Childs

Formatter: Brea Alepou

✿ Created with Vellum

Warning and Triggers

Break me Daddy is a mafia MM romance that includes but not limited to: violence, death, explicit scenes, and dub-con.

Prologue

Six

I SHIVERED AND PULLED MY JACKET AROUND MY SHOULDERS MORE tightly. Florida was my home at one point and while I loved the heat, I hated the unusual cold that had settled in. I dragged the space heater across the marked up floor and slammed the heel of my hand against it.

The machine grumbled and rasped before the barest bit of heat shot out. I shoved my palms right up against it, no longer giving a damn if I burned myself when the thing inevitably decided it was time to work right again. For now, I needed to be warm because I couldn't satisfy my growling stomach. I had to pick a struggle.

I need to find work asap.

Ty, an old friend from high school, had given me some cash. I was grateful for it and I'd been able to get out of Georgia, but I was still too close to the Bianchi's. Thinking about them made a shiver run down my spine. It was stupid to steal that money, but it had been sitting right there. All of that cash in that huge, flashing casino and I was being hunted down like an animal over a few thousand dollars?

Okay, maybe not a few but they were rich as hell! They shouldn't even have noticed it was missing. You'd think they would give up by now, but I knew how the Bianchi's were from the rumors. I'd only laid eyes on Amadeo once or twice, but he wasn't the kind of man you screwed with. And I had bent him over and shoved a stick up his ass.

I'm dead.

There was no way in hell I could keep running forever. My original plan had been to flee to the other side of the country, but I hadn't counted on having to pay motel fees every night, how much it cost to eat when you didn't have a kitchen, and how little you slept and how exhausted you became when you couldn't close your eyes without hearing every little noise around you just waiting for someone to put a bullet in your head.

I can't think like that or I might as well jump off the roof of this building right now. I can get away. A job, some money in my pocket, and I'll be able to get a plane ticket at least. Hopefully.

My stomach growled and I knew I couldn't put off eating again. It had been a day and a half and my stomach was trying to eat itself. Glancing around the dumpy little apartment I'd rented with its worn floors and discolored walls, the depression came hurtling back to me.

I'd fallen so far.

"Fuck this." I stood up and kicked the space heater. It started pumping out more heat and I sighed. "Yeah you better work. And you better still be working when I get back."

I snatched up my wallet and key and shoved them into my pocket. There was a convenience store a few blocks away and I was sure they would have something I could eat. I was tired of canned soup that was still cold by the time I tried to warm it in the tiny pot on the impossibly small stove. Right now, I needed something heavy, but I wasn't sure what was going to be available at one in the morning.

Tugging my hood up over my head, I stepped out of my apartment and fear hit me in the chest. I looked around me quickly searching for any sign of the men that had been chasing me down in Atlanta. My heart drummed against my rib cage and I shivered trying not to think about worst case scenarios.

It wasn't like I couldn't fight, hell I had taught myself after getting my ass kicked one too many times in school before a friend helped me learn more a while back. But these men didn't come with fists, they came with guns. And that was something I didn't have.

When I was sure there was no one in the dingy hallway with its flickering light, I sighed and my shoulders dropped. *Okay, I'm fine. I'll get some food, come back home, and...stare at the wall for the rest of the night.*

Groaning, I started walking to avoid how miserable this was going to be. I couldn't have a phone because I was worried they would be able to find me somehow. What I did have was a burner that I'd picked up after ditching the old one but it was for emergencies only. There was no TV, no computer, nothing to do but think about every point in my life where I had royally screwed up.

I shoved my hands into my pockets as I walked down the street. If I dwelled on all of my mistakes, I would be up and miserable all night. Instead of doing that I was going to grab a beer or two and go to sleep. Tomorrow I would let reality return and deal with all of the bullshit I had to face.

The convenience store came into view and I picked up my walk. It wasn't a luxury meal, but I could grab a hot dog with all the fixings, some chips, and a few beers without burning a hole in my pocket. It wasn't a steak, but food was food and I wanted my belly to be full.

I walked into the store and looked around, nodding at the cashier before I disappeared down the aisles. I grabbed my snacks first, loading them onto the counter before I sat the beers next to it.

"I'm gonna grab a hot dog."

"Whatever man," the guy behind the counter said as he scrolled on his phone.

I shrugged and went back to grab my meal. I picked out two hot dogs and piled them high with chili, cheese, jalapenos, fried onions, and sauerkraut. The ketchup and mustard packs were shoved into my pocket by the time I returned to the counter.

"This it?" the guy asked, scratching his acne covered cheeks.

"Yeah, that's it," I said as I opened my wallet and dug out a few small bills. "Thanks."

I grabbed the bag and my change and left to the jingling sound of the bell over the door. My stomach growled again and I salivated over my impending meal.

"Hey!"

I turned on my heels, my heart pounding in my chest. A guy leaned against the brick wall of the convenience store. He looked me up and down as he ran his hand over his scruffy beard. Everything about him yelled trouble.

"Where you going?" He asked.

I backed up. "Home."

The man grinned. "Aww, why? Come here for a second, I want to talk to you."

As he spoke, two other men joined his side. *Shit.* He didn't look like one of the Bianchi's men, but he could be just as dangerous. I took another step back as I prepared to run.

"Yeah, no thanks."

The smile faded on the man's lips. "Come here!"

"Fuck that," I muttered as I turned and ran.

Cold wind whipped past my face as I raced back for my place. It was just my luck that I would run into some lunatic while I was hiding out. I turned the corner and ran into something firm. My eyes flickered up as I stumbled back.

Oh, shit.

My heart raced in my chest as I stared up at the man dressed in a dark suit. His eyes narrowed at me. *That seems like a Bianchi.* I turned on my heels, ready to run for the hills when a hand grabbed my shoulder and yanked me back.

"Move," he said. "Stay behind me."

I stumbled as I was moved to his back and another man grabbed me. He held me in place or I would have kept running. When I tried to move away, he sneered at me.

"If you keep squirming, I'm going to break your leg," he said flatly. "Boss's orders."

Boss's orders. Yeah, I was screwed.

I watched as the guns came out. My heart skipped a beat. They could easily use that on me and I didn't want to get shot. Who did? I glanced around, trying to see if there was a way out, but I had nowhere to go.

"I suggest you leave," the man in front of me said. "Now."

The three men who had chased me looked from me to them and decided I wasn't worth it as they turned around and left. Relief flooded me and I sighed. Finally.

Now I just need to get away from-

"Six, don't even think about it," the man holding me growled.

"Go easy on him, Luka. You know our orders are he doesn't get hurt."

The one named Luka nodded. "I remember."

I stared between the two of them. What the hell were they talking about? Whoever they were, they definitely worked for Amadeo Bianchi. My instincts screamed to run but I couldn't force my feet to move.

"Get in the car," Luka said as he nodded toward the car that pulled up.

That was enough to make me move. I turned and ran. I would take my chances getting shot in the back before I would get into that car. The sound of heavy footfalls behind me made me speed up, but no matter how hard I ran I could hear them getting closer and closer and-

I grunted as I was snatched.

"Get off of me!" I snapped. "Fuck off!"

"Shhhh," a voice whispered against my ear. "Time to sleep."

A sharp pinprick of pain blossomed on my neck. I slapped at the spot on instinct but nothing was there. I took two steps before my head started to swim and I couldn't focus anymore.

Shit.

My body started to relax as my eyelids drooped. I realized they had jabbed me with a needle and I wasn't going to be on my feet for very much longer. When I wavered, arms wrapped around me and I felt like I was floating as I was lifted up.

"Let's get him to Amadeo," a voice said. "He's waiting."

I opened my mouth to speak, but my tongue felt like it was ten pounds. I wanted to scream not to take me there, but my head lolled and my eyes closed. When I opened them again I was in the car, staring up at the ceiling before my eyes fluttered shut again.

I'm going to die.

Chapter One

Six

My body protested when I tried to move and I groaned. *Why was my throat so dry?* It felt like I'd spent the night eating sand. I tried to push my hand against the bed to lift myself up, but my arms wouldn't move. *Am I sleeping on them?*

I rolled over and willed my eyelids to open. When they did, it felt like there were ten-pound weights on each lid. I groaned again and stared up at the ceiling.

This isn't the apartment.

The realization hit me in the chest like a ton of bricks. I shot up and instantly regretted it as my head throbbed and I had to wait until the dizziness faded away so I could move. I blinked a few times and took in my surroundings.

"Shit."

I was in a small room that was barely big enough to walk around in. A cot was on one side which I sat on and how sad was it that the cot was more comfortable than my apartment with the sleeping bag on the floor? My eyes ran over everything else in the room, which was empty. The floor was cold, my feet were bare and in front of me, there was a big, steel door that was dirty and worn.

"Okay, they definitely got me," I mumbled. "Shit."

My heart started racing and I tugged at my arms. They were tied together tightly, rope digging into my wrists and burning my skin. I rubbed my wrists back and forth. The burn increased and I gritted my teeth as I tried to ignore the pain and focus on the goal.

I need to get the hell out of here.

I forced myself to calm down. I didn't want to pass out before I could escape. One thing these guys didn't know was that I was damn good at running away. And if I could get out of this room, I was gone. I didn't care if I had to hitchhike across the country, I was getting out of Dodge.

"Not bad," I muttered as I inspected the door. I squatted and looked over it carefully. "Lock is old as hell. I just need something..." I muttered to myself.

There was a window at the top with bars over it. Clearly, that was so they could look in. At the bottom of the door, there was a smaller one that was probably big enough to slide in food. I didn't want to think about where that food was supposed to go because there was no bathroom. I shivered.

I gotta get the hell out of here.

My wrists protested as I continued moving them back and forth and tried to hold my nose at the same time. The room had the damp, musky scent of a basement and there was so much dust it was crowding my nostrils. I had to keep my head clear but whatever those bastards had injected into my neck was still pumping in my veins and it was hard to focus.

Get it together, bitch!

I could get out of anything and everything. That was my specialty. Give me a problem and I found a way to slip free and move on with my life. Hell, I'd done it my whole life and I could do it right now. I stood up and looked around to the cot. Turning around, I maneuvered the thin mattress off and tossed it to the side eventually, my muscles screaming from moving while I was still restrained.

My chest rose and fell and I fought a wave of nausea while I wavered on my feet. *I really want to make that bastard pay.* The big goons that had snatched me needed to be punched for making me feel like crap. I didn't have time to give in and puke or pass out. Both of those were too embarrassing to contemplate. I wasn't going to end up being dumped in a river somewhere when they decided to slit my throat.

I saw a piece of metal jutting out from the cot and my eyes lit up. *Bingo.* Moving to the cot, I squatted down until I could feel the jagged piece scrape against the ropes. Slowly, I moved my wrists up and down. If I moved too fast I was going to cut open a vein and bleed out in this little jail cell from hell.

"Come on. Come on."

Footsteps echoed and I stopped breathing. My lungs burned and my heart pounded so loudly I could barely hear. I took a slow, deep breath and when I could focus on the noises outside the door again the footsteps were retreating. My eyes stayed fixed on the window on top of the door just waiting for someone to look in and discover what I was doing.

Seconds passed. Minutes. It felt like fucking hours, but I knew it hadn't been that long. Once I was sure no one would return, I started on the ropes again. I could feel them giving, the fibers snapping and releasing me bit by bit.

I swear if I get out of this alive I'll never do anything stupid again. Yeah, I'll stop fighting, I'll get a good job, I'll work hard. I'll get a fucking house and two-point-five goddamn kids and a good husband if I can just get the hell out of this. Please, please, please.

I wasn't the praying type, but I was hoping someone or something heard me because otherwise I was screwed. Once I left this room I still had to figure out where I was, where the guards were, and how to slip out without being detected.

I can do it. I don't have a choice.

Right, if I didn't want to end up on the news as a missing person escaping was my only option. *If anyone even missed me.* I had to keep it together. There was no time to overthink because if I did I would be frozen, unable to get myself out of this trap.

"Yes!" I hissed.

The ropes snapped and I pulled my arms in front of me. Both of my wrists were inflamed, all covered in bright red rope marks and patterns that had been dug into my skin from them. I took a moment to rub each of them and get the circulation going. My fingertips were faintly blue. *How long had I been tied up?*

Too long. Especially for someone who hated to be tied down.

I turned and examined the piece of metal I'd used to secure my freedom. Grabbing it, I tugged and it gave a little. *My luck is finally changing.* I snatched off my hoodie and the t-shirt underneath. Wrapping the shirt around my hand, I grabbed the bar, put my foot on the cot, and tugged.

I almost yelled when it came free with a loud clank and I stumbled back just able to stop myself before my back slammed into the door. Once more I paused and waited for any sound of approaching footsteps, but there was nothing. At least now I had a weapon and I wouldn't hesitate to smack one of those bastards with it if they came. It wasn't the biggest thing in the world, but I prayed the element of surprise would be mine and I could use that to my advantage.

Putting the rod down, I yanked on my hoodie again before I grabbed my weapon and went to work on the lock. I closed my eyes and listened to the door as I pushed around in the lock. There wasn't much I couldn't break into or out of. And this was no different. I just had to be patient, take my time, and...

Click.

The heavy sound of the door disengaging made a shiver of delight run right up my back. Yes, that was the sound of sweet, sweet freedom. I still didn't have any shoes, but I would just have to deal with the cold January ground and get over it. Once I was out of whatever hellhole I was in then I could work out the details of what to do next.

I grabbed my shirt and stuffed it into my pocket. What I was wearing might be the only clothes I could afford for a while because there was no way in hell I was going back to that apartment to collect anything. Going there would be a death sentence.

Staring at the door, I took a deep breath and readied myself. Whatever was on the other side was the line between life and death and I wasn't ready to die. Maybe I was only alive out of spite, just to throw a big middle finger up to the world, but that was as good a reason as any to get out of bed each morning so I was going to keep using that for motivation.

Turning, I fixed the mattress back onto the cot and nodded. There, no one needed to know I was gone before I was ready for them to know. Turning on my heels, I faced the door and sucked in a breath before I stepped toward it.

I pushed against the door and it swung out with a loud squeak. I winced and looked around wildly, but there was no one in sight. Slipping out, I gritted my teeth as I pushed the door closed again. I needed to buy myself as much time as I possibly could.

My head swiveled back and forth. *Where do I go?* The smell of the basement seemed to intensify now that I was out of the cell and I held a hand up to my nose. As I walked, I noticed there was a row of cells. When I walked past some of them, I heard noise or whispering. My heart sped up again and I walked faster.

I need to get the hell out of here.

There was no time to stop and help anyone, not that I would. I would break my good luck streak and wind up dead for trying to be a good samaritan. Hopefully, these guys' luck turned around like mine did. I tiptoed down the hall and glanced out the door at the end. There was another hallway, but at the end, there was a door that looked like it might lead outside.

All I can do is try it.

Summoning every ounce of my courage, I opened the door all the way. There was no cover out there, nowhere to duck and hide if someone came in and saw me standing like a deer in headlights.

As I stepped outside the door, a hand gripped my shoulder and I was yanked backward. I lost my footing and a grunt left my lips as I hit the dirty floor. My back flared in pain and my anger ignited.

So much for luck. Fuck my life!

I wasn't going to lie on my back and die. Growling, I glared upward ready to jump to my feet and fight until I couldn't anymore. If I was going to be taken down then I was going to fight every step of the way.

My eyes focused on the person who'd grabbed me and my blood ran cold. Standing over me, his coat resting only on his wide shoulders, the first three buttons of his black shirt undone, and his hair slicked back was the monster I had been trying to escape. His deep green eyes flashed and there was a frown on his lips.

I'm fucked.

Chapter Two

Amadeo

"And where do you think you're going?"

Six. I'd been looking for him for a few weeks and I had to admit it was satisfying to stand over him while he practically pissed himself. He deserved it for making me take time out of my day to come down here and drag some truth out of him. But on top of that, he had the nerve to almost escape. It was a good thing I'd come down to question him personally instead of making one of my men do it.

It's not like I would have let one of them touch him anyway. He's mine.

Ever since I'd laid eyes on Six, there had been a spark, a draw like ship in a storm to a siren's song. The first day I'd seen him he'd been all cocky arrogance and charming smiles. I'd watched as he personally charmed his way through half my staff at the casino in the blink of an eye.

What the hell makes him so special?

I couldn't put my finger on it, but I was just as bad because this boy screamed for my attention without ever saying a word. I needed to know more about Six than what I could read online.

Six scrambled back trying to get away from me and I stepped forward following him as his eyes darted around. He looked like a frightened bunny.

I tilted my head. "If you run and I have to chase you down, you'll only be making this harder on yourself. Stand up. Now."

He swallowed hard and I watched the way his Adam's apple danced up and down. Instead of doing what he was told, he leaned back on his palms and stared up at me.

"What if I don't?"

My lips twitched and I raised a brow. "Do you think it's wise? Testing me?"

"I think you probably won't shoot a man if he's on the ground."

"You're mistaken. I would shoot a man in the back if he stole as much money as you took from me." I pulled my Sig Sauer from its holster and slid off the safety. "So which would you prefer? On your feet? Or on the ground?"

An anguished sound left Six's lips and he scurried away from me further. "Neither," he said, his voice wavering. "I prefer to live."

"Then do as you're told and stand up," I growled, my patience wearing thinner by the second. "I do not ask things twice."

"But you just did," he pointed out.

I blinked at him. *Does this boy have a death wish?* I'd done my research on him and I had to say it looked as if every report I had was true. But he was even more reckless and crazy than I thought.

"Do you know who I am?"

Six nodded. "Amadeo Bianchi. Head of the Bianchi family."

"Yes. And you know what I do?"

"Kill people," he said, his breath shuddering. "A lot of people."

"That's right." I walked over to him and crouched down until my face was close to his. "So, when you face me and talk to me, maybe you should remember that, hmm?" I reached out and grabbed a fistful of his hair. It was greasy. He desperately needed a hot shower, but not yet. Not until I got what I wanted. "Do you understand me?"

Six's tongue darted out over his lips, wetting them. He nodded quickly, his head bouncing up and down as he looked up at me with those deep, chocolate eyes. Except they weren't just filled with fear. There was a fire blazing behind them as if he wanted to punch me.

Oh, I dare you.

As if he could read my mind, Six sucked in a shaky breath and glanced away before his eyes landed on the gun. I could see the goose bumps on his exposed forearms and he quickly tugged the sleeves down of his worn and dirty hoodie. When his gaze flickered back up to meet mine, there was a steel resolve there that I wanted to break.

"Stand. Up."

This time, I didn't have to say another word to him. Once I was on my feet, Six followed. He was only a few centimeters shorter than me but he kept his head up. I wasn't sure if he was brave or just stupid.

I guess we'll see.

"Follow me. My men," I nodded to the two men who flanked me on each side, "will follow you. One wrong move and they won't hesitate to put a bullet in you." I shoved my gun back into its holster. "Let's talk."

"About what?" He muttered as he followed me.

"Anything and everything." We entered a back room and he immediately gagged. "Is something the matter?" I asked, glancing over my shoulder.

"It smells like death in here."

"There *is* death in here." I glanced around the room. "Lots of it. Sit in that chair."

The room we were in did indeed smell like death, but maybe I had grown used to that. It was a small space with a drain in the floor and plain white tiles. It was easier to clean the blood up that way. Above the chair was a hook that was useful for suspending people if necessary and a huge hose jutted out of the far wall. If you wanted to get answers, this was the room to do it in.

I turned and realized Six still hadn't sat down. When he didn't move, one of the guards shoved him forward. I clenched my jaw. *Why did that tick me off so badly?* Six sat down and I swept it away as he glared up at me.

"So? What do you want to talk about?" he asked. "The weather?"

"Don't be a smart ass." I took my coat off and passed it to a guard. "Leave us."

"Are you sure?" one of my men asked. "This one is tricky. He's given us the slip-"

"I understand that all of you are incompetent," I growled. "Why you would want to remind me of that pertinent fact is beyond me. Get out!"

"Yes, sir," he said quickly.

They both scurried away like rats and I stared after the closed door for a minute envisioning exactly how I was going to snap their bones later. How was it that I was surrounded by idiots? I turned back to Six who was looking around wildly.

I snapped my fingers. "Don't even think about it. You even move wrong and I'll break your ankles."

Six shoved himself back in the chair. "Shit, relax!"

I raised a brow and stepped toward him. "Put your arms behind you, around the back of the chair."

"Kinky. Do I at least get a safeword?" When I stared at him, his grin fell and he cleared his throat. "Sorry, I'm real nervous."

"You should be."

Six hesitated and I was across the space between us and in his face in seconds. I grabbed a handful of his hair and he gasped, the breathy sound going right to my balls as they tightened. *That sound should be illegal.*

"You're going to keep testing me until I lose my patience. Aren't you?"

"N-no, no I'm not," he breathed and shoved his hands around the back of the chair. "I've just got a really dumb mouth. That's what my mom used to say anyway. It runs when I don't want it to and trust me I'm not trying to keep talking I just can't stop when I start and then I always say something crazy and I end up kicking myself. Like now. Right, this moment I really want to shut up but

I can't. It's a curse or a disease or something. Shit. Sorry. I'll shut up, I swear."

My mouth twitched again and for the second time in a twenty-minute space, Six had almost made me grin. Almost. He was annoying as hell and I really wanted to smack some sense into him, but there was something about him that I couldn't shake.

"Stop talking."

"Yeah, good idea. Stop talking. I can do that."

"Can you?" I growled.

He let out a squeak as he pressed his lips together. "I'm fuckin' trying!"

I shook my head as I released his hair and walked over to a table along the far wall. Picking up a pair of heavy, metal handcuffs I walked back over to the chair and stepped behind it. As I gazed down at Six, his chest rose and fell. I knew his heart was beating out of control and I wanted to stare at that fear a little longer.

Instead, I pushed his wrists closer together and secured the cuffs. As soon as I took a step back, he shook them and groaned.

"Really fucking hate being tied down," he muttered. "I could sit here and talk without this you know."

"No, you couldn't." I grabbed another chair and dragged it across the floor before I sat down. "You would have tried to run, my instincts would kick in, and I would end up shooting you. We can't have that. So, how'd you steal my money?"

Six paled under the low overhead lights. "Oh you wanna talk about that," he said nervously.

"What else?" I asked shortly.

"Anything else." Six's eyes darted to the side avoiding my gaze.

I sat there staring him down, unwilling to repeat my question. Daring him to keep defying me.

Six blew out a heavy sigh and frowned. "You really want to know?"

"Yes."

Six chewed his bottom lip briefly. "It wasn't that hard if I'm being honest. Everything's on a schedule and the guards can be easily distracted. It was easy to slip in, break into the room, and grab the cash. When I left, I walked out. No one even knew. Must have been another stupid camera somewhere I missed."

There were many cameras that he had missed. My casino was constantly getting new and improved security tech. It was my utmost priority to make Bianchi's a fortress in each and every room. So, when he'd taken the money, I had been alerted damn near immediately. But he'd been faster, slipping out of frame and getting out of the casino.

"Why did you take it?" I asked. "You had to know you'd be caught."

Six looked at me and shrugged. "My brain doesn't really work that way. It tells me to do something and I just...do it." His shoulder rose and fell again. "I don't exactly think out the consequences. I needed the cash."

My jaw ticked. "Why?"

"I owed some guy money. You wouldn't want to owe the guy five bucks and he'd kicked my ass real bad a few weeks before I did it. Listen, I didn't have a choice. All of the interest he laid on top of that loan killed me."

"So you thought you would take *my* money?"

"Not like you'd miss it," he huffed.

I reached forward and grabbed the edge of the metal chair before I dragged him closer. His eyes went wide and he shivered as I rested my foot on his crotch and pressed a bit. It was barely any pressure, but it was enough to make him straighten up.

"Sorry," he muttered. "It will never happen again, I swear! An-and I can pay you back. Every dime."

I searched his face and all I could see was a lost, misguided man that needed a firm spanking and an attitude adjustment. Six was only twenty-one, but he had a whole heap of trouble on him already. Getting into bed with a loan sharking asshole? That was probably one of his biggest mistakes.

Until he stole from me.

"I should kill you," I said as I reached into the pocket of my pants and pulled out a pack of cigarettes. I lit one up before I pushed the pack away again. "But I have a proposition for you. As you said, I don't really need the money. But it's the principle of the thing, you know?"

"Yeah, yeah I get that," Six said with a nod. "So, I can pay you back, right?"

"All four hundred grand of it?"

Six winced. "Was it that much?"

"Probably a bit more, but I'm rounding down." I blew smoke out and leaned forward, putting a bit more pressure on his crotch. He groaned and I could imagine that face moaning for me. "But enough of your talking. I want something from you."

"What?" He asked quietly.

"I'll forgive your debt if you become my companion."

"Companion?" He scoffed. "Do you really mean whore? Because I feel like you mean whore."

I glared. "In a sense, yes. If you stay with me, do as you're told, spread your legs for me, then I'll drop it. But I need something else on top of it. I need you to call me Daddy."

Six blinked at me before he burst out laughing. "You're fucking with me, aren't you?"

My face turned to stone. Did it look like I was joking? From the moment I'd laid eyes on Six, I knew he needed someone to take control of his life and I wanted someone who would call me Daddy, obey me, and give me what I needed. My lifestyle didn't afford me mistakes and the high-priced whores I'd hired in the past to play the role of boy had been a far cry from the real thing. No, I wanted a boy of my own.

That boy was going to be Six.

Chapter Three

Six

I STARED AT AMADEO.

"What the fuck are you talking about? Are you crazy?"

No, because he was joking. *Right?* There was no way in hell that all he wanted was for me to be his private whore and call him Daddy. Did he realize there were people out there who would do that for a fee? *So why me?*

"I'm trying to decide if you're stupid or just crazy," Amadeo said leaning forward, his foot pressing down harder. "Which is it?"

Grinding my teeth, I tried to keep back the cry that lingered on my tongue. *Shit.* The bastard was really rubbing me the wrong way. Normally, I would have kicked his ass. But since I was strapped to a chair and he was toying with me, there was no way out. I had to take it.

"I-I don't know," I finally spat out.

Amadeo tilted his head. "Right now I believe it's stupidity," he said as his foot pressed down more and I cried out. "So, why don't you watch your mouth? Hmm?"

"I hear you!" I groaned when he released some of the pressure and tried not to glare at him. "But I don't understand what you want from me."

"Exactly what I just said. You stay with me, pay off your debt, warm my bed." He reached out and tilted my chin up. "And call me Daddy."

I swallowed thickly. Searching his face for a trace of a lie or a joke, I frowned when he continued to be stone-faced. Out of every possible scenario I had in mind, this had never been one of them.

Nervousness welled in my chest and I had to bite my lip to keep from laughing. *Stupid nerves.* I was on the brink of cracking up because my heart was thumping too hard, my face was hot, and I wanted to hide.

It was so much worse that Amadeo was staring right at me, those deep green eyes not glancing away for even a second. The feeling of his hand on my chin was overwhelming. I tried turning away, but he stopped me, his grip tightening.

What is wrong with me?

"Well?" Amadeo asked.

I blinked at him. "Well, what?"

"Do we have a deal?"

No way in hell. Amadeo Bianchi was as crazy as people said he was. There had always been rumors, things whispered behind closed doors about him. I'd heard he was a murderer, a kidnapper, that he enjoyed torture, that he was cold and heartless. But I had never personally met him and I dismissed the rumors. Everyone liked to make people out to be more than they were, especially some rich dude who glared more than he smiled.

But it turns out Amadeo is as bad as I'd heard. His eyes swept over me and I squirmed in the chair. Damn. I should have run a lot further.

"Six."

"I'm thinking."

Amadeo growled and that sound shot straight to my cock making it stiffen. *Don't get a boner. Don't get a boner. Don't get a boner!* I'd always had a thing about fear; the way it made my heart race, my head spin, and my blood rush? It was a turn-on. And if Amadeo wasn't who he was I probably would have offered to blow him the first chance I got. The man was insane, but he was hot.

"What is there to think about?" Amadeo asked, interrupting my ridiculous thoughts. "You can either take the deal or face the consequences."

"Considering you want to be my Daddy, how bad could the consequences be?" I mumbled. "What? Do I get a time out?"

Amadeo's grip on my chin tightened, his nails digging into my skin and forcing an embarrassing whine from my lips before I growled right back at him. *Okay, he's hot but he's pissing me off. Take your goddamn hands off of me.*

"Do not growl at me again," he ordered.

The stupid part of me was tempted to ask him or what? What else could he possibly do to me that hadn't already been done? My life was one giant shit show and it continued to spiral out of control even now. So, what could he do to me that would be worse? Kill me? That would be a vacation at this point.

"And you're right, the consequence will be a time out." He leaned forward and I tried to pull away, but there was nowhere to go. "You can spend it right back in the cell you woke up in. Except this time you can stay in there until I feel like being gracious and opening the door."

I shivered. I'd had my fair share of crappy places, but that tiny room was the worst. All I could think about was being trapped in that space, the damp smell filling my nostrils and making me feel clammy and gross. No, I didn't want to do that.

But calling him Daddy...

My brain couldn't wrap around it. It's not like I had anything against people who did the whole Daddy thing, my friends were all over in terms of who they were and what they liked. But I wasn't into it and I didn't want to do it.

"We can figure something else out," I said. "Like I said I could pay you back. You're right, it's your money and I shouldn't have taken it. So, let me replace it. I can get a job or you can make me work for you for free."

Amadeo quirked a dark brow. "Why would I ever allow you to step foot in my establishment again? You robbed me once."

"And I would never do it twice," I informed him, nodding hard. "Trust me, I have learned from my mistakes and I am ready to make amends. What do you say?"

He removed his hand from my face and pushed his fingers through his jet-black hair. "I think you're leaning more toward delusional than crazy or stupid at this point."

"Is that better or worse?" I mumbled.

"Does it matter?"

"I'm hoping it does."

Amadeo shook his head at me. "You have one deal and that's it. So, which are you going to choose? Go with me and repay your debt or stay down here and suffer?"

"Listen, here's the thing. I'm not into the whole Daddy situation. I won't yuck your yum, I'm not an asshole, but I don't have any urge to call a man Daddy. Hell, I've never even referred to my own father that way. So, let's do something else. I can cook. Oh! I'm a great cleaner. What about a driver? Do you need a driver?"

The man stared and blinked at me. I watched as he removed his foot from my crotch before he stood up and adjusted his sleeves. He rolled them up before he stalked toward me and I nearly pissed my pants.

"Okay, okay!" I yelled. "Shit, calm down man. I-I told you I don't know how to shut up!"

"Learn," he snapped.

"Fine! But I mean it. I can do a hell of a lot of other things okay? Let's figure out wha- What are you doing?"

Amadeo had walked behind me and not being able to see him made my fear shoot through the roof. I tried to glance back at him, but he shoved my head back around. My heart sped up to the point I could barely breathe and I squeezed my eyes shut waiting for the finishing blow. Would I even feel it when he put a bullet through my brain?

The handcuffs clicked and my wrists were freed. I brought them around and rubbed them one after the other before a hand wrapped around my upper arm. Amadeo hauled me to my feet and started walking.

"Where are we going?" I asked, the panic rising in my throat as we left the room and walked back down the hall.

"I believe you already know that."

No, I didn't want to go back into that room. But Amadeo's offer? I didn't want that either. If he was looking for a few good fucks and then he would release me, fine. But I had a feeling he wanted something more than that and I don't do commitments.

Amadeo opened my cell door and released my arm. "Go inside."

I stared at the confines of the room and frowned. "Can we-"

"You and I have nothing further to discuss. When you have come to your senses then we can have a conversation."

He pushed me forward and my hands shot out, clutching each side of the door as I dug my feet into the concrete. *Shit, he's really going to lock me up isn't he?* I glanced over my shoulder and his lips were in a straight line.

Amadeo was serious.

Fear laced up my spine and bile rose in my throat. There wasn't a hint of remorse in his eyes and it fueled my anger all over again. Who was he to lock me up? Yes, I had stolen from him, but I would give it back or find some other way to repay him. Why did it have to be on his terms?

"Go," Amadeo said with a nod. "Now."

It took everything to pull my hands off of the doorframe and take a step into the room. The door slammed behind me, the sound echoing through my bones as I shut my eyes and forced myself to take in a deep breath.

This is fine. I was able to get out once and I can do it again.

"You, stay on this door. If he escapes again, it'll be you in that room."

"Yes, Boss!"

Amadeo knocked on the door and I spun on my heels. He peered at me through the window and tilted his head. "You let Angelo here know when you're ready to talk."

"Fuck you!"

I shoved my middle finger up at him and he only pulled away and disappeared. My stomach churned. Shit. I moved over to the cot and sat down, every inch of me shaking as I faced how screwed I really was. Being confined? That was worst than death.

I drew my legs up onto the cot and rolled onto my back. The ceiling was thrown into shadows, that stupid light overhead shining in my eyes. I laid my arm over my face to shield myself from it and tried to calm my racing mind.

Amadeo Bianchi was the biggest asshole on Earth. It didn't matter how hot he was when he was a bastard. The moment I found a way out of my cell, I was going to get far away from him and never look back.

Chapter Four

Amadeo

I STARED AT THE MONITOR, MY EYES TRACKING EVERY MOVEMENT Six made. Right now, he bounced from one wall to the other, mumbling to himself. He wasn't speaking out loud because I would have heard every word, but rather only his pink, plump lips were moving.

"How long are you going to resist me?"

It had only been three days, but Six looked as if he was going crazy being in there by himself. When he was let out to use the bathroom and returned, he only got more pissed off. So far he'd called me every kind of son of a bitch in the book, but he still wouldn't break.

Keep fighting me. It'll be even better when you give in.

Six couldn't stand me, but I was enamored by him. He was strong, courageous, daring, and an absolute pain in my ass. Once I'd left from our little chat, I had fired everyone on the floor and in the back rooms of the casino and replaced them all. It was an easy feat. People wanted to work in my casino and since Six had shown me it was the people who were flawed, not the tech, they all had to go.

The little box beside my desk came on and a blonde woman smiled at me. "Mr. Bianchi, your family has arrived."

I pressed the button. "Thanks, Darla. You can let them in."

I switched to the security cameras and tracked my brothers and cousins as they walked into the casino. No one could see we weren't related. All of us had the trademark Bianchi jawlines, the same dark hair, and the same sense of power and control. They were men who bowed to no one.

Except me.

I switched back to the other screen and traced the outline of Six. *Why am I obsessed with him?* Maybe it was his reckless stupidity that drew me in. If I were anyone else and Six had stolen from me, he would have been dead by now. My methods might be harsh, but in reality, I was saving his life.

And he owed me for that.

"Yo!" Gabriele was first through my door as loud as he always was. When I stood up, he dragged me into a rough hug, his palm slamming against my back before he pulled back and grinned at me. "How's shit going?"

"Fine," I said, waving a hand to a chair. "Sit down. Where are the others?"

He jerked a thumb over his shoulder. "Right behind me." He leaned over my computer and raised a brow. "Who is that?"

I tapped a key and the screen went dark. Gabriele straightened up and I swore his eyebrows were going to crawl off of his forehead if they shot up anymore. He stared into my eyes, but I wasn't backing down. Six was nobody's business but mine. I wasn't sharing him, not even with my brothers.

Mine.

As the others filed in, Gabriele continued to stare me down as if he could pry the truth out of me. We both knew I didn't talk unless I wanted to. Gabriele might be skilled at extracting truth with that withering glance, but it wasn't going to work on me.

"We interrupting something?" Riccardo asked, the shape of him moving in my peripheral. "What's wrong with you two?"

"They're in a pissing contest," Niccolo whispered. "If they were dogs, there would be lifted legs and all."

"Disgusting," Dario chided his brother. "Can you at least pretend to be civilized?"

"Nah," Niccolo laughed. "That shit's boring."

"You want to tell me what's going on?" Gabriele asked.

"No. Sit down."

He stood there and crossed his arms over his chest. "You've been squirrely the past few weeks and I don't like it. Who was that?"

"I said no one. Now sit the fuck down before I make you sit down," I growled.

"Leave it, G," Dario said.

"He's hiding something and I-"

"Leave it," he repeated. "Come on, sit down. We've all got stuff to do and I'm not wiping up blood when he loses it and socks you in the face."

Gabriele finally broke eye contact and glanced away, a swear on his lips as he uncrossed his arms and sat down. He was always the one that gave me the most trouble, but then again what did I expect.

I took my seat afterward and looked at each of them. They were the most trusted people in my organization. Gabriele was my second in command for good reason. He was a smart ass and could get bossy, but he was loyal to a fault. Riccardo had a resolve made out of steel, but he needed to when he was the one looking after our sex workers. Niccolo, my cousin, was insane, but he was good with a gun and ran them without getting taken down. Which wasn't easy to do. And Dario? He was a good five years older than me but he had no desire to run anything. His expertise lay in cooking books and laundering money. Each of them played a role and I couldn't run things as smoothly as I did without them.

"What's going on, Ama?" Riccardo pried.

"Two more of our warehouses were hit last night."

"Shit," Gabriele frowned, our impasse forgotten. "What was taken?"

"Guns, drugs, contraband." I shrugged. "The list is endless but my men are compiling the damage the best they can."

Dario frowned. "They don't keep better records of what goes in and out?"

"Of course they do," I said, pinching the bridge of my nose. "You know we're more organized than that. But when they attacked the warehouse, they lit them both on fire on the way out. There's no telling what's there, what isn't there, and what *was* there when all the records were burned too."

"I told you we needed backup of all inventory on something other than paper," Dario said with a shake of his head.

"And I told you nothing electronic is completely secure. Both methods have their risks, but I choose to do things the way my father did. Everything written down, encoded and kept safe. This is an unfortunate event, but don't think you can get away with criticizing how I run my shit."

Dario threw up his hands. "Geez, you're wound up today. I was only pointing something out to you."

"He needs to get laid," Niccolo said with a nod. "He has that grumpy, horny look on his face."

I glared at him.

"That one!" Nic grinned as he pointed at me. "That's the look right there."

"If you weren't my cousin I swear I would shoot you."

Nic's grin only grew. "Does that mean you love me?"

"Is it the Irish?" Gabriele cut in, ignoring Niccolo.

I shrugged. "I wish I had answers, but so far I don't. Of course, I believe it's those bastards. Conor Kelley has been screwing with me for too long."

"Maybe we need to have a little meeting," Riccardo said. "We've always screwed with each other, but this is taking it a bit far don't you think? Even with our pissing contests, we try to respect each other's trades."

"Exactly," I said with a nod.

Gabriele nodded. "I'll get a meeting set up soon. If this was his guys, then he needs to put a leash on those mutts."

There was that look in Gabriele's dark eyes like he was going to murder someone. If I was an average bystander and I saw that I would probably pass out.

"Yeah, but do it calmly," I told him. "We're not trying to start a war, we're trying to negotiate and get everyone on the same page again. That's all."

Gabriele groaned but nodded. "Fine."

I nodded. "Good. Now, update me on what's going on with you guys."

They went one by one giving me information on how everything was running. Some of them had problems and I helped them work through them or moved around guard details on my tablet. I didn't trust certain aspects of my business online, but this was simply organizing my employees and that was all it would look like if anyone ever gained access to our files.

"Is that all?" I asked once they were finished speaking.

"Yes," Dario nodded. "No. Nonna Emilia wants to know if we're coming home for dinner this weekend."

"What's she making?" Riccardo asked.

"The usual, but Caponata is involved so *io sono lì*," Dario said.

"Count me in too," Gabriele said.

I wanted to join them, but by this weekend I planned to be with Six. They all looked at me expectantly.

"I'll see."

"Mom's gonna lose it if you don't come," Riccardo pointed out.

"I said I'll see."

Gabriele groaned. "She's gonna be on our ass. You better get there."

My eye was on the verge of twitching. "Hey, I know. Why don't all of you get the fuck out of my office before I lose my damn temper?"

"See? He needs dick," Niccolo whispered.

"Out!"

Niccolo laughed, but he ran out of my office like his heels were on fire. *Bastard.* One day I was going to end up punching him in the face. Out of all of them, he and Gabriele got under my skin the most.

We said our goodbyes and I shook my head at the door as I closed it. I loved my family but damn they drove me crazy. Sitting at my desk again, I turned my computer back on and stared at the video.

I picked up my phone and called Angelo who was standing guard at his door. He picked up on the first ring.

"Yes, boss?"

"How's the prisoner?"

"Pissed off, hungry, and weak." I watched as he peered into the room before he walked off again. "He should be more willing to talk now."

"I'll be there shortly."

I hung up and shoved my phone into my pocket. Work could wait, I wanted to see the boy that made my pulse race. I grabbed my jacket and threw it on before I stepped out of my office.

"Mr. Bianchi, you have a meeting in-"

"Move it," I said as I breezed past Darla. "I'm busy."

"Yes, Mr. Bianchi, but this is the last time it can be moved."

I turned on my heels and glared. "Don't start with me today."

Her jaw ticked. "No, you don't start with *me*. If I don't do my job, you're the one that yells at me so as I said I can move the meeting, but it is the last time it will be moved."

"You're breaking my balls."

Darla smiled. "Happy to do it, Sir, if it means this place runs like a well-oiled machine." She turned back to her computer. "Let me know where you would like your lunch to be sent. Enjoy the rest of your day, Mr. Bianchi."

I stared at her, but she paid me no mind. Darla was the one employee I hadn't fired when I did a clean sweep and I never would. She was a pain in my ass, but she did her job and asked no questions.

Turning on my heels, I left it alone. Darla was fearless even in the face of a family full of mobsters. There was nothing I could possibly say that would shake her confidence or make her change the way she spoke to any of us. I'd grown up around strong women and every last one would stab you before they let you disrespect them. Maybe I was just used to it by now.

I climbed into my car, my mind back on Six. As soon as the door was closed, I opened the surveillance camera on my phone and gazed at him. He looked exhausted as he laid on the cot.

Don't worry, I'm going to fix everything, Six. And you're going to be mine.

Chapter Five

Six

MY BODY HURT. LYING ON A TINY, HARD COT DAY AFTER DAY would do that. The feeling of it being better than the floor had worn off and the reality was that I hated this room. Every once in a while the light flickered, but it never went off. And there was no window to the outside world so I had no idea what time of day it was. That chilly, damp smell was everywhere now and I was slowly losing my fucking mind.

I've been in worse situations. Can't think of any, but I'm sure I have. Right? No, pretty sure this one is the worst. Held prisoner by a psychotic mob boss? Yeah, I'm positive this is the worst thing I've ever gotten myself into.

I was still pissed off at Amadeo, but slowly the blame was pivoting to me. That money should have stayed where it was and out of my greedy palms. If I had listened to that little voice in the back of my head that screamed *walk away*, I wouldn't be where I was now. Self-pity crawled into my chest and I groaned as I ran a hand down my face.

"I am the stupidest person alive," I announced to the ceiling. "Seriously, I will stop being such an asshole if I can get out of this room."

The confined space was starting to mess with me. I wanted out of this damn locked box and I would do anything to be free. I threw my arm over my face, the scratchy five o'clock shadow on my face rubbing against my skin and irritating it. Every little thing was getting on my nerves. There was no noise in the room except the sound of my breathing and beating heart. When they fed me small meals, all I could hear was my own annoying chewing. Even now there was very little I could hear even outside of the room.

I turned around and faced the wall. It was better to pretend the door didn't even exist than to stare at it and pray it opened. The small moments of freedom I received weren't nearly enough. Today I found my feet dragging when I was marched back to my cell from the restroom and I hadn't wanted to go inside. But one look from the thug outside my door and I knew he would hurt me if I didn't.

Okay, I mean it this time. If I get out of this, I'll behave. Seriously. I'll think things through and stop being impulsive. I'll get a real job and never steal again. Just get me out of here!

The heavy sound of the lock clicking jarred me. I shot up and turned to the door falling off the cot in the process. The cool floor greeted me and I hissed as I hit the ground. Two Italian leather shoes stepped into view and I slowly looked up at Amadeo.

"I could get used to seeing you on the ground for me."

My heart skipped a beat. Why did that happen every time I laid eyes on him? I pushed myself up onto my knees, but when I tried to get up, he laid a hand on my head and shook his.

"Don't move. I told you, I like seeing you on the ground."

My cock jumped and I wanted to yell at myself. Seriously, was I that fucked in the head that I found that hot? A chair was brought in and Amadeo sat down before he reached out and grabbed my chin.

"Are you ready to talk?"

I opened my mouth with the words fuck you on my tongue and quickly snapped it shut. My stomach growled and I was glad I had stopped myself. Even if I wanted to hold out and get this man away from me, I was starving. *Play along. I can make a run for it later.*

"Yes," I nodded.

Amadeo grinned and it took my breath away. He was hot all broody and frowning and glaring, but this? It was so much better. My body flushed and I leaned into his touch without even meaning to. He was too powerful for his own good.

"That's what I like to hear." He released my chin and his fingers danced along my jawline. "And have you considered my offer?"

Tingles ran over my scalp and I had forgotten to talk as he touched me. How long had it been since I had anyone touch me anyway? *Way too long. This is what people mean when they say they're touched starved. I'm letting a crazy man pet me.*

"Yes."

Amadeo tilted his head. "Oh, you're so quiet now. Perhaps this room did you some good." He stroked one warm finger down my cheek. "So, you're ready to be a good boy for Daddy?"

Why did he have to say it like that?

Honey dripped off of the word Daddy when he said it. I pressed my thighs together and realized I was doing it. Quickly, I forced myself to relax He searched my face, and when I didn't immediately answer he gripped my chin again and a stupid whimper left my lips.

"What will I have to do?" I asked quickly. "What does that mean? Being your good boy?"

Amadeo sat up and looked down at me. I watched as he pulled out a pack of cigarettes like he'd done before and lit one up. He blew smoke out before his eyes rolled over me and I felt like I was being inspected from head to toe. It made me want to crawl into a corner and hide from that withering gaze.

"It means you do what I ask when I ask." He blew out more smoke and leaned forward. "Have you ever heard about this type of relationship?"

I shook my head. "No."

"How do I describe this?" he asked himself, his eyes taking on a far-off look before he gazed down at me once more. "It is basically a need I have inside of me for control. Of course, that's simplifying it, and I'm sure many other Daddies have many other ways of defining it, but that's what best suits me." He waved a hand. "I'm getting off track. I have a need for control and also care. I like being in charge and guiding a boy to where he should be in life."

I chewed my lip so hard it throbbed. "Can I ask a question?" I finally blurted out.

"Yes."

"If you want something like this, why not just find someone who can fulfill it? You have to have access to the kinda guys who would love to call you Daddy. Why me?"

"None of them need me the way that you do," he said simply. "I could see it in your eyes the first day I saw you. There was something broken in you and I wanted to fix it. Besides, yes, I can pay for the fantasy, but it is far from real with them and I grow tired of the illusion of submission. It's like bad porn where you just want the actor to shut up because it's too much and not at all good."

"And you want me? But wouldn't I just be playing a role too?"

Amadeo frowned so deeply that I pulled away from him even further. *What was that expression?* I couldn't read him sometimes. It was like a stone wall replaced his emotions and I was lost for words.

"Perhaps," Amadeo answered. "But I want to try. That's the deal I have to offer you. Stay by my side, be a good boy, earn your freedom."

"I don't know about that good part," I mumbled.

"You'll have to try."

I fuck up everything I touch and he thinks it's as easy as just trying? Yeah, that will go over well. He's setting himself up for disappointment.

But that was his problem, not mine. As long as I went along with what he said, I could get out of this room. All I had to do was fake it. I gazed up at him and searched his face. Something about Amadeo unnerved me. If he was anyone else, I would probably agree to anything and everything just to find a way away from him later. But when I looked into Amadeo's green eyes, I felt as if chains were locked around my limbs and when I said yes there would be no escaping.

"How long?" I asked.

Amadeo ashed his cigarette on the floor. "How long what?"

"How long would I have to do this? When will my debt be paid off?"

Amadeo looked me over. "Six months."

Six months. *Months.* I was going to be a prisoner for a long ass time.

If I can't get away. But I will find an out.

"Six months and I'll be free?"

"Yes," Amadeo said, a heavy sigh on his lips. "How many times must I repeat myself?"

"Just wanted to make sure I understood." I blew out a breath and nodded. "Okay fine. I'll do it."

Amadeo stepped on his cigarette and put it out. "You'll do it, what?"

I stared at him, completely lost. What was he talking about now? He stared at me expectantly and I searched my brain until the realization dawned on me.

Right. The Daddy thing.

"I'll do it. Daddy."

The smirk that curled his lips did something to me, tingles running all over my body like I'd been shocked by a live wire. He reached out and took my chin in hand once more before he tilted my head this way and that. His thumb ghosted over my bottom lip and I resisted the urge to bite him just to be spiteful.

"Let's get you cleaned up. You smell terrible."

My eyes widened. "You locked me up in this...this...fucking dungeon! Of course, I smell terrible!"

Amadeo gripped my cheeks hard. "Lower your voice. Now."

"Okay, okay," I backed off quickly.

"Say you're sorry."

He's already getting on my last nerve.

Amadeo's eyes challenged me as if he was waiting for me to screw up. Instead of giving in and doing what I do best, which is putting my foot in my mouth, I sucked it up and nodded.

"Sorry."

"Sorry what?"

I growled. "Sorry, Daddy!"

He clicked his tongue. "We'll break you of that attitude eventually, but for now, good enough." Amadeo released me and stood, towering over me. "Angelo, we're going to go. Six, Angelo will be your new personal guard. Follow me."

"Yes, Boss," Angelo said with a nod.

My heart raced as I stood up and followed behind them. *Finally.* I never wanted to see the inside of that room again.

"Oh, and Six?" Amadeo stopped and glanced over his shoulder at me.

"Yes...Daddy?"

"If you try to escape. If you piss me off. If you do *anything* that steps over the line, I will put you right back in that cell until you're ready to behave again. Do you understand?"

No words formed no matter how hard I tried. I nodded and he turned on his heels. I stole one final look at my prison and sped up. No way was I going back in there again. Whatever he wanted, whatever I had to do, I would make sure I stayed free.

Chapter Six

Six

THE BUILDING AMADEO LIVED IN WAS HUGE. ALL OF THE LIGHTS gave off warm glows and the pristine lobby was all but empty. *What time is it?* There was a clock on the wall, but it was too far away for me to read it. I gave up and gazed at Amadeo. No one looked directly at him when he stepped inside and I stared in awe. *Did they know what he was?*

They certainly looked right through me. I glanced down at myself. A dirty, ripped t-shirt, ill-fitting pants, and no shoes. If I saw a wealthy man with a guy that looked like me, I would either think something sinister was going on or he was being a good guy and helping out a homeless man. As I passed by a mirror and took in my greasy hair and skin, I grimaced. *Yeah, I definitely look homeless.*

"Don't fall behind, Six," Amadeo said as he glided to the elevator.

I nodded and picked up the pace. We stepped inside and I held my breath as the elevator went up. As each number ticked by it felt like an eternity. Soft music played in the background and I shifted from foot to foot staring at Angelo's huge back as he stood in front of us.

"Be still."

I glanced up at Amadeo and he was staring at me. "Sorry," I muttered. "Can't help it. Fancy places make my skin itch." I scraped my nails over my neck and shivered.

"Stop it. You're making me itch now."

"See? Fancy shit does that to you."

"Didn't you grow up wealthy?"

I stiffened and turned to him. "How do you know that?"

"I know everything about you."

"Creepy."

"Intelligent," he countered. "The person who knows the most in a room is always the most dangerous."

His green eyes looked right through me and I turned around again. *Okay, so he's obsessive and nuts. Noted.*

The ding of the elevator drew me back to the present. We all stepped out and were admitted into Amadeo's place. Right away I stood in the entranceway stunned by the size of it.

"This is your house?"

"No," Amadeo shrugged off his coat. "This is my loft. It's where I go when I have meetings and things of that nature. You'll get to go to my place tomorrow, but not until you've had a bath and I have things put into place properly."

I blinked at him. "What things?"

"Stop asking so many questions." He rolled up his sleeves and I saw peeks of tattoos on each of his forearms. "Take those clothes off."

"Right here?"

Amadeo's eyes narrowed and I took a step back involuntarily. He was downright terrifying when he made that face. Which was odd because I wasn't scared of him all the time, not even after locking me up in the basement of a warehouse. But his sharp green eyes on me like that I could see the killer beneath the man.

"Bathroom," I blurted out. "I need a bathroom."

I was careful not to make it a question, sure that he would snap if I did. Amadeo nodded and pointed to the stairs.

"The main one is off the bedroom. Angelo will take you," he said as he sat at the bar. "There will be fresh clothes laid out for you by the time you're done."

I nodded and made a beeline for the bathroom. *When did I get shy about being naked in front of people?* I'd stripped off all my clothes in front of friends and strangers before and it had never bothered me. But being under Amadeo's watchful gaze felt different, more intimidating.

I might as well get used to it. I have to sleep with him.

Right, that was going to come up sooner rather than later. I pushed it away, not wanting to think about it. Instead, I walked into the bathroom and froze.

"Itchy," I muttered, scratching at my skin. "It's too damn big!"

I had gotten used to the simpler things in life ever since my family lost all their money when I was still in high school. The mansions and expensive cars had been traded for second-hand clothes and tiny houses. It had been humiliating going to the same school as my friends wearing the clothes they had probably donated after wearing them once. Funny how you didn't realize the extent to which money influenced things until you had none and suddenly you had no friends either.

I stripped out of my clothes and tossed them to the floor. As I stepped away from them, I left those memories behind as well. Once I figured out how to work the shower, I turned it so hot the bathroom filled with steam in moments. I couldn't hop into it fast enough.

"Fuck, that feels good."

I braced my hands on the wall and let the three different jets hit me with hot water. The grime and dirt washed off of me and I stared at the murky water that swirled around my feet and disappeared down the drain. Water dripped into my face, but I didn't care. This was the best I'd felt in weeks.

Glancing around, I found body wash, shampoo, and conditioner. When I opened the body wash and took a whiff, heat swept over my flesh. Amadeo. It smelled exactly like him. I took one more long inhale before I dumped some into the palm of my hand and slid my hand over my body.

"Food will be ready in thirty minutes," Amadeo said, his voice too close to be on the other side of the door. "Hurry up."

I poked my head out and jumped when he blinked at me. "Holy shit, how did you get in here without me hearing you! Are you trying to give me a heart attack?"

Amadeo raised a brow. "I move silently. Get used to it."

Creepy.

I shoved my head back into the shower before I said that out loud and caused more trouble for myself. Amadeo, the bastard, had wrecked my peaceful mood and I couldn't get it back. Instead, I focused on cleaning up and getting out of the shower. My stomach twisted and I touched it, groaning.

Gotta get some food inside of me.

Food in my personal hell had been scraps mostly. There was nothing substantial to put in my body and now it felt as if my stomach was eating itself. I rinsed the shampoo and conditioner out of my hair before I stepped out and grabbed a towel that had been left out on the counter for me. As I glanced around, I noticed my clothes were gone.

"Hey, where's my stuff?" I called.

"I had them thrown away," Amadeo called back.

Anger shot through me and I clenched the towel tightly. Yes, my things were ratty and horrible, but they were *mine*. I stormed over to the door, ripped it open and there he sat on the edge of the bed, staring at me with a drink in his hand.

"Excuse me?"

"I believe you heard exactly what I said."

"That was my shit!"

"All of it was disgusting. You will get new clothes," he nodded to the dresser. "There are more in there and the closet. But I already left you some on the bathroom counter." His eyes rolled up and down my body and suddenly I was very aware that I was naked and wet. "But if you'd like to begin your contract now, we might not need the clothes at all."

The shiver that danced up my spine made my mouth clamp shut. Amadeo's eyes looked like a wolf who was stalking his prey and I was in his crosshairs. I took a step back and he stood up. Every move I made away, he stepped closer until his arm shot out, his hand wrapping around my throat.

"Are you going somewhere?"

"To get dressed," I whispered.

Amadeo leaned forward and pressed his nose against my shoulder. My eyes flew open when he took a long, slow inhale and a strangled groan left his lips.

Let me go. Let me go. Let me go!

If he kept looking at me like that, touching me, and smelling me, I was going to get hard. He would think I actually wanted this when that was the furthest thing from the truth. I did not want to sleep with Amadeo Bianchi, no matter how much my stupid body insisted that was exactly what I wanted.

Amadeo released my throat and his body pressed against mine. Slowly, his lips ran up my neck to my ear. I stopped breathing when his teeth grazed my flesh before he whispered right into my ear.

"I suggest you get dressed if you would like to eat because if you're naked for five more seconds I'm going to throw you on the floor and fuck you until you have rug burn." His fingers feathered over my chest before he grabbed one of my nipples and pinched. When I cried out, he chuckled. "Move, boy."

As soon as he pulled back, I looked anywhere but at his face. My skin was on fire and if I looked at him, it was only going to make the blaze worse. I closed the bathroom door and locked it as if that would do something. There was no doubt that he would and could get inside if he really wanted to.

Hands trembling, I reached out and snagged the clothes he had left for me. I dropped the shirt three times before I swore under my breath, snatched it up, and shoved it down my body. *What is wrong with me?*

Amadeo was not someone I should be lusting after. He was the monster that lurked in the dark, the boogeyman that grown men feared. I was not going to get caught in his wake, thirsting after a man who could just as well slit my throat and throw me away when he was tired of me. And I would exhaust him quickly. I knew myself. I was not a long-term thing, just a fleeting few nights of pleasure before I was either dropped or I ran away.

"He does not own me." I gripped the edge of the sink and stared into my dark eyes. "Remember that."

I shoved away from the sink and stopped looking at myself before I saw something I didn't want to see. Quickly, I tugged on the black sweats he'd given me. They hung off my hips a bit, but I didn't care because they were warm and soft. Even though they were only sweats, they probably cost more than anything I'd had in the past five years. I slipped on socks and they were just as soft and pleasing as the sweats. My entire body felt like it was wrapped in a hug.

My stomach rumbled again and I couldn't avoid leaving the bathroom. Food. I needed something or I was going to pass out. When I stepped out of the bathroom this time, it was Angelo who greeted me. He had a face that might have been attractive years ago, but his eyes had dark bags underneath and his nose had clearly been broken in more than one place. He was huge, wide as hell, but when he looked at me he grinned a little.

"Gotta feel a lot better being here than the dungeon, right?"

I blew out a breath. "You have no idea."

He chuckled. "Come this way. The boss had to step out to make a phone call, but he told me to get you set up with some food."

"What time is it?" I asked as we descended the black stairs to the floor below.

"A little after seven."

"That's it?" I scratched my head. "I really lost track of time."

"Yep, that's what the cells do to you. We never realize how much we need to know the time until it's endless." He waved a hand to the table. "Have a seat. I'll grab the food."

"Thanks."

While he stepped away, I looked around. The whole place had a modern feel, but it seemed...empty. There were no family photos, not a shoe or glass or tie out of place. It was cold, like the cell I had been in before but more lavish with its black, white, and silver colors. This didn't feel like a home. Not that I knew what one of those felt like in the first place.

Angelo walked in and my stomach growled. He placed a plate in front of me with pasta and steak on it, shrimp on the side. When he disappeared, he came back with a big salad bowl, a bowl of bread, butter, and he poured me a glass of wine.

"Holy shit," I stared up at him. "All of this is for me?"

"Yes, but the boss will be joining you," he said as he poured a glass of amber liquid from a heavy glass decanter.

I grabbed a piece of bread and shoved it into my mouth. Even the news that my kidnapper was going to be joining me for dinner wasn't enough to put me off my meal. I looked at Angelo when he came back with Amadeo's plate and fixed him a salad.

"You're not so bad," I said. "I thought you were an asshole in the dungeon, but you're cool."

"We all got jobs to do," he said with a shrug. "I'm not a waiter either, but if the boss says serve the food, you serve the food. He says watch the prisoner, you do that too."

I frowned. "What if he'd asked you to kill me?"

His gaze flickered up. "You'd be dead. Do you need anything else?"

I stared at him, too stunned to form words. Just like that. If Amadeo had told him to pull the trigger, I would have died in that room and no one would know or even cared. Did my family wonder where I was right now? Would they have mourned me if I never showed up again?

"Don't take it personally. Like I said, it's a job," Angelo said with a wave of his hand.

I nodded, but I had no more words left in me. When he walked away, I stared at the food in front of me, my stomach now churning for a completely different reason.

Am I that disposable? Is that how little these people care about others' lives? I clenched my fist, my dull, broken nails digging into my flesh and sending pinpricks of pain over my skin

"Is something wrong?"

Amadeo stood behind his chair at the table and frowned. I searched his face. *Would he have killed me? Just like that?* I couldn't even look at him. I went back to staring at my plate, pushing around the food there with a fork.

"Six," he said sternly. "What is the matter?"

I didn't answer him. Fuck him. My eyes stung and I wanted to laugh at myself. What the fuck was this? Was I going to cry like some goddamned child at the fact that this guy would have killed me? He still could at any moment. The comfort I had fleetingly felt for five seconds was gone. I had traded in one prison for another.

"If you don't speak to me, I'm going to get pissed off," he growled.

"Nothing," I spat out and stabbed a piece of shrimp. "Lay off."

"Do not tell me to lay off."

I looked up at him and wanted to push every button he had. *Fuck Amadeo*. He didn't get to treat me like I was trash. I already knew what I was. If he was going to kill me, he could just do it and get it over with.

"Get fucked," I said.

"Angelo!"

As the man walked into the room, my heart started to race. This was it. He would have his goon do the dirty work and I would be dead. I gripped the edge of the table and looked between the two of them wildly as my throat closed.

"When I left he wasn't in a bad mood." Amadeo sat down. "What happened?"

"He asked a question and I answered it, Boss."

"What question?" he asked as he picked up his glass.

Angelo told him our exact conversation and I made a note to never tell Angelo anything ever again. Of course, he had to tell

Amadeo every word. If he didn't, he would probably be dead himself. I stared at Amadeo as he nodded at Angelo.

"Put your hand on the table, Angelo."

The man's features darkened, but he laid his hand on the table. "Yes, Boss."

"We don't need to go telling everyone our business, do we?"

"No, Boss."

"And you don't need to fuckin' scare him either. Do you?"

"No, Boss," the man said with a shake of his head. "I said too much. It won't happen again."

"I'm sure it won't."

I choked as Amadeo slammed the glass decanter on Angelo's hand. He picked it up and did it again the sound of glass against bone forever imprinted in my ears. Blood stained the bottom of the glass, but Angelo didn't so much as whimper as he pulled his hand back and blood dripped onto the floor.

"Get someone to clean that up," Amadeo said as he picked up his drink again. "Next time, I'll take your tongue out."

"Yes, Boss."

"You're excused for the night," Amadeo said with a wave of his hand. "Get that hand patched up."

"Of course. Goodnight, Boss."

I stared at Amadeo after Angelo left the room. The place was eerily silent except for the sound of the ice that clinked around in his glass. Amadeo sat it down, his eyes met mine, and he tilted his head.

"What?"

"What?" I repeated. "What the fuck? You didn't have to do that to him!"

"He upset you."

"So what!" I snapped. "He upsets me so you fuck up his hand? You probably broke something."

"Maybe," he said with a shrug before he picked up his utensils and started eating.

I stared at him, my heart racing. He didn't see anything wrong with that, did he? The man said a few words to me and I had gotten him injured. I licked my lips and tried to think of something to say that wouldn't turn into me freaking out.

"You didn't need to do that," I repeated. "Just because he said something stupid that wasn't necessary."

Amadeo looked up at me and put his fork down. "This is my world, Six. What is and isn't necessary is entirely up to me. He made you upset, he was corrected, he won't fucking do it again," he said as he laced his fingers together. "Where do you think you are? Do you think this is a place of constructive criticism and golden stars for participation? I'm not a good man, Six. It would serve you well to remember that."

He went back to eating as my stomach twisted and I couldn't tear my eyes away from him. Yes, I had my violent side, but it was never that bad. Was it? I shook my head. No, no damn way. Amadeo was a psychopath.

I'm going to die if I stay with him.

"Six?"

I stared up at him. Amadeo had that look in his eyes again, like he could pounce at any moment and I'd be done for. Instead of answering him, I just waited.

"Let that be the last time you tell me to get fucked or disrespect me again, hmm? Next time I'll punish you."

"Why not now?" I challenged.

"You haven't had enough sleep or food. I'm assuming you're delirious. Tomorrow, you'll come to your senses."

Jokes on you, asshole. I never had any sense to begin with.

Chapter Seven

Amadeo

Six crammed food in his face like it was going to disappear if he didn't. I left him to eat and walked into the kitchen while a woman cleaned up the blood. I did the same to myself, cleaning off the specks of crimson that had been left behind when I crushed Angelo's hand. It rinsed off my skin and swirled around the drain before the pink water was whisked away.

I took a second and dried my hands as I stared off into the distance. Six had looked genuinely upset when I hurt Angelo. *He's a lot more delicate than I thought.* I had to rein in my temper or I was going to make him terrified of me.

Isn't that what I want?

The question remained, but the truth was that I didn't know what I wanted when it came to Six. I knew I wanted *him* but I switched from desiring fear to adoration and back again. He was a complication. I should turn him loose and go about my life if I wasn't going to punish him for stealing my money. But I couldn't bring myself to do it.

I tossed the dish towel down and walked back into the dining room. As soon as I walked in, Six tensed up and his eyes flickered up to meet mine. He looked like an animal out in the wild ready to protect his meal at all costs. But I wasn't going to take the food from him. He needed to eat.

He narrowed his eyes and something in me shifted. I was trying this whole patience thing, but the boy was getting on my nerves. He really did need someone to watch over him and put him in his place or he was going to end up pissing off the wrong person.

"Fix your face. Don't glare at me."

Six's eyes narrowed more. *Does he have a death wish?* I knew grown men who wouldn't look at me the way he was and here was this twenty-one-year-old punk staring me down like he wanted me to lose my shit. *Maybe he did.*

"Come here, Six."

Six straightened up and stared at me, searching my face for something. He snatched up his glass of wine and downed it as if it was the last drink he would ever have. Maybe he thought it was, but I had no intention of killing him. Six was interesting and he had no idea just how much he had me wrapped around his finger even if I didn't show him that.

He was upset about Angelo, but the man had deserved it. Why he would say something to rattle my boy was beyond me, but he would never do it again. The pain was a constant, steady reminder of what *not* to do, and when Angelo returned we wouldn't have to have a damn conversation because we already knew what went wrong.

"Six."

The boy shot up out of his chair. "I'm coming."

He huffed and stalked around the table. I tried not to grin, amused at his tough-guy act. Did other guys get scared when Six walked their way? He looked like he could cause some trouble, but all I could see was a boy who needed someone to care for and guide him. To break and reshape him. He stood in front of me.

"What?" he asked.

"Don't be stupid."

"Yes," he growled. "Daddy?"

"Good boy," I cooed, reaching out and grabbing his hand before I yanked him forward. "Pull your pants down."

Six hesitated. "What?"

I stood up and gripped the hem of Six's pants. They slipped down his thighs and his face flushed as he stared up at me, his jaw unhinged. I reached out and grabbed his upper arm, dragging him into the living room before I sat down.

"Lay over my lap."

"Wait," Six said, hopping from one foot to the other. "Just wait!"

"I will not wait another minute. Lie over my lap. Now."

Six must have seen the seriousness in my eyes before he swallowed hard and cursed under his breath. But he moved closer to my legs before he hit them and slowly lowered himself over my lap. His pale ass screamed for a tan and a whole lotta red marks. I could give him at least one of those things right now.

As he stayed draped over me, I took in the curve of his ass that led to his long legs. My hand slipped down the curve of his back before I let my fingers dance along his skin. He was soft to the touch, but his hands were rough and calloused. How had he gone from upper-class royalty to this?

"What are you going to do?" he muttered.

"I'm going to spank you."

Six scoffed and turned to look up at me. "You can't be serious? How old do you think I am? I don't need a goddamn sp- Fuck!"

My hand crashed against his ass and the sting vibrated over my palm. Immediately, my hand started to grow hot, but it was pleasant. Six's chest rose and fell against my thighs, his breathing sporadic before he glanced back at me again.

"You were serious."

"I was," I said as I raised a brow and ran my hand over his ass. "And I'll do it every single time you act out. I can take a bit of resistance, but you're going to respect me. If it gets too much and you can't take it anymore, you can say red and I'll stop."

"This is bullshit," he growled.

Six clearly wasn't ready to be on the same level. I raised my hand again and the smack echoed through the living room. His skin turned pink before welts started to form and raise along his flesh. I ran my fingers over them before I smacked him again. And again. And again.

He was quiet at first, holding back any sound that tried to escape his chest. I could feel it against my legs, the way he stifled the sounds he made and kept them from leaving his lips. He gripped my thigh, his fingers digging against my slacks.

Did he know how good he looked stretched across my legs, ass in the air, pants down around his ankles? He shook his head, dark hair moving back and forth as he bounced on his toes. I could feel him trying to squirm away, but I was far from done with Six. I laid a hand in the middle of his back to hold him down and slapped his ass again.

"Okay!" he shouted, his voice trembling. "Okay, okay!"

"Okay, what?" I asked. *Smack.* "What are you okaying?" *Smack. Smack. Smack!*

"Goddamnit," he groaned. "Fuck I'll stop."

I grinned as he tried to dig his nails into my skin, but it just felt good. *Smack.* "You'll stop what?"

"Everything!"

"Will you be a good boy for me?"

"Yes...yes, Daddy!" He panted, his body writhing on my lap. "I'll be a good boy for you!"

That was what I wanted to hear. Six needed someone to reel him in, to smooth those rough edges that were too sharp and jagged for the world. I smacked his ass again and he cried out this time, his body trembling under my palm.

I lowered Six to the floor and he panted as he stared up at me. His dark eyes were filled with frustration, but there was something else there as well. A heat that had nothing to do with pain or anger. No, this was pure, wild, lust. I gazed down and he quickly snapped his legs shut after shoving his hand over his cock.

I grabbed his chin and tilted it up so he was forced to look me in the eyes. "You can obey or be punished, Six. That's the way this arrangement works." I ran my sore palm over his stubbled cheek and he frowned. "So, you can do what Daddy says or I can drag you over my lap again and spank you until you get the point. Which would you like?"

"Neither."

I nodded and did exactly what I said I would do. Dragging him over my lap, I made sure he was situated before I smacked my hand against his ass again. This time, I didn't hold back. Every strike was rough and Six shouted and cursed and squirmed, but his cock grew against my thighs. I felt his pre-cum stain my slacks and my body burst into flames.

Calm down. Not yet.

As much as I wanted him to straddle my lap and take my cock, I knew it wasn't time yet. Six needed to be tamed a bit more before I could give in and enjoy him the way I truly wanted to. My hand slid over his skin, soothing the burn before I struck him hard and he cried out, his breathing shaky now.

"Red," he cried, shaking his head. "No more. I'll be good!"

I stilled my hand mid-air before I laid it on his ass gently. Six still squirmed, but he wasn't talking back or spewing nonsense so I rubbed his skin to soothe the burn. Finally, his body relaxed and his shuddering breaths began to smooth out.

"This is me being nice, Six," I said as I ran my hand up and down his body. "But if you get too out of hand, know that I'll skip the spanking next time and put you back down in that cell. I don't have the patience for someone back talking me day and night, Six. I need you to honor your part of the contract."

Six was silent. I moved him to his knees again and he looked everywhere but at me until I tilted his head up. Six's eyes were low, his breathing uneven. I stared at his bottom lip, so soft and pink and plump and waiting to be kissed. I ran my thumb over it and he sat there, not moving or speaking.

"Do you understand?" I asked. "I need to hear an answer, Six."

"Yes." His voice was barely a raspy whisper.

"Yes, what?" I asked.

Six swallowed hard. "Yes, Daddy."

I pushed my fingers through his hair. "Good boy. Are you still hungry?"

Six stared up at me and shrugged. "I don't know."

"Yes, you do. This is an adjustment. I know that, but you'll be okay. If you don't want to eat then get some rest. Which would you like?"

"Food," Six muttered.

I nodded. "Okay, come on."

I helped him stand up and he quickly yanked up his pants but I had already seen the truth. Six might deny it, but he was turned on from that spanking. I wanted to tell him it was okay, but I knew he would rebel against it. Six was the type of guy to go left if you said go right. I had to take my time as best I could but I knew that Six was supposed to belong to me.

As he sat at the table and winced I sat across from him. My heart refused to stop racing and I couldn't take my eyes off of him. Six was sparking something deep inside of me that I thought was dead long ago. He was stirring feelings I thought had gone. But when I looked at the boy I was even more enamored than I was before.

I'll keep you safe no matter what.

Chapter Eight

Six

Amadeo hadn't touched me.

For three days he came home, we ate dinner together, he tried to talk and when I didn't respond, he spanked me. Afterward, we would go to bed but I slept on the very far edge and Amadeo kept his distance. Every nerve in my body was on edge. What was he waiting for? Why hadn't he fucked me yet?

I was allowed to watch his expensive TV while he was gone, but the moment he came home, Amadeo always shut it off. That drove me crazy. No matter what I was watching, he grabbed the remote and ended it before telling me to sit at the table. Like I was a damn child. *I'm losing my mind in this place.*

Glancing up at the wall I looked at the time. It was almost seven. Amadeo was going to be home soon and he'd drag me off to the table to have dinner together. I looked back at the television before my eyes flickered up once more to the ticking clock before they slid down again.

What the hell am I doing? Waiting for him?

Amadeo had my head all messed up! I groaned and shook my head as the door opened. I sat up straighter, but it was Angelo who walked into the loft. His hand was bandaged and I didn't want to know what his hand looked like underneath.

"The Boss wants you to come with me."

"Where am I going?" I asked.

"His other home. Your room is ready."

I blew out a breath. "Of course it is. Let me put on my shoes." I snagged them and tugged on the expensive sneakers Amadeo's men had dropped off the day after my arrival. "Why isn't he here?"

"He had a meeting that might run a little long so he sent me."

I glanced up at Angelo and tilted my head. "Hey, um I'm really sorry about your hand. I didn't know I would get you in trouble."

He held up a hand. "It wasn't your fault. As I said, it's all part of the job. Besides, nothing's broken. Don't worry about it."

"Are you sure?" I asked, frowning.

Angelo nodded. "Positive. But we should get a move on. Amadeo isn't a patient man."

"Tell me about it," I muttered under my breath.

I grabbed the hoodie that smelled like Amadeo no matter how many times I asked for it to be washed and pulled it over my head. His scent suffocated me, but I ground my teeth and ignored it. Once I was ready to go, Angelo made me walk beside him and led me to the parking garage. We climbed into a waiting car and pulled off.

"What's his other house like?" I asked, unable to stop myself from talking to fill the uneasy silence in the car.

Angelo glanced out the window. "It's a late nineteenth-century revival. Pretty big. There's a garden and a pool so I'm sure you'll be comfortable."

I nodded, but I wanted to scream that I couldn't get comfortable. Not because of the size of the loft, but because I was a prisoner. How was anyone supposed to relax when they knew they were being held against their will? I was silent for the rest of the drive trying not to spiral into despair or more self-pity, but it was already hitting me.

The car left the city behind and we entered an upscale suburb. We passed a huge set of iron gates and slid up the driveway before the car came to a stop. I stared at the house.

Pretty big. Angelo had said the place was "pretty big," but that was an understatement! The house was enormous, with two floors that extended far and wide. There were even stairs leading up to the front of the house and another set that wound up to the door. A fountain stood in front lined on either side with sprawling flowers and bushes. It looked like something out of a Greek textbook.

"Goddamn," I muttered.

"We should move a little faster," Angelo said gently. "Amadeo has already arrived it seems."

I nodded and followed him up the stairs. When I reached the second set, there was Amadeo standing at the door. His eyes roamed over me and my heart all but stopped. He pushed his fingers through his hair and his gaze tracked me. Once more I felt like prey, but I kept my head up and refused to let him see me as that.

"What took so long?" Amadeo asked.

"The most direct route was taken, Boss," Angelo said. "Here he is."

The moment I was near him, Amadeo grabbed my arm and dragged me into the house. I glanced over my shoulder and Angelo shrugged before he trailed us at a safe distance.

"Where are we going? I can walk on my own you know," I said with a huff as he led me up a flight of stairs to the second floor. "Amadeo!"

He turned on his heels. "What did you call me?"

I swallowed thickly. "Daddy. Where are we going, Daddy?"

Amadea searched my face before he turned around again. I followed along because I had no choice. We walked down a hallway and he opened one of the doors and let me inside.

"This is your room."

It was huge. The bed was made up in lavish black blankets with gray pillows and the whole room was done in those shades. Gray, black, cream. It was sophisticated without being too over the top and I had to admit that I liked it. It might be a jail cell, but it was a nice-looking one.

"I believe that's yours," he said, nodding to a bag in the corner.

I walked over to it and dropped to my knees. "My duffle!" I pushed through it and found the last of my possessions. I had been sure I would never see any of it again. Glancing up at Amadeo the words thank you were on the tip of my tongue, but I didn't know how to say it. Instead, I dug into my bag.

There were a few clothes that Amadeo hadn't thrown away, which I was happy about. Underneath them, there was a small book of photos that I kept with me at all times. That was the most important thing out of all of them. My phone had been confiscated, but I wasn't surprised at that. However, my favorite ring with a huge letter S was still at the bottom of the bag and I slipped it on.

"What's the ring?"

I glanced up at Amadeo. "It was my gift from my friend."

"What friend?" he growled.

I moved back a little and stood up. "An old one in high school."

The frown on Amadeo's lips intensified. "Why is he giving you jewelry? Were you two dating? Are you still in contact?"

I sighed. "You're worrying for nothing. I haven't seen Ty in a few months now, doubt I'll see him anytime soon either," I mumbled under my breath.

"A few months." He stepped forward, his eyes narrowing.

There was that look on his face again. It screamed *danger* and I wanted to retreat and fight him at the same time because I didn't owe him a damn thing. Not who I knew or who had bought what for me. This was a temporary six-month arrangement and then we would be going our separate ways.

"Let's drop it." I ran my hand over my hairy cheeks and grimaced. "Can I get a razor today? I need to shave."

Amadeo stared me down a while longer and I could see the wheels turning in his head. "The bathroom is right here," he said as he walked over to another door and opened it for me.

I stepped in and looked around. The bathroom was done in the same sophisticated colors as the bedroom, but at least it wasn't overly huge. I could enjoy this one. I walked over to the counter where Amadeo was crouching down and emerged with a razor, shaving cream, and a towel.

"Sit on the counter."

I stared at him, my brow rising. "Why?"

"Because I told you to," he snapped. "Counter. Now." When I laid my hand on it, he stopped me. "Take off your clothes first."

I swallowed thickly and searched his face for any sign that he wasn't serious. But Amadeo was always serious. I gripped the hoodie I wore and hesitated.

"Is there a problem?" he asked.

Shaking my head, I steeled myself and tugged off the hoodie. "No, Daddy."

"Good boy. Strip all of it off."

What is he going to do? I had gotten used to him making me get rid of my clothes for spankings, was this that? It didn't feel like it. As I pulled off my shirt and pushed the rest of my clothes down my hands shook slightly and I tried to force them to be still. Amadeo didn't rush me however, he simply stood there, watching. Finally, I straightened up and he patted the counter. I hopped up on it and sucked in a deep breath.

Amadeo undid his sleeves and rolled them up his forearms. I caught sight of one of his tattoos, a skull, gun, and rose. I stared at it before my eyes ran up the length of his muscled arms, veins protruding against his olive skin. Mesmerized, I completely forgot that I was naked until he laid a hand on my thigh.

"Open your legs."

My mouth went dry. "Why?"

"You ask too many goddamn questions," he growled before he squeezed my leg. "Open them. Wide."

"Yes, Daddy."

I tried to force them open, but my body kept resisting the order that my brain gave. Amadeo stood there, watching me patiently. I expected him to lose his temper, but he didn't. Closing my eyes, I snapped my legs open and Amadeo immediately took up residence between them.

"Hold still."

I opened my eyes as he began to slather my cheeks with shaving cream. He picked up a straight razor and I sucked in a breath. Amadeo with a dangerous weapon in his hand? Yeah, that wasn't exactly where I wanted to be, but it didn't seem like I had a choice.

The blade slid against my skin and I held my breath trying to stay as still as I possibly could. Every swipe of the razor against my flesh made my heart race. It didn't help that the only thing I had to look at the entire time was Amadeo. His face was flat as he concentrated on shaving me.

He's not a bad-looking guy at all. Amadeo's hair was so thick and dark that I was itching to touch it. The strong line of his jaw that was covered in hair and his smooth cheeks begged to be traced. As I stared, something stirred in my belly and I felt heat sweep over my body. Amadeo's green eyes flickered up to me and he glanced away quickly.

What was that about?

"Lie down," he said.

I looked around us. The counter was definitely big enough to hold me. I looked at him once more and when he didn't budge I gave up and laid down. The coolness of the counter made me shiver and I watched as Amadeo picked up the shaving cream and put more on my pubes before he picked up the straight razor again.

"Hey, hey, hey! What the fuck man?" I panted, shaking my head. "Whose dick do you think you're going near with that goddamn thing?"

"Do you not trust me?"

I stared at Amadeo. "Fuck no I don't," I spat. "Are you insane? Just use a regular razor."

"No, I want to use this one." He pushed my legs apart and his eyes roamed over me hungrily. "Hold still and it'll be fine."

My heart skipped a beat. I was going to die. I sucked in a breath as he lowered the straight razor and slid it over my skin. He kept his fingers on my skin, pulling it taut as he shaved me slowly. Amadeo leaned closer, his breath ghosting over my cock. The heat made it twitch and I flushed as an embarrassing noise that sounded a hell of a lot like a moan left my lips.

Amadeo glanced up at me. "See? Is that so bad?" He ran his thumb over a smooth patch of skin. "Be a good boy for Daddy and I'll take care of it."

I stared at him, my chest rising and falling fast, but I finally nodded. Amadeo cast one of those rare grins my way before he went back to work. I laid still, watching him as he took his sweet time shaving me. Amadeo was still a huge bastard, but there were moments like this when he was so soft and gentle that I sometimes forgot what a monster he was.

Why is he being so nice to me?

"Ah!" I hissed as he nicked me and glared at him, the illusion shattered. "You cut me," I growled.

"Slip of the hand," he said as he picked up the towel, wet it, and wiped the area. He inspected it and my eyes widened as he leaned down and kissed the nick. Amadeo's tongue darted out and he licked it in one quick swipe, my blood on his tongue as he moaned.

Fuck.

In that moment I forgot how much I hated him. Our eyes connected and my pulse tripped. Amadeo leaned over and his lips pressed against mine hungrily. My mouth opened up accepting his tongue as the taste of blood danced on my tongue. I tried to moan, but he swallowed it with his kiss, his hand gripping my inner thigh roughly.

I want this man to fuck me until I forget what any other cock has ever felt like.

The thought was so involuntary but violent that I was shocked by it. I pulled away from Amadeo, panting as I shoved a hand against his chest. He growled and I shoved away from him even more. Amadeo blinked, his eyes losing that blazing inferno and returning to normal.

"We're almost done. Lie still."

I nodded when he didn't tear his eyes away from mine and he finally went back to work. My lips still tingled from the forcefulness of his kiss, the iron taste of blood lingering on my tongue. Amadeo finished up his shaving and he tapped the blade on the sink before he began to clean me up. He inspected me closely, but the nick had stopped bleeding almost as soon as it had started.

"Are you okay?" he asked.

He...cared about how I was? What was this? Some sick mindfuck?

But when I looked in Amadeo's eyes I didn't see deception, just curiosity and a hint of worry. His jaw was tight and I wanted to reach out and touch it.

"Yeah."

"Are you sure?" he asked. "I didn't mean to hurt you. Not like that."

"It's fine," I whispered, still shocked by the way he was acting. "I'm okay."

Amadeo let out a heavy sigh. "Good." He wiped me down one last time and nodded. "You're done." He held out his hand. "Come on, I'll help you up."

He pulled me into a sitting position and before I could gather myself his lips were on mine again. Amadeo's hand pressed against the back of my head, keeping me close before he grabbed my hips and yanked me closer. He rubbed his clothed cock against mine and I groaned.

What is he doing to me?

"Shower and get prepped," Amadeo whispered against my lips before his eyes met mine. "I plan to collect on our contract tonight."

A shiver ran through me, but I nodded. There was no way out of it, might as well get it over with. "Yes, Daddy."

"Good boy." He lifted my hand. "Take this goddamn ring off before you come back in the room."

"Yes, Daddy."

Amadeo graced me with another grin before he walked out of the bathroom. Once he was gone I finally released the breath that had been burning my lungs.

What the hell had I gotten myself into?

Chapter Nine

Amadeo

What am I doing?

I pushed my fingers through my hair as I stared at the bathroom door. Six was right on the other side, the water running as he went to take a shower. I left him to it and walked through the double doors that led out to his balcony. Sitting at the table, I took out a pack of smokes and lit one up before I tilted my head back.

"Fuck."

He was so goddamned hot I had almost bent him over and fucked him over the counter. The way he'd gasped when I licked his blood, the look in his dark eyes that begged for more. I shook my head.

This was a six-month agreement, but I was already getting attached. How could I not? Everything about Six seemed as if he was made for me. His attitude, the way he moaned, the taste of his lips against mine. I was losing control. All I wanted to do was go back in there, wrap a collar around his throat, attach a leash, and keep him locked up in a cage.

What was it about Six that made me so...soft? I could see it from a mile away, but I couldn't stop.

My phone rang, dragging me away from my thoughts of Six. I sat the cigarette in the ashtray and looked at the number. *Great.* I stabbed the answer key.

"This had better be fucking good."

"Sorry to interrupt you, your majesty," Gabriele answered. "But no one in the family has heard from you since Monday. What the fuck, Ama?"

I wiped a hand down my face. "Something came up."

"Something or someone?" Gabriele asked. "Because I hear you've been spending your time with someone in your loft."

I had picked up my cigarette and it broke in my fingers when he said that. "Who the fuck has been talking about me?"

"Don't worry about it. Who is he? What are you up to?"

"You're too nosey for your own damn good," I growled. "Back off."

"Ama..."

"I have everything under control, okay? Why are you so worried about what I do in my own home?"

"Because you have a tendency to get too invested," he stressed. "One look and you're obsessed and then what happens when you get your heart broken? You go off the deep end and I'm the one left picking up the pieces while you're off on a killing spree." He sighed and I could imagine him pinching the bridge of his nose. "I don't have time to clean up a city-wide blood bath, so please, please be careful. Questo è tutto ciò che chiedo. Okay?"

I sighed. "You're a pain in my ass."

"Yeah, I love you too, asshole. I better go." I heard a commotion in the background and Gabriele shooting off rapid-fire Italian to someone in the background. "The fight is starting. I'll talk to you later."

"Tomorrow," I said sternly. "I've got shit to do tonight."

"Are you following Nic's advice and getting some ass?"

The bathroom door opened as I lit another cigarette and Six walked out, water rolling down his body. I tracked water droplets as they slipped over his skin and he turned, our eyes locking. He had taken off the ring and he had a towel in hand, drying himself off before he looked away from me.

"Something like that," I muttered to Gabriele. "Gotta go."

"Remember what I said, Ama! Seriously, don't-"

I hung up and shoved the phone back into my pocket. Gabriele could wait until tomorrow. He wasn't in any trouble. More than likely he was happy getting to watch some bloodshed. And I was happy to watch Six.

He moved around the room elegantly and I could see the old world money that he had once come from. There was a noble air to everything he did without him even realizing it. He might have denounced wealth and everything to do with it, but he was still born and bred from money and it was easy to see.

I stubbed out the cigarette and walked back into his room, transfixed as he dropped the towel on the floor. He looked nervous, his usual bravado silent now that he was faced with the actual possibility of sleeping with me. But I wanted that feisty, fiery boy that I had first become enthralled with.

"Pick that up," I said, nodding toward the towel.

Six glanced down at it. "Does it really matter?"

"Do it, boy, or I'll start tonight's activities off with a long, hard spanking."

I saw the words on his lips. *Do it.* Oh, he wanted to say it so badly but he was holding back, trying to control himself. I loved watching him struggle with himself.

Six snatched it off of the floor and balled it up. "Happy?"

I grabbed a handful of his hair and he moaned as our lips crashed together. As much shit as he talked, he was putty in my hands. Why did he think he could resist me? It was almost entertaining if it wasn't so infuriating.

Stepping forward, I kept moving until he hit the bed and tumbled into it. Six moved back slowly and I followed him, crawling over the bedspread as I leaned down and took his lips again. He arched his back, pressing up against me as his tongue tangled with mine.

"You hate me so much, but you kiss me like you're starving," I pointed out as I traced his bottom lip with my tongue. "Why is that?"

"Fuck you," he spat.

"Watch it." I tilted his head to the side and attacked his neck, kissing and sucking his skin until he cried out. "Don't piss Daddy off."

Six's moans were intoxicating. I could listen to them all day long and never get tired of them for a second. Biting his bottom lip, I sat up on my knees and gazed down at him. I finally moved off of him and sat on the bed.

"Take my shirt off."

He took his time climbing off of the bed and standing in front of me. When he looked up at me I grinned.

"Hurry up," I taunted.

Six huffed. "Has anyone ever told you that you're a real asshole?"

"Yes, everyone including you." I tilted my head. "Why should I be nice?"

"If you were just a *little* nicer, maybe I wouldn't want to punch you in the face every day," he muttered as he reached out and began to unbutton my black shirt.

"You want to punch me?" I asked. "Do it."

Six looked as if he was honestly contemplating it and that just made me want him even more. Instead of taking me up on my offer, however, he went back to undoing my shirt before he opened it up and his eyes searched my chest. I knew he was taking in the myriad of tattoos there and I let him.

Reaching out, I grabbed the back of his thigh and he blinked at me. I couldn't stop touching him. Everything about Six felt so much more real than anything else in my life. Being who I was, it wasn't easy to let anyone in and I didn't even want to. People always found a way to get close to you before they stabbed you in the back. I had learned that very early on. But when I looked at Six, I yearned for all of the things I'd lost when I became head of the Bianchi family.

"What's wrong?" Six asked.

I frowned. "What?"

"You looked..." He ran a hand down my chest. "Sad."

Did I? I reached up and touched my face trying to see if I had let some emotion slip while I was deep in thought. Six had clearly seen it. I was getting too close to the boy, showing parts of myself that needed to stay hidden for me, for him, for everyone I protected.

"Pants," I said. "Take them off."

Six nodded. "Okay."

"When are you going to get that right?" I asked. "Not okay."

"Yes, Daddy," Six said with a barely hidden roll of his eyes before he shivered. "It's insane."

"But you like saying it," I mused. "I can tell."

Six shook his head. "You're crazy! I have never said I liked saying that shit." He undid my pants and none too gently yanked them down my thighs before he pulled them and my boxers off completely. "You're making things up."

"I can see it," I countered. "Whenever you call me Daddy, you get so turned on you get flustered."

"I don't do flustered," he grumbled.

"No? Then what's this," I asked as I grabbed his cock and gave it a squeeze. "Then why are you so hard for me?" Before he could answer I pulled him on top of my body and rolled us both over until his back pressed against the soft blanket. "Hmm? Why is your cock so rigid in my hand?"

"Because..."

I tilted his head and forced him to look at me, my hand releasing his dick to hold his chin. "No, there's no looking away. I want your eyes on me the whole time."

Six swallowed hard. "I...I can't," he muttered. "I never do. Just," he squeezed his eyes shut. "Put me on my knees and fuck me like that," he whispered.

I stared at him and felt the rush of anger take hold, squeezing my heart. "What the fuck? What moron would screw someone that looked as beautiful as you from behind?" I ran my hand over his cheek, my thumb dragging over his bottom lip. "You are far too intoxicating not to take in every sigh, moan, and gasp that I'm going to pull from your lips."

Six's eyes opened and I saw more beneath the anger and lust he usually displayed. Was that fear? Uncertainty? I wished I could read his mind, but I was left to grasp at straws as I gazed at him.

I was telling the boy entirely too much and I had to remind myself that this was all a fantasy. Six months. That was all the time I had before I would keep my word and turn him free because if nothing else, I was a man of my word. My heart would shatter when he walked away, but we were already on this treacherous road and I didn't want to turn back. I had been numb for so long.

I just wanted to feel *something*.

"You think I'm beautiful," Six mused, shaking his head. "I think you're delusional."

I grinned. "Maybe a little. For you."

He frowned. "Why me? There is absolutely nothing special about me."

Six was so wrong about that. At the casino, I had watched him for months. I saw the way people flocked to him, his charm and easy-going laughter. He was smart, cunning, but wild, and maybe even a little dangerous too. The darkness in him screamed for the monster in me and I was going to protect and keep him safe no matter who I had to kill or what I had to destroy. Even if the thing I destroyed was myself.

"Just keep your eyes on me," I said to him, unable to voice what I felt. "Okay?"

"Yes, Daddy."

The words made my heart squeeze and I wanted to sink my teeth into his flesh and tear into his bones. Yes, Daddy. Two words, so simple, but when he said them like he meant them, I was on top of the world. It was a high that I never wanted to come down from.

"Good boy." I watched the way his eyes lit up. Did he realize that happened whenever I praised him? "Lay right here. I'll be right back."

Six nodded and for once he had gone quiet. I rolled off of him and went to the nightstand to gather the lube and condoms. After I had crushed Angelo's hand, I was afraid that look of terror would forever be etched on his features when he looked at me, but it wasn't. More than anything I saw the conflict in his eyes and I knew that he felt something. Maybe he wasn't as far as I was, but it was growing.

He wanted me.

I turned back to the bed and Six was watching me. Smiling at him, I moved back onto the bed and tore into the condom with my teeth. I spit the wrapper out and slipped the condom free before I rolled it up the length of my hardened cock. As I poured lube into my palm, I glanced down at Six and he still stared at me.

"Are you nervous?" I asked.

He bit his lip. "This shit is new to me," he sighed. "So just...hurry up and get it done already."

"No," I said. "I'm going to take my time."

Six growled. "Why the fuck do you have to be such a dick all the time?"

I shrugged. "It's in my DNA." I ran my hand over my length before I worked some over his hole. He sucked in a breath and I grinned. "Relax. You'll be fine."

"Does it matter? You're paying for it so what I like doesn't mean shit."

I stiffened at his words. Six looked up at me before his eyes cut to the side and my chest tightened painfully. He was right. It was all an illusion, one that was going to shatter. But I wanted to hold onto it for a little while longer.

Moving between his thighs, I pressed my cock against his entrance and drove forward. Six gasped, his arm wrapping around the back of my neck as I rolled my hips and pushed in deeper.

"A-Ama...Daddy, please," he cried out.

"If I'm paying you and don't give a fuck about you, why should I go slow?" I growled at him. I wiped my lube slicked hand in the blanket before I thrust forward sharply. "Since that's who you think I am, I won't try to change your mind."

Six cried out, his nails digging into my back. "Fuck you!" he snapped, his hips moving on their own as he met my firm thrusts and he glared up at me. "You think this is the roughest I've ever been fucked?" he spat. "This is nothing."

I grabbed his wrists and slammed them against the bed. Just like that he was back to infuriating me. Six had a way of getting under my skin and I detested it. I slammed into him and his back arched up from the bed as his mouth opened, but no sound left it.

"I'll show you just how much of a monster I am, Six," I whispered against his ear. "I'm going to make it so that your ass can only ever feel pleasure from my cock. Even when you finally walk away, all you'll dream about is fucking me."

"Never," he spat. "I fucking hate you."

"Hate me harder," I demanded as I snapped my hips forward and dragged a choked moan from his lips. "That's right, baby. Take Daddy's big cock and know that you will never get away from me."

Six's eyes watered. "Asshole," he ground out as his head tilted back exposing his glorious throat. "I'm going to kill you!"

"You can try," I chuckled. "So many people have." I leaned down and nipped at his throat making a gasp twist from his lips. "No no, don't stop moving your hips now. Move harder. Faster. Come on, I want you to get me off."

"Fuck you!"

"Just like that," I groaned as he clamped down around me, his body bouncing on its own. "Tell Daddy you love it."

"Ah," Six panted, shaking his head. "Fuck I just..." He pulled his hand free and it fluttered down before he wrapped it around his cock. "I love it, Daddy. Fuck me harder!"

I chuckled as his eyes glazed over and I knew he meant every word. He couldn't escape from me this way, not the way he could if I had put him on his belly. Right now, there was nowhere to look but at me, nowhere to escape when I kept drawing him back to reality.

"You're doing so good," I moaned as I nipped his bottom lip. "I don't think I've ever felt this amazing."

Every inch of my body felt like it had been set ablaze. Six clenched; I moaned. He rolled his hips, I squeezed his wrist tighter to the bed. And when his eyes gazed into mine I all but broke apart into a million little pieces.

"On my knees," Six moaned, shaking his head. "Please, Daddy."

"No," I growled. "You're not getting away from me."

All of Six's fire was fizzling out and in its place was the boy I knew was underneath it all. He cried out and moaned, shook his head, and tried to draw me closer while pushing me away. But I wasn't going anywhere. Every part of Six belonged to me. Maybe he didn't know that yet, but he would soon find out.

I slowed down and took in the way his body moved, the way he gazed up at me with half-lidded eyes. Leaning down, I captured his lips and slipped my tongue into his mouth. Our tongues tangled and heat ran over my body in waves.

"Daddy, I'm so full," he moaned. He looked so high I couldn't help but grin. "Please, it's enough."

"Almost there, baby." I left a trail of kisses over his smooth jaw. "Can you take a little more for Daddy? If not, you can call red and I'll stop. So can you take more for me?"

Six nodded hard. "Yes...yes, Daddy!"

"Such a good boy. You're doing so well." I leaned down and took one of his nipples into my mouth. When he cried out, I drove inside of him harder and moaned. "You have to cum, don't you?"

"Yes, Daddy," he panted.

I sat up so I could look at him. "Ask nicely."

Six gritted his teeth and I saw him battling with himself once more. My cock jumped. There was something addictive about making him fight himself. He licked his lips, closed his eyes, and then opened them once more. I saw the resolve in his eyes and I knew he had made up his mind.

"Can I cum, Daddy? Please?"

There it was. I picked up the pace once more and left a trail of kisses and bites down his left shoulder to match the right.

"Yes," I moaned. "Cum for me, boy. Fuck, you're squeezing so tight." I pressed my forehead against his. "Just like that. God!"

Six bit into his arm as he tried to muffle his moans. I grabbed his arm and pulled it away. He fought to try to get it back into his mouth, but I refused to let him.

"Give me all of your moans," I growled. "You will not hold *anything* back from me. Do you understand?"

"Yes, Daddy!"

I barrelled toward my orgasm at breakneck speed as I grabbed Six's hips and thrust inside of him wildly. He stopped holding back anything and I watched as he let loose, writhing on my cock as I shoved in deep. I threw my head back and groaned as pleasure tore through my body.

Next time I'm cumming inside of him and nothing can stop me.

I wanted to feel my load filling up his insides, embrace the heat of his ass, and watch the way my cum poured from his hole. For now, I had to settle with what I had and I wasn't complaining, but next time I would have *everything*. I braced my hands on either side of Six's head and panted as he gazed up at me.

I could stay like this all night.

Six licked his lips. "Is that it?" He mumbled, closing his eyes. "Are we done for the night?"

I stiffened and stared down at him. "Was it that awful?"

"Yes," he snapped, his eyes flying open. "So if you're done, get off of me!"

I glared at him. "If you had never stolen from me, I wouldn't pay to be inside of you. Reel it in before you pay off the rest of your debt in your own personal cell."

Six shoved his hands against my chest. "Get off of me." He hit me again and my eyes widened. "I said get off!"

Anger rose in my throat and choked me. *Ungrateful little bastard.* I pulled out of Six swiftly and he cried out before he flopped back onto the bed. Without another word, I tossed the condom out and yanked on my pants before I stormed out of the room, slamming the door behind me. I walked down the hall to my office and poured myself a drink with a trembling hand.

I hit a key on my computer and typed in the password before the screen showed a video of Six. He laid in his bed, his hands pressed against his face. I turned up the volume and heard...sniffling.

Had I done something wrong? Six had been just as into it as I was, right? Suddenly, I felt clammy. Had I crossed the line?

I brought the glass to my lips, but the amber liquid tasted like rust in my mouth. I threw it. The glass crashed against the wall and shattered, whiskey raining down on the hardwood floor. I closed my eyes and opened them again to stare at Six.

You need to run away from a monster like me, Six. Get the hell out of here.

I should have just turned him loose, but I couldn't let him go. Especially not now, not when we had shared a moment. I dug my nails into my scalp and reeled in the scream that threatened to break free.

Why couldn't I be normal?

Chapter Ten

Six

Amadeo Bianchi had broken my brain.

How could I have fallen for that shit?

Why did it feel so good?

Last night was burned into my brain. Every kiss and caress was permanently seared into my soul and I couldn't get that monster of a man out of my head. The way he grinned at me, the growl in his voice. It was like I was still there, still wrapped in his arms as he took me apart.

I had tried to keep up my walls, to keep him at bay, but he had crossed the line making me look at him. Making me *feel* things I didn't want to feel. The word Daddy had slipped out of my mouth so easily and it had felt right.

I dragged myself out of bed as the sun hit my face. Groaning, I took a step and felt soreness lace up my backside. My hole throbbed and I reached back to run a finger over it. Immediately, I thought about Amadeo. How he'd pinned me to the bed and fucked me feverishly. My face heated and I quickly snatched my hand away.

"What the hell is wrong with me?"

Amadeo had exposed something in me. Every one of his sweet nothings and good boys and whispered praise had ripped off the plaster that covered my emptiness and he had touched raw emotion. I hated him even more for it. For the first time in years I had cried and it was all because of him.

I made my way to the bathroom slowly and turned on the shower. As steam filled the room, I glanced at the marble counter and imagined lying up there again with his lips pressed against my skin. My cock stirred and I swore under my breath.

He's in my head.

I dug my nails into my palms and forced myself to take a long, deep breath before I blew it out. All I had to remember is that Amadeo Bianchi was a son of a bitch who killed and maimed without blinking an eye. That's it. I had a debt to pay off and if I had to keep screwing him, fine. But I wasn't going to let him get to me.

God, I hope he's not here.

Right now, I needed some distance between me and Amadeo. I prayed he was at work and I could get some time to myself. I leaned against the shower wall and ran a hand down my body. Right away, my skin ignited and I groaned. It was only a flash, but I imagined Amadeo pushing me up against the wall and taking me roughly.

"What the fuck? What moron would screw someone that looked as beautiful as you from behind?"

His words played on an endless loop and I groaned as I thumped my head against the wall. The man was nowhere near me and I was still being tormented. Why couldn't he just fuck me on my knees and go about his business? Why did he have to say such stupid things to me?

I slammed my hand against the wall and snatched up a bottle of body wash. "Stop it," I lectured myself. "You're letting yourself get caught up by some guy because he talks pretty? Come on, wake up. This is clearly Stockholm Syndrome."

Right, that was all this was because there was no way in hell I had anything but hate for Amadeo Bianchi. I washed up and lingered in the warm water until my skin felt like it would boil right off. Finally, I stepped out of the shower and dried myself off. When I walked back into the room, I froze.

Lying in the middle of the bed that had been stripped of the sheets and blankets from the night before was a stack of clothes neatly folded and waiting for me. I glanced around, my heart skipping a beat as I expected Amadeo to be sitting in some dark corner, staring at me. He was nowhere in sight, but I still felt as if his eyes were on me.

Walking over to the pile of clothes, I picked up a pair of new boxers and slipped them on. They were warm as if they had just come out of the dryer, all of my clothes were. I tugged on the sweats and t-shirt before I grabbed the hoodie.

Instantly, my mistake hit me. Amadeo's scent was everywhere as I tugged the garment over my head. It was like he was standing right beside me, that frown on his lips that twitched into the most ludicrously sweet smile.

Why does this damn thing always smell like him? And why am I not ripping it off of my body?

Instead, I lifted the front of it and took in a short whiff. Yes, it was definitely his cologne; a combination of woodsy and clean that I could inhale all day. I quickly dropped the thing and shook my head before I focused on the bed.

Underneath the clothes, there was a note and a bottle of pain pills along with a water bottle. I opened the pills first and swallowed two so I could dull the ache of my ass. It had calmed down after the shower, but it was still there. *I should be a hell of a lot angrier about that.* Shaking my head, I picked up the note.

Meet me for breakfast downstairs. It's the first door on the left. Unless you would rather stay in your room to eat in which case I'll have someone bring something up for you.

Amadeo

Blowing out a breath, I threw the note on the bed. "Asshole."

There wasn't so much as an apology for him fucking me the way he had. Or for the things he'd said. I knew I was his whore for the next six months, but he didn't have to make me feel as if...

As if that's all it is? That's exactly what this arrangement was when we made it. Suck it up.

I pushed my fingers through my still damp hair and growled. *Fuck that.* I wasn't going to hide in the prison cell that he was calling my room as if I was too afraid to face him. Looking through the drawers I found a pair of socks and tugged on my sneakers. I had one goal today: Find any weaknesses in his security so I could get the hell out.

When I entered the door, I found a dining room and a huge table. At the head of it was Amadeo. My heart sped up and I swallowed thickly. He was in one of his classic tailored suits, but this one was a deep crimson, his tie gold. It was flashy. Did Amadeo do flashy?

His green eyes flickered up from his phone and he tilted his head at me. I felt his gaze slide up and down my body and felt exposed all over again. He pushed his fingers through his hair and gestured to a seat.

"Sit."

Immediately, I snapped back to reality and growled. "I am not a dog."

Amadeo stared me down. "Sit down or skip breakfast. It's up to you."

"I changed my mind," I said as I turned on my heels. "I'll eat upstairs."

"You will sit down! Now."

A shiver ran up my spine and I moved on autopilot, turning and walking toward the table like a man possessed. I stopped short of actually sitting down. *How the hell did he do that?* It was like he was controlling my stupid brain.

"Not that chair," he said, calming down again before he pulled the one out beside him. "This one."

I sighed and walked over to the chair. This seat had a cushion in it. I glanced at the others and there wasn't one in them. Amadeo's eyes stayed trained on me and he searched my face for god knows what before I finally sat down. My ass was grateful not to have to sit on anything too hard right now and I settled in.

"What would you like for breakfast?"

I glanced at him. "I don't know."

He raised a brow. "Fine, then I'll choose for you." He typed on his phone and sat it down after a minute or two. "It will be ready shortly."

I blinked at him. "What did you do, order in?"

"No," he shook his head. "My chef is in the kitchen and has a screen set up so I can order without having to go into the kitchen. She likes her space and I like mine," he said before he picked up his coffee mug. "Do you want coffee?"

"Yeah."

Amadeo stood up and picked up the coffee pot that had been left on the table. I wanted to argue with him that I could pour it myself, but he was on edge and I didn't want to set him off. I looked at how tight his jaw was, how stiff his shoulders were.

What's up with him? I should be the irritated one.

He poured me a cup of coffee and I declined the sugar and cream. I took a sip and the bitter cup of black coffee warmed me. I hummed happily. The one thing I never wanted to live without again was coffee.

"Is it okay?"

I opened my eyes and glanced at him. *Why is he being so nice? What the hell does he want?*

"Yeah," I said. "It's fine." He nodded and went back to looking at his phone, but I caught him stealing glances when he didn't think I was looking at him. I couldn't take it anymore. "Why the fuck are you being so nice to me after last night?"

Amadeo sighed and sat the phone down. "I wasn't mean to you last night."

"Yes, you were," I growled.

"How?"

I searched his face, looking for the anger I thought would be there, but it didn't exist. Amadeo's face was completely passive, but... *Is he genuinely asking?*

I licked my lips. "Nevermind."

"No, tell me," he said sternly. "What did I do wrong? This is what you agreed to, isn't it? So, how was I mean?"

You made me feel like a cheap whore and part of me loved it. The other part of me fucking hates you for it.

I couldn't tell him that. It felt too real and raw and we were only a passing thing, something I would forget about years from now. Grabbing my coffee cup, I picked it up and drank more of the hot liquid trying not to melt under his withering gaze.

"Six." When I didn't answer, he growled. "Look at me and talk to me, boy. Now!"

I glared at him. "Fuck off."

Amadeo's eyes darkened. I swallowed thickly as he stood up and walked toward me. With every step he took, my breathing faltered. I was going to pass out.

"Fine," he said as he towered over me. "Enjoy your breakfast."

That's it? He breezed by me and I could breathe again as he walked out of the dining room. I stared at the door for a while, my pulse still racing, but he didn't return. A woman walked in and sat a plate in front of me before Angelo joined me.

"Boss told me to give you this," he said as he laid a phone beside the plate. "It only dials two numbers; mine and his. He said if you need anything to let him know."

I snatched up the phone and glared at it. "Why is he being so nice?"

Angelo shrugged. "Beats me."

"You've never seen him like this before?"

The man glanced around before he lowered his voice. "No, it's weird. But let's not talk about him. I would like to continue to use my other hand."

I swallowed thickly and nodded. "Right. Sorry." I sat the phone down and picked up my fork.

The breakfast Amadeo had prepared for me was something an old person would eat. Fruit, egg white omelets, turkey sausage, and whole-wheat toast. *Is this what he eats? I mean no wonder he looks that good but gross.*

"Can I have something else for breakfast?" I asked Angelo.

"Anything you want. There's an app on the phone where you can order."

"Thanks."

I picked up the phone and was about to find the app when I saw a text. Daddy. I rolled my eyes at my phone. He had to have programmed the damn thing himself.

Daddy: You are to eat your breakfast. If you don't like that one then choose something else. But you'll also take the vitamins I'll have brought to you and drink plenty of water. You're underweight.

I scoffed. "I am not asshole!"

Daddy: For today you can stay in the house. I don't trust you on the grounds just yet, but soon. By the time I return I want you to realize that we WILL be talking and you'll be more respectful than this morning.

I gripped the phone hard and raised it, ready to smash it against the table before I stopped myself and took in a calm, deep breath. Slowly, I sat the phone down just as the woman from before came back with a cup of pills and some more water. My eye twitched and I threw the pills across the room.

Six: Fuck you.

Six: Just because I let you fuck me doesn't mean I have to listen to you.

Daddy: No? Alright, I will remember that when I return home.

Six: You're an asshole.

Daddy: I'm an asshole...what?

Six: You're an asshole Daddy.

Daddy: Good boy.

This time I slammed the phone against the table before I tossed it into a corner of the room. Breathing slowly, I stood up and grabbed my plate. Angelo was staring at me so I smiled at him and pushed back the anger that boiled in my veins.

"I'm going to eat in my room."

"That's fine. I'll get you another phone."

My smile widened. "No, thank you. Amadeo can shove his phones right up his ass and it can gag him when it comes out of his big, stupid mouth!" I pressed a finger to my temple. "He's driving me nuts. That's what he's doing. I won't let him get to me," I muttered as I walked away shaking my head. "Just ignore his bullshit. That's what I'm going to do."

But as I made it to my room, I couldn't let it go. Amadeo was going to pay. I might not be as strong or as dangerous as him but I would make both our lives hell.

I PUSHED through his closet and dug around. There was a huge safe in the back, but it was the advanced kind with an electronic lock. *Wish I could hack stuff.* The door had been easy, but the safe was impossible.

Picking up the pair of scissors from the dresser I snipped through his ties one by one. Not a lot, just the first two inches of each one. I smiled as I pushed through the huge walk-in closet and made sure I didn't miss a single tie.

"What are you doing?"

I jumped and nearly pissed myself. When I turned around, however, it wasn't Amadeo standing in the doorway. He did kind of look like Amadeo. He had the same height, the same smirk, but his eyes were lighter and more playful whereas Amadeo was all seriousness.

"Shit." I fumbled with the tie in my hand and it fell to the floor. "Shit. I uh was..."

Nope, I had no explanation for this.

"Who are you?" I asked instead.

"Gabriele. Bianchi." He held out a hand. "Nice to meet you."

"Yeah." I shook it. "Six."

"Six. Is that short for something?"

"Not a thing," I answered before I picked up the tie and returned it to its rightful place.

"Can I ask why you're cuttin' up all my brother's ties?"

"Oh uh he asked me to," I lied

Gabriele folded his arms over his chest. "He asked you to?"

"Yeah, he wants to go shopping for new ones."

His grin widened. "You're lying your ass off." Gabriele walked over and pulled out another drawer. "These are the best ties. Special occasions only."

I zeroed in on them. "Really now?" I walked over and picked one up giving a long, low whistle before I snipped it. "That's too bad." I chuckled under my breath before I gazed up at Gabriele. "Why are you helping me destroy your brother's things?"

"Oh I'm going to deny I ever did," he said as he shook his head and leaned against the wall. "What are you to Amadeo?"

I thought about lying, but then I decided I didn't care. Amadeo was the one that had locked me up here. And he was the one that could deal with the consequences.

"Your brother kidnapped me and I can't leave," I said with a shrug as I went back to cutting. "So, I guess you could say I'm his prisoner." I paused and glanced at him. "No chance you'll let me out is there?"

"No way in hell," he said. "Nice try though." He pushed off of the wall. "What did you do to him?"

I frowned. "I might have stolen a little bit of money."

Gabriele whistled. "That'll do it." He shook his head. "If you really wanna mess with him, go for the books."

I put the last tie away and instead focused on the bookshelf in the next room. The place was way too damned big. A bed was all you really needed, but there was a tv, a table, a bar, and on the other side a door leading into an office. I had already been through it, but the computer was password protected and there were just a bunch of boring papers on his desk. But the books, those were apparently important to him.

Crossing over to the office I stepped inside and looked around. The bookshelf was immaculate with not even a single dust bunny. I ran my fingers over the spines and noticed they were all in alphabetical order.

Grinning, I started moving them around. Yeah, it was childish, but I wasn't going to be the only one that had to put up with bullshit. I looked over my shoulder and Gabriele watched me, amused. His phone rang and he dug into his pocket.

"Yeah. Yeah. Well, you should have told me what the hell was going on. Don't worry about how I got past your guards, I have my ways. Hold on." He held out the phone. "He wants to talk to you."

I nodded. "You can tell him to go fuck himself."

"He says you can go fuck yourself. Word for word." Gabriele held it out toward me again. "He says if you don't answer right now, you're going back."

I snatched the phone. "What?"

"Where are you?"

"Around. Why?"

Amadeo growled. "Go back to your room. Now."

"Or what? You're not even here and your brother is cool." I pushed another book into place and turned another one the wrong way out so you could see the pages. Opening one up, I dog eared it in a random place and put it back.

"Six, you have two minutes to get to your room from wherever you are. If you don't, I will put you right back in that fucking cell."

"Ooh, Daddy's angry."

"One. Two. Three..."

"Shit." My heart raced and I knew he wasn't kidding. The time to play was done. I raced out of his room and went back, pulling Gabriele with me as he laughed. Once we were out of Amadeo's room and everything was closed up, I skittered to my bedroom. As soon as I was inside, panting, he stopped counting. "Wait, can you see me?"

"No. Do you want me to see you?"

"Fuck no." Gabriele walked in and I sat at the table on the balcony.

"Take your vitamins and drink your water. Gabriele's already there so I guess it's alright if he keeps you company, but keep your hands to yourself."

"What do you think I'm going to do? Hit him?"

"Something like that," he growled. "Do what you're told."

"Yes, Daddy," I said sweetly.

"Don't be a smart ass and you can't embarrass me. So call me Daddy louder."

My cheeks burned. *Shit backfired!* I glared and wanted to tell him to go jump from a rooftop, but his chuckling in my ear made me grind my teeth together and swallow it.

"Watch yourself, boy. Let me speak to Gabriele."

I held the phone out and Gabriele took the phone. They talked for a minute, but I ignored it. *He's a demon.* Was there really a way to get free of Amadeo?

"Come on," Gabriele said as he waved a hand at me. "He'll let you wander around as long as you're with me. Why don't we have a drink on the back patio?"

"As long as it's something stiff," I muttered, getting up and wincing a bit as the soreness reminded me of last night's activities. "Really, really stiff."

Chapter Eleven

Six

"This is bullshit. Why do I have to go?"

Amadeo walked over to me and yanked me close. I forgot how to breathe as I looked up at him and swallowed thickly. He ran a hand over my cheek before he grabbed the back of my head and brought me close.

"Because you can not be trusted to be alone!" he snapped.

It was unnerving being so close to him when he was angry, but part of me, the insane part, had to stop myself from laughing. Amadeo had been pissed when he discovered the ties, but I heard him yelling from down the hall when he discovered the dog eared books. My ass still stung from him dragging me over his knee and spanking me until I had to call red.

"You could always let me go get my own shitty apartment and I could just come to you when you want to do stuff."

"No." He released me. "Put on your shoes and let's go. I have a meeting."

"Asshole," I huffed as I bent over to grab my shoes and he smacked my ass hard. "Hey!"

"Stop complaining," he growled. "You did this to yourself. If I can't leave you in the house alone, you're going to be right by my side."

I grumbled under my breath and tugged on my shoes. Amadeo had decided that my usual sweats or jeans and a t-shirt weren't acceptable for the casino. Instead, he'd bought me a number of suits that almost made me pass out and break into hives when I saw the price tag. There were also expensive new shoes and a plethora of ties that I refused to wear.

"You have to wear it," Amadeo said as I tossed it on the dresser.

"Listen," I snapped. "I'm going with you, but I am *not* wearing that thing! I feel like I'm back in school in those stuffy uniforms and tight ties. I'm not doing it."

Amadeo walked over to me and I backed up against the dresser. He reached beside me and I kept my eyes on him, unwilling to look away as he stared at me. Fabric wrapped around my throat and Amadeo pulled the tie tight, a gasp leaving my lips as my hand shot out and gripped his arm.

"You will wear the fucking tie or I will fuck you until your legs no longer work." He leaned forward, his lips brushing over my ear as he tightened the material. "And then I will make you wear it anyway."

My heart flip-flopped in my chest and all of the steam and bravado disappeared. He released my neck and I breathed heavily, panting as I tried to draw in air. Amadeo draped the tie around my neck and proceeded to fix it before he kissed my lips.

"Try to be a good boy today, hmm?"

Eat me.

I followed him out of the house and even though I didn't want to go to the casino, it felt good to be outside again. The last few days I'd been locked up in my room. Of course, there was the balcony, but it wasn't like being in the city. The sights, the smells, the people; I loved all of it. Leaning back in the car I stared out the window while Amadeo typed away on his phone and Angelo drove. I turned around and his intense gaze was fixed on me.

"What?"

"Nothing," he said shortly.

I pulled a face. "Weirdo."

"I'm not in the mood today, Six."

"You're the one that was staring at me," I muttered, but I left him alone. He really was in no mood to deal with me it seemed. "What's crawled up your ass anyway? Why are you so on edge?"

Amadeo's face went even more serious. "Don't worry about it. I can handle my own business."

I rolled my eyes. "Whatever you say."

The tension in the car was so thick it was choking me more than the tie was. Once we rolled to a stop I was grateful to get out of the car and put some distance between me and Amadeo. I followed him into the casino, my hands in my pockets as I looked at my old stomping grounds. But every face was new.

Except one. "Morning, Six." Darla smiled at me. "Coffee?"

"I'm good," I muttered as I strolled into Amadeo's office. "Thanks though."

"Of course, hon. What about for you?"

"Yes," Amadeo nodded. "The usual and we'll have breakfast here. We were a little late today."

There was accusation in his eyes and I shrugged as if I had no idea what he was blaming me for. He shook his head at me and a muscle in his jaw ticked. *If he keeps clenching that hard, he's going to break a damn tooth. It would be a shame. His teeth are perfect.*

"Sit down," Amadeo said as he moved to his desk and sat down.

I looked around his office. The place was huge. Chairs sat in front of his desk and there were more pushed along a wall. A big, leather couch took up another wall and there were two doors. I had no idea where they led.

"What am I supposed to do?" I asked as I plopped down on the couch. "Stare at a wall all day?"

"You could have been at home watching TV, but you decided to act out. Remember?"

I rolled my eyes. "That's not my home, it's yours. It's the same thing as being here. All of it is a prison cell."

"I could re-introduce you to a real one if this is a problem," he said, his eyes flat as he stared at me. "Is that what you need?"

Snapping my lips shut I looked away from him. *Bastard.* He was always threatening to throw me back into that hole and I was sick of it. I almost wanted to tell him to go ahead and do it. But then I remembered the way it smelled, the dampness, the tiny space and it was too much.

I stared at the wall. Every once in a while I looked over at Amadeo, but he was into his work, whatever his work was that didn't involve killing people. Whenever I stared for too long, he looked up at me and I stopped staring at him.

What is wrong with me?

Amadeo finished his coffee and I hopped up from the couch. Scooping up the mug I nodded toward the door. "I can go get more. I remember where the kitchen is. Well, the main one if you have another one."

He raised a brow. "I do, but why are you so eager to get it for me?"

"I'm going out of my mind sitting here. At least let me walk around." When he frowned I groaned. "Angelo can follow me around."

"Fine," he sighed. "But if you wander off anywhere, remember that I have cameras and I'll see it. My meeting starts soon. I want you back before we're in that conference room," he said as he pointed to it. "Understand?"

"Yeah."

"No," he said shortly. "Answer me correctly."

"Fuck, you're such a pain."

Amadeo glared and started standing. "Let's try this again."

"No, no okay. Yes, Daddy!" My heart skipped a beat. He looked at me and sat back down, smoothing his tie down.

"Good boy. Go on."

I hate him.

God, he got under my skin like no one I had ever met before. Every time I called him Daddy it continued to scratch some terrible itch in me and I wanted to give in again and again. I detested everything about that. How he made me feel, how he made me think about him. *I need to get away.*

"Darla, where's the boss's kitchen?" I asked.

"Oh, come along. I'll show you." She walked down the hall and waved a hand. "I can't believe you're back here. Amadeo was pissed when you stole that cash. I guess that's why you're working for him now."

"Something like that," I muttered.

"Well, you just mind yourself. He has enough trouble on his plate with the damn Irish breaking into stuff and doing god knows what," she muttered as she put in a code and pushed a door open letting me into a lavish kitchen. "Coffee's over there."

I walked over to the pot and frowned. "The Irish?" I asked her.

"I'm saying too much." Darla sighed. "Just keep your head down and do your work. Two sugars and cream. Lots of cream," she added. "He likes the hazelnut one the best."

"Thanks," I smiled at her. "Maybe he won't be such a pain in my ass."

She chuckled. "Doubt that, hon. I need to get back to my post."

I nodded. "Angelo is staying with me. Don't worry about it."

"Alright."

Darla excused herself and I went to make Amadeo's coffee. I was about to add the sugar when my phone buzzed in my pocket. I slipped it out.

Daddy: Hurry up.

Daddy: What's taking so long?

Six: I wasn't aware that I was on a time limit.

Daddy: You are so hurry up.

Six: You know I agreed to fuck you, not be bossed around by you.

Daddy: Seeing as how I've only fucked you once I would say you're failing miserably at your job.

I stared at the screen and clenched my teeth. *What the hell?* He was the one that hadn't come into my room at night, trying to climb on me for the past three days. How was this my fault? I scoffed and shoved the phone into my pocket again before I picked up the sugar and put it down. Instead, I grabbed the salt dispenser and shook and shook and shook before I stirred it up.

One day I'll find a way to hurt him that's not a childish prank. One fucking day.

Until then, I was going to keep doing it. It made me feel better. Once I had his coffee, I followed Angelo back to the office and stepped inside. There were a few men inside now and I moved past them and sat his mug on his desk.

"Here you go." I smiled. "At least I can do this job right."

Amadeo picked up the mug and stared at me. I could see the fire in his eyes and yeah, I was going to pay for it later. But this was now. And I liked to live in the moment. He brought the mug to his lips and took a sip before he spit coffee everywhere.

I pressed my lips together and held down the laughter that threatened to tear free. Amadeo's green eyes tracked up to mine and he looked murderous. My cock twitched *Damn. I need therapy.*

He was up and around his desk without a word as the eyes in the room watched his every movement. Amadeo's hand wrapped around my upper arm and he dragged me into the conference room.

"One moment, gentlemen. I need the conference room before we settle in for our meeting." He closed the door and continued pulling me along until we reached the conference table in the empty room. Amadeo shoved me and I went down with a grunt before his fist was in my hair, dragging me between his legs once he sat down.

"What are you-"

My eyes widened as he gripped my hair with one hand, pinpricks of pain dancing along my scalp while he freed his cock with his other hand. Amadeo dragged me forward and shoved my face against dick as he growled. I took in his heady scent, how hard he was as precum glistened on the tip of his slit.

"Open your mouth."

I shook my head. "No." I stared up at him. "Daddy," I added quickly. "No, Daddy."

The growl turned long and deep and electricity ran up my spine. "If you don't, I'll make you suck it."

I licked my lips, my body erupting into flames. "Make me."

Amadeo's eyes flashed and I saw it again. Darkness tinged with spectacular fire. As much as I hated him, those eyes were mesmerizing. And hell, maybe I wanted his cock in my mouth, but I didn't want to admit that. I would never let him think I wanted him. His ego was already huge, how much would it grow if he knew my dirty little secret? That he made my cock hard and my mouth water?

He glared at me and shook my head roughly. "Open your fucking mouth before I hurt you."

I challenged him for only a second before I opened my mouth and he shoved his cock down my throat. Amadeo shoved the heavy conference table away as he stood and gripped the back of my head with both his hands. He fucked my mouth hard, a gag tumbling from my lips as I stared up at him and my eyes watered from the intrusion.

Daddy.

There was more monster than man on his face right now as he took me relentlessly. Amadeo might have spanked me the past few nights, but he had been tiptoeing around me, trying to *speak* to me as if I wanted to visit emotions. I didn't need to feel, I just wanted to at least enjoy the way he fucked me. Hard and fast, no regrets, no lovemaking. Amadeo could have my body.

But he would never own my heart.

His hips snapped forward and I pressed my palms against his thighs. But I didn't push him away. Instead, I gripped his thighs and yanked him forward, my eyes rolling up as he completely filled my throat. *Breathe through the nose,* I reminded myself as he picked up speed. When I opened my eyes, he was staring down at me, panting and moaning like a man possessed. He pulled free and I coughed, saliva rolling down my chin as I panted.

"They're going to hear you." I grinned up at him.

"Let them fucking hear it." He grabbed my hair and tilted my head up. "Then they'll know who you belong to."

I shivered. "I don't belong to you, Daddy." I shoved him away from me and wiped my mouth with my wrist before I backed up. "Don't touch me."

I knew my taunting would only rile him up more. He took one glance at me before his eyes went to the tent in my slacks. I ran my hand over my cock and he closed the space between us again before his cock was back in my mouth, pushing into my already aching throat.

Yes, take me. Don't take no for an answer.

Closing my eyes I groaned, the vibration traveling up his cock and making him groan. Amadeo's big hands held onto my head firmly, his nails digging into my scalp as he face fucked me roughly. My cock throbbed and I squeezed it.

"Don't touch what's mine," he growled. "Take your fucking hands off of my cock, boy."

My eyes fluttered open, and as desire dripped off of every word he spoke, I squeezed his thighs tightly. His mouth fell open, a shudder wracking his muscled frame as he hissed my name.

"Six."

Just that one word and I desperately wanted to free my cock and stroke myself until I had some kind of relief. *Did I miss this? No, there's no way.* This was inevitable, the need to cum and feel some kind of stress relief. It had nothing to do with Amadeo and absolutely everything to do with my need to calm down.

Knock. Knock.

"Boss? Everyone's here. We're ready."

"Fuck!" Amadeo snarled and I almost grinned at how animalistic he looked. Until he pulled his cock free from my lips. Sighing, I started to stand, but he shoved me right back to my knees. "Did Daddy say you could get up? You're going to suck my cock throughout this meeting."

My eyes widened. "But...everyone will see me?"

"So fucking what?" he asked as he tugged my head back and growled at me. "Even if the whole world was to watch you're still *mine*. My property."

I swallowed thickly. "I am not you..." His eyes challenged mine and I backed down. *Shit, he's not playing.* "Yes, Daddy."

"I want more of that when we get home," he said before he pressed a rough, demanding kiss to my mouth. He pulled back and whispered. "I like when you tell me no Daddy. It's fucking hot."

My skin flushed. I knew exactly what he meant though. It was hot. The way he took me even when I tried to push him away. Amadeo fixed his hair, tugged the table back into place, and then sat down. He moved closer and grabbed the back of my head before he shoved me against his crotch. All I could do was take in his scent and lap at the base of his cock and his balls until he released me.

"Get to work, boy."

"Yes, Daddy," I panted as I readjusted myself and took his cock into my mouth.

"Come in," Amadeo called. "Let's get this meeting started."

The door opened and my eyes slid to the ground as pairs of shoes moved into place around the table. I held my breath, my pulse skyrocketing as they took their seats. Amadeo grabbed a handful of my hair, forced me down his length and I choked before my face flushed.

Bastard! He's doing that on purpose!

"Mr. Bianchi? Is uh...something going on?" a man asked.

"Nothing of consequence," he said before he removed his hand. "Let's start with the numbers and we can go from there. Dario should be here shortly and I can give them to him."

"Alright, sounds good."

They launched into some boring talk about numbers, money, and warehouses. I hesitated for a moment before I closed my eyes and lost myself to worshiping Amadeo's cock. It really was a work of art. He was thicker rather than longer and I remembered the way my hole burned when he shoved it inside of me. I reached behind me and pushed my fingers into my pants. Pressing a finger against my hole, it clenched and demanded I shove something, anything into it.

I moved my finger and tried to pull free from Amadeo's cock, but he didn't allow it. He pushed me back down his length and I wanted to groan in frustration, but I was too worried about someone looking under the table and seeing me. Instead, I opened my mouth and let saliva drip onto my fingers.

As soon as they were wet enough, I reached back and shoved my finger inside of me without hesitation. Once I pressed against my prostate, I sucked Amadeo harder, licking and lapping at his length whenever I needed to pull free to breathe. As long as I didn't stop, he let me switch it up and rest, but damn did it feel like the meeting was droning on forever. My cock was so hard, I *needed* to cum, but I couldn't.

How would anyone know?

I fumbled with my pants and tugged my cock out. It sucked having one hand occupied because nothing was inside of me anymore and that empty space throbbed with need. But I wrapped my hand around my shaft regardless, squeezed, and then stroked myself as quickly as I could without making a ton of noise.

The danger that anyone would look down and see what I was doing fueled me. I panted gently against Amadeo's cock and he thrust forward, claiming my throat again. But it was as if I wasn't even on the man's dick. He spoke flawlessly, his voice not even wavering. That pissed me the hell off.

What? He doesn't think I feel good? I'm a fucking boss!

I doubled my efforts, sliding my mouth up and down his length as I caved my cheeks in. My hand moved faster, stroking me into a frenzy.

"What about our east loca-Fuck!"

"Are you okay, Mr. Bianchi?"

"Just fine," Amadeo growled. "I was asking about our east location and operations there."

I wanted to laugh out loud, but it would stop the amazing fucking job I was doing. Amadeo thought he was the only one that would imprint himself on someone's brain and make them crazy? I would make it just as difficult for him to ever forget *me*.

Shutting myself up, I came hard, my body jerking and shaking as I spilled my cum on the floor. My head spun and I wanted to groan. *Shit, why was that so good?* Amadeo pushed me away a moment later and did his pants up. He chatted and shook hands and I stayed put, too fucking high to move even if I wanted to.

"Dario, I'll speak to you a little later."

"Right." The man stopped. "Is that your um...guest underneath the table?"

"Yes."

"Gesù Cristo," he groaned. "Get it together."

"It's always been together," Amadeo said coolly. "You can go. Send my men back in."

"Whatever you say, Boss."

The door closed and Amadeo yanked me from underneath the table. He reached down and came back up with my sticky cum on his fingertips.

"Did Daddy say you could cum?"

I shook my head. "No, Daddy."

"You're going to pay for that and making me stumble over my words." He turned me around and slammed me against the table before he yanked my clothes down my hips and I gasped. He touched my hole. "Why is this wet? Were you touching what was mine?"

I let out the most embarrassing whimper, but I couldn't answer. After cumming, I felt more docile than I did before and the man was goddamn intimidating. A hand landed on my bare ass and I cried out.

"Yes, Daddy!" I answered quickly.

"Were you horny for me?" he asked. "Did you think about my cock being stuffed inside of you while you fucked yourself?"

Damn it, why was he in my head? My tongue darted out, running over my lips. When I didn't immediately respond, I earned another sharp slap and I shuddered.

"Y-yes Daddy," I admitted, hating myself a little. "I couldn't help it!"

"Good boy," he growled against my ear, tugging the lobe between his teeth. "For telling the truth, I'll give you a present. I'll let you cum again while my cock is shoved deep inside of you."

I groaned. "Daddy, please. I can't take more that quickly."

"Deal with it," he whispered, his lips leaving a kiss on my shoulder. "Spread your legs."

I did it on instinct alone and he spread me open. My entire body heated knowing that he was examining my hole. He pressed his thumb against it before he spat on it and I almost blacked out from how turned on I was.

And then my world crashed and burned.

The door swung open and there was Angelo with a few more of Amadeo's men. All of them stopped in the doorway and stared at me and then Amadeo.

"Pay him no mind," Amadeo said before he nodded toward the door. "Angelo, there's a white bottle in the right drawer of my desk. Bring it to me."

"Yes, Boss."

I wanted to scream at the man not to do it, but there was no way in hell he was going to listen to me over Amadeo. The rest of the men filed in and most avoided my gaze. But every once in a while one of them would glance my way and my face burned hotter than a five-alarm fire.

Angelo came back and passed the lube to Amadeo as I shook my head no. The man didn't give a damn. He squeezed some onto my hole and I cried out as he sank inside of me, his fingers digging into my hips.

"I need you to beef up security at our east location," he told Angelo. "We need more men on it in rotating shifts. If one more warehouse gets fucked, I'm going to lose it."

"Yes, Boss."

How can he carry on a conversation when my knees feel like they're about to give out? I clung to the table as best I could, my breathing turning into desperate pants as he drove against my prostate with every stroke. It was like he knew exactly how to find the damn thing!

"Daddy," I groaned. "Wait."

"No," he said, grabbing the back of my neck and pinning me to the desk. "Be quiet. I'm in a meeting."

Shit. Does he know how hot that is?

I let myself go and gave into the pleasure that wrapped around my body and refused to let go. My eyes fluttered half-closed and I pushed back against him, needing more of Daddy's cock. I wanted him to defile me, to turn me into the empty-headed husk he was so good at bringing out of me.

"You," he growled and my eyes snapped open thinking he was talking to me before I noticed one of the younger guys at the table looking like a deer in headlights. "If you look at what's mine much longer, I'm going to pluck your eyes out and have them made into novelty cuff links. Redirect your fucking gaze from my property."

I came so hard I saw stars.

"Dismissed," Amadeo called. "I'll send out more info as it comes."

They all walked out and the moment they were gone, his cock disappeared. He tossed me onto the table as if I weighed nothing and shoved his cock back into me. My legs were pushed against one of his shoulders and he fucked me hard, his face a mask of pleasure.

"Bad boy," he groaned. "Again? What, you like hearing how you're my property?"

I shook my head. "No, no I don't like it."

"You do," he said as he shoved in roughly and I cried out. "You can lie to yourself, but you can't lie to Daddy. I see it in your eyes. Give in, Six."

I hated him. God, I hated him so fucking much, but I couldn't shake how good he made me feel. My back arched up from the table and he grunted as he thrust forward sharply. I realized a minute too late that he wasn't wearing a condom and I was flooded with his load. I bit my wrist to keep from crying out as he panted and gazed down at me. He maneuvered us until he could take my mouth in an Earth-shattering kiss.

"Good boy. You did so well, taking Daddy's cock."

I stared back up at him, speechless as my stomach fluttered. One stupid compliment and I felt like I was alive. He cradled my cheek and I shuddered.

Who am I becoming?

Chapter Twelve

Amadeo

I watched over him as he slept curled up in his bed. Sitting on the edge of it, I leaned over and pushed the hair out of his face. When we returned home, I had been insatiable. Six had taken my cock so many times over until he was a cum stained mess of a boy, too exhausted to go on. I smiled at the memory before the smile dipped.

What does this mean?

He had been acting so petulant lately, but now he was calm and docile and asleep. The way he'd called me Daddy while I screwed him on every square inch of his bed still made me groan inwardly with delight. I just wanted to wake him and do it all over again.

Leaning down, I pressed a kiss to his temple. Six stirred and I pulled back slowly so I wouldn't wake him. He'd passed out underneath me, my cock still firmly in his ass until I'd had to pull out slow and watched my cum slide out of him.

Now, he was firmly tucked beneath a heavy comforter with a water bottle, pain killers, and fresh clothes sat out for when he woke. Instead of sleeping, I had spent all night by his side. Watching him.

I finally stood up and picked up his hoodie from the chair it was draped on. Carrying it out with me, I took it to my room and lightly spritzed it with my cologne. I brought it to my nose and made sure it was just enough; not too strong or too weak. I slipped back down to his room and placed it with the rest of his clothes before I left one more kiss on his forehead and walked away.

The boy made me weak, I knew that. Where I should be focused on my problems, I was enamored with him and I didn't know why. I kept expecting things to fall apart at any moment and to be back at square one, lost and alone. But every day, there was Six challenging me, fighting me, giving in to me.

My heart squeezed and I gripped my chest as I walked out of his room. *Please, don't let this end in disaster. I couldn't take that. Not with him.*

I never prayed, but I wanted to do it to keep him. Didn't matter who was listening, as long as they realized that I would do anything, burn heaven or hell for what was *mine.*

Stepping back into my room, I took a shower even though I didn't want to wash off the scent of my boy. I hurried up and came out, dried off, and dressed in my casual clothes; a pair of dark jeans and a button-up. I fixed my hair, my phone on the dresser beside me so I could watch over Six.

Crash!

I jumped and immediately growled. "What the fuck was that?" I stared at the phone and Six rolled over, groaning before he fell back asleep. "Fuck."

Snatching up my phone, I jogged down the stairs. I turned the corner and found one of my men picking up pieces of porcelain. He stopped and glanced up at me.

"Sorry, Boss. I was bringing some things in for the chef and bumped this vase. It should be cleaned up in-"

My fist collided with his face. He stumbled back, his eyes wide before I hit him again. Blood dripped from his nose, but as he rose his hands to defend himself, I dared him to *keep* them up with a single glance. Other guards watched on as my fist crashed into his jaw and he fell to the floor with a cry. My fist throbbed, but I didn't give a damn.

"You're careless. Senseless," I said as I walked up to him and he tried to drag himself away. My hand tangled into his blond hair and I yanked his head up. "Get the fuck out of my house before I slit your throat and make your friends clean you up. Now!" I barked.

The man scrambled to his feet and didn't look back as he fled the house. I watched until he was well down the driveway before I turned to the rest of the men. "Keep it down. No one is to disturb Six. Am I understood?"

"Yes, Boss!"

I looked at each of them making sure they understood the seriousness of what I was saying. Pulling out my phone, I checked on my boy and he was still passed out, sprawled over the bed and snoring now. The corners of my mouth ticked up before I brought back the calmness I always exhibited and put the phone away.

"Get this cleaned up," I said. "And keep the noise down."

"Yes, Boss!"

I turned and walked away from them. "Idiots," I mumbled.

When I was halfway up the stairs I realized my feet were bleeding. Pain blossomed out of nowhere and I hissed as I sat on the stairs and saw the porcelain in my feet. I grabbed a piece and yanked, forcing myself to shut up as it pulled free of my flesh.

"Shit," I muttered.

"What are you doing?"

I turned and stared up at Six wrapped in a robe. His black hair was all over his head, those dark eyes still bleary with sleep.

"What are you doing up?" I asked. "You're supposed to be asleep."

"I had to pee." He yawned and moved around me. I tried to hide my foot but he moved faster and grabbed my ankle. "Shit, what have you been doing?"

"Nothing." I waved him off. "Go back to bed." I grabbed another piece and yanked it free as I swore under my breath.

"You're so fucking stupid," he huffed. Six lowered himself beside me and grabbed my foot. He winced. "This looks bad." He paused and grabbed my bloody hand. "So does this. What the hell?"

"It's nothing."

"Don't tell me it's nothing," he snapped. "What? You think I'm a moron?" He held up a hand. "Don't answer that. Is there a first aid kit in your room?"

I nodded. "Under my sink."

"Come on." He stood up and offered his hand. When I stared at him, he snapped his fingers. "Let's go already."

"Boy..." I warned.

"Yeah, yeah I'll be punished later. I've heard it all before. Let me help you up."

He helped me to my feet and I walked on the sides of them trying to avoid forcing the porcelain in deeper. We made our way to my room and I opened the door before he helped me to the bed. Six sat me down before he disappeared into the bathroom and returned with what looked like a black toolbag, but were actually medical supplies. Six sat them on the bed before he grabbed peroxide and poured it on my foot.

I hissed. "Son of a bitch! What the fuck are you doing?"

"Don't yell at me," he snapped. "I'm trying to help your stupid ass." He grabbed my ankle and forced it in place before he poured more peroxide on my flesh and I had to snap my teeth shut. "Almost done. Give me the other one."

I stuck my foot out and he gave it the same treatment. Once he was done and I was over wanting to curse him out, he took out a pair of tweezers and started pulling out pieces of porcelain. I gripped the bed tightly, my veins bunching underneath my skin as I tried to keep an even temperament.

"I thought blood bothered you."

Six glanced up at me before he focused on his work again. "I don't mind blood, never have. Hell, I've been in my fair share of scrapes." He shrugged. "It was more so seeing you damage an innocent man's hand that had me riled up."

"And now?" I pressed. "Seeing my hand like this, what do you think?"

He glanced at it. "Oh yeah, give me your hand too." He poured more peroxide and checked out my hand before he went back to pulling out porcelain. "I think you're a bastard, but...it's your business. Not mine."

I stared down at him as he worked. Six wasn't freaking out about it. He was...accepting it almost. That had to be a good sign right? Maybe I wasn't the monster I thought I was in his eyes.

"How do you know how to do all this?" I asked. "Patching yourself up?"

Six shrugged. "I have a friend that's a boxer so I've had to do it for him before and..." He trailed off before he cleared his throat. "My mom was always in the bottle, especially in the end when we were losing everything. You have no idea how many times she would drop a bottle and step in the glass shards. I was the youngest, but I was also the only one that gave a shit. While they were all off pretending our world wasn't ending, I took care of her the best I could."

I frowned. "I'm sorry."

His head snapped up. "I did not ask for your pity," he spat. "I don't need it!"

"Hey." I held up my hand and shook my head. "I never said you did, Six. Calm down."

Six deflated a bit and went back to treating my foot. "Anyway, it's all old news. They might not be rich, but they're middle class now and just as snooty as always."

"Do you talk to them?" I asked. When he gave me an exasperated look, I corrected myself. "I mean before you were with me."

He twisted a hand back and forth. "Sometimes. Usually, it's if they need something. Or they might call and check-up, but honestly? They don't care. I mean do you see me plastered all over the news as a missing person? Trust me, no one gives a shit except for maybe Ty."

I growled. "Who the fuck is this Ty? That's the second time you've mentioned him."

"Well yeah, I miss him, you asshole. He's a friend. You don't have any friends?"

"Of course I do. My brothers and my little sister."

Six rolled his eyes. "Those are siblings, not friends. Ty is like my brother, that's how close we got. Now, he's got his own Daddy and is living the high life." He paused. "I want to see him." Six glanced up at me. "Can I?"

I swallowed thickly. Allow Six into the outside world? My nerves were set on edge instantly. What if he told someone what was happening? What if he was taken away from me?

"Nevermind," he muttered. "I can see the answer on your face." He pulled out a piece of porcelain aggressively and I hissed. "Sorry," he snapped. "You're done."

"Six..."

"It's fine." He reached into the bag and brought out gauze. In silence, he wrapped both of my feet and then my hand. When he pulled away, I grabbed his arm and yanked him close. "What?" he asked, his face passive, hiding the emotions I knew existed under that mask.

"We'll set it up, okay?" I found myself saying, almost desperate not to lose this side of him, the sweet one that I never got to see.

"If you want to see this friend of yours then fine. You can."

Six blinked at me, his eyes wide before he frowned. "Are you lying to me?"

"No," I said, shaking my head. "A friendly visit can't hurt anything. As long as you keep your mouth shut about our little arrangement."

The boy threw his arms around my neck and leaned back enough to kiss me. My eyes widened before I wrapped him in my arms and kissed him back. Six stayed in my arms for what felt like an eternity and it still wasn't enough by the time he pulled away.

"Thank you," he said, a smile forming on his lips. "Daddy."

My heart fluttered in my chest and I dragged him in for another long, deep kiss. There was so much that needed to be discussed with my boy but now wasn't the time. He was being compliant, open, and I wanted to reward him for that. I rolled us over and straddled him in my bed.

"Spread your legs."

Six groaned. "Really? Again? There's something wrong with you."

"A hell of a lot." I grinned. "Now do what I say."

"Yes Daddy," he purred. "Whatever you say."

A shiver worked its way through my body and I stole another kiss. Six was coming around and I wouldn't allow him to pull away again. The closer he grew to me, the more I knew that releasing him was an impossibility.

The boy was *mine.*

Chapter Thirteen

Six

"Are you sure this is what you meant to order for breakfast?" Amadeo asked as he joined me at the dining room table.

I tilted my head. "What? You don't like it?"

"It's...pizza. You know this is pizza, right? And not even good Italian pizza, it's Americanized crap."

I flipped him off. "Fuck you! Nothing wrong with good old US of A pizza!" I snagged a slice and bit into it. Pepperoni, mushrooms, bacon, and pineapple was my favorite combination. I devoured an entire slice before I grabbed another and only stopped when I realized Amadeo was staring at me, grimacing. "What?"

"Disgusting," he said.

I fake gasped. "How dare you? You know what? Now you have to eat it." I shoved the slice against his lips. "Eat it."

"No thank you."

I stood up and moved closer. "Eat it!"

"Six," he growled.

I ignored the big, growly man and forced the slice into his mouth, sauce, and grease smeared all over his immaculate face. He shot up and I burst out laughing, licking my thumb as I backed away from him.

"Hope you enjoy eating your breakfast with a sore ass," he said as he snatched up his napkin and wiped his mouth before he threw it to the table again. I refused to tell him there was still sauce on his nose. "Come here."

"No!" I yelled as he chased after me and I ran for my life.

Amadeo grabbed me and marched me to the couch in the entertainment room. As soon as the door was closed, my shorts were down and his hand collided with my ass. I braced my palms against the floor and moaned as he spanked me hard and rough, his hard cock pressing against my body as he did.

"You are really getting out of control, Six," he said as he slapped my ass, and pain radiated over my skin. "Do you understand me?"

I nodded. "Y-ah! Yes, Daddy," I panted, humping my hard cock against his thighs as I held onto him. "Sorry, Daddy. I'll be good for you."

He growled and I knew it was an approving sound rather than his disapproving growl. Amadeo loved when I called him Daddy and caved to him. Usually, he could only draw that out of me when he was fucking me, but I loved toying with him at times, saying it just to mess with him.

And I like it. I like calling him Daddy.

I brushed that thought aside. That was a whole can of worms waiting to be opened that I didn't have time to face right now.

Instead, I screwed my eyes shut and pressed back into his firm, calloused hands. Every strike released a part of my pent up mind until I felt free.

Amadeo pulled me into a kiss. "Calm down when we're eating," he said sternly.

"Yes, Daddy." I batted my lashes at him. "Do I get a present if I do?"

"What?" He sighed.

"A phone that can dial more than you and Angelo." He pulled away and I panicked, grabbing his hands and holding them in mine. "Please, please let me have this. We both know I'm not going anywhere until this contract is up."

Amadeo frowned and searched my face. "Fuck," he swore and stood up. "Is this why you've been acting so nice lately?"

I shook my head. "Have I been acting nice?"

Thinking about it, I could see what he meant, but I hadn't planned it. Seriously, it was tiring to fight someone all day every day and those little moments of peace stilled my mind. Especially because I was starting to see there was more to Amadeo than the monster, even if it was hard to see.

"Ama," I said.

He glared at me.

"Daddy, please," I begged. "I've been locked up here for what feels like forever! I just want to talk to and see my friends while I pay you back. That's all. We both know If I ran you would find me without even trying. Right?"

He nodded slowly. "Yes."

"Then that's all I'm asking, to see my friends."

"We'll see."

Amadeo stormed away from me and I sighed. He still didn't believe me, but seriously, where the fuck could I go? I had already tried to map out my escape a thousand times and came up short. Honestly, it was better to give in and pay off my time, and then I would be free. But I wanted at least the semblance of my past life.

"Six, come and eat!"

I stood up and fixed my clothes. Glancing at the door, I turned and looked out the window. It was right there; I could probably disappear without anyone seeing me. But my stomach churned and I turned back toward the door, moving through it so I could finish my breakfast with an aching ass and a mind full of unanswered questions.

"Mr. Bianchi has asked me to drive you to dinner."

I looked up from the bed where I was sprawled out and cocked a brow at Angelo. "Isn't dinner just downstairs?"

The man laughed. "Not tonight. Apparently, there are reservations and I'm supposed to take you to it." He took out his phone. "The boss wants you to dress nice."

"Would you get in trouble if I showed up in sweats and a beater?"

Angelo winced. "Probably."

"Shit," I groaned. "Fine, I'll put something nice on."

"Thanks."

I looked at his hand and nodded. "How's it feeling?"

Angelo flexed it a little. "He was nicer than you'd think. It's fine, just a bit sore. I can still drive and shoot, so no problem."

I nodded. "Still feel bad for that shit."

"Don't," he said. "Just get dressed."

I saluted him. "Yes, sir!"

Angelo shivered. "Shit kid, don't let him hear you joking like that. He'll think something is going on with us. Get ready."

"Sorry," I said quickly and popped outta bed. "I'll be down in thirty minutes. That okay?"

"Yeah, but not much longer than that."

"Okay."

I watched him leave before I thumbed the heel of my hand against my head. *I need to be careful.* Sometimes Amadeo felt so normal that I forgot he was a psychopath, but Angelo was right, the man would for sure kick his ass or kill him if he thought for even a second that we were close.

Gathering myself, I focused on the task ahead of me. A quick shower and I grabbed a razor and began to shave. As I glanced into the mirror, my hand on the countertop I vividly remembered the way he shaved me with a straight razor and licked my blood. A shiver ran over my body and I quickly refocused and shaved my face clean before I stepped into my room. *This is not the time to be thinking that kind of thing. Keep it together.*

I walked to the closet and rifled through the clothes until I decided on something that hopefully wasn't too formal. Black slacks, a gray button-up shirt, a gray tie, and a black vest on top. I finished it with the expensive loafers he'd brought me and looked at myself in the mirror.

Hell, I hardly recognize myself. I turned my head this way and that checking out how I looked. Ducking into the bathroom, I grabbed some hair stuff and slicked back my black locks until they swooped back and I felt like a brand new man. Checking myself out, I grinned until the smile fell.

What the hell is he doing to me?

I was more confident than I had ever been, but look at me! No rebelling, no fighting. I had dressed with him in mind to be sure it was an outfit that he would appreciate and I worried that he might not like it even now. Amadeo was changing me and it was terrifying.

"Six?" Angelo knocked and called through the door. "Are you ready?"

"Yeah, shit, sorry!" I called taking one last look in the stand-up mirror and shaking my head. I crossed the space to the door and yanked it open. "Sorry, I'm ready."

Angelo looked me up and down. "You look good. He'll approve."

That statement took a load off my shoulders. Nodding, I followed him down to the car and climbed inside. As we pulled away from the trees, the suburbs, the quiet nothingness of my life now I was all too excited to be in town and not stuck in my room.

We pulled up to a small restaurant and I was surprised that it wasn't something flashier. Angelo opened the door for me and I stepped out before I was escorted inside. Soft piano music played and I looked around, freezing when my eyes landed on Amadeo.

He glanced up from the menu and his eyes trained on me. At that moment, I forgot how to breathe. Despite all that he was, the man was breathtaking. I stared and the corner of his lips twitched up into a grin before he nodded and I walked to him like a man possessed, ignoring the hostess altogether until he stood and pulled me into his arms.

"Wow," he said as he checked me out. "You look amazing."

The lump that had been in my stomach since we left the house lightened. "Yeah, you think so, Daddy?" I asked.

He chuckled. "I do." He reached out and caressed my cheek. "Damn good."

The flattery shot straight to my cock and my heart skipped a beat. Amadeo pulled a chair out for me. Normally, I would have argued with him that I was perfectly capable of doing it myself, but I suppressed the urge and sank into my chair.

As he walked back to his, I glanced around the room. The restaurant was mostly empty and we were off to ourselves in a corner. While the outside had been beautiful red brick, the inside was white with a pretty chandelier in the middle of the room and soft lighting. A candle flickered in the middle of our table and I felt like I was being taken on the best date of my life.

"What is this place?" I asked.

"One of my favorite restaurants," Amadeo said as he gazed at me. "It's a little mom-and-pop Italian place. I know, you're probably getting sick of Italian food when it's all I ask for when it comes to dinner..."

I shook my head. "No, I like this place. I think it's nice."

Amadeo lit up in a way I'd never seen before. "Yeah?"

"Yes," I smiled. "Who knew you gave a shit about mom and pop shops?"

He stopped with his glass halfway to his lips. "I give a shit about a lot of things." He frowned. "What? Just because I do what I do I can't care about things?"

Instantly, I felt like crap. "That's not what I meant," I said before I swallowed my pride. "Sorry."

Amadeo waved a hand. "It's okay. Not your fault," he sighed. "I'm just on edge."

"The Irish?" I asked.

"Welcome to L'ultima Cena." A woman bounced over and smiled at us. "What can I get you to start tonight?"

I picked up my menu and stared. At first, I was pretty sure I was having a stroke before I realized it was completely in Italian. I laid the menu back down and stared at Amadeo for help.

"Inizieremo con l'antipasto misto del leccio seguito dalle tagliatelle ai funghi porcini. Per il secondo vitella al forno e tiramisù per dessert."

The woman nodded. "Sounds lovely. I'll get this right in for you. Any drink orders?"

"Wine," Amadeo supplied. "For both of us and keep it coming."

"Yes, Mr. Bianchi."

My jaw dropped and Amadeo looked at me. "That was hot," I blurted. "I mean I knew you were Italian but damn that was so hot. What did you order? Is it good? I want to hear you speak Italian again."

Amadeo burst into laughter. "Calm down, *ragazzo*."

I tried, but I couldn't stop thinking about how hot the words sounded from his lips. "Um, what did you order?"

He chuckled. "The appetizer is an assortment of cold meat, bread, and cheeses. Followed by tagliatelle with porcini mushroom sauce, roast veal, and for dessert tiramisu. Sound good?"

My mouth was salivating for completely different reasons but I nodded. "Sounds great."

Amadeo smiled at me and I forgot how to breathe. He turned all of his attention on me and tilted his head. I watched the way his eyes moved, his jaw tightened, and his fingers laced.

"How do you know about the Irish?"

I opened my mouth to tell the truth but snapped it shut again. Darla might get in trouble if I said anything. Instead, I shrugged.

"Just heard it around."

"Hmm," he said looking me over before he glanced around and leaned forward. "Yes, that's part of my stress right now. Things keep coming up...messed up or missing. I'm doing a lot of clean-up lately and it's tiring."

I frowned. "What can be done?"

"I'll have a talk with Conor."

"Conor?"

"Yes." Amadeo picked up his glass after the wine was poured and the waitress disappeared again. "He's the head of the Kelleys. We used to have somewhat of a relationship."

I stared at him. "Relationship?"

"Yes," he said.

"What kind of relationship?" I pressed.

"Does it matter?"

Something in me stirred and I snatched up my glass. Wine wasn't usually my thing, but I downed some of the red and ignored the tartness that made the back of my jaw twinge.

"No."

Amadeo grinned. "Are you jealous?"

"No!" I snapped and reeled it in before I huffed. "You really know how to rile me up."

"At this point, I consider it a talent," he said with a smile as he drank more wine and refilled our glasses. "But Conor and I were never like that. Rivals, school friends, accomplices. We've held all of those titles, but we have never been romantically involved."

Relief filled me and I sighed. "Oh, okay."

"Were you jealous?" he asked, prodding at me.

"I told you no," I growled. "Calm down." I picked up bread and cheese once it was delivered and ate some, enjoying the sweetness of the bread and the tanginess of the cheese. "If you two are friends then why would he be attacking you?"

Amadeo frowned. "It's complicated."

"Then explain it to me."

He looked at me before he sighed. "We *used* to be friends, but not anymore. Our lives won't allow for that," he said with a shrug. "And we've always played these games with each other. He steals my guns, I steal his girls. He improves his drugs, I corner the security market. Back and forth. It's like a dance."

"Not a good one if you're stressed about it now."

Amadeo's frown deepened. "Lately it's been going beyond good-natured. I'm losing profits, losing men, and losing my grip on goddamn reality," he muttered, wiping his hand down his face before he looked at me. "Shit. How do you get me to say so much?"

I picked up my glass. "I'm not a threat, that's why. All of this stuff is over my head, but...I can listen to you while you talk about it. That's about it. I barely passed high school because of how rarely I went. Trust me, I'm not going to be in your business."

"School means shit when it comes to intelligence," Amadeo pointed out. "And I already have a feeling someone is feeding information to the outside."

I scoffed. "Are you accusing me?"

"No," he said before he turned stern. "No, Six. You have been with me and closely monitored. Besides, this started happening before you even disappeared. I'm not accusing you of this."

My shoulders relaxed a little. "Okay, good." I sighed. "It must be stressful. This life."

"It is," he said quietly before he laughed bitterly. "Stressful and lonely."

I frowned. "I'm sorry."

Amadeo shook his head but smiled. "You say those words to me so rarely. I'm sorry."

Did I really? Well, I usually thought Amadeo was a bastard, but as we sat there talking, I was starting to see that he wasn't so bad. Yes, he was still a kidnapping, monster, but he was under a hell of a lot of stress.

"What about your family?" I blurted. "Can't they help?"

Amadeo sat up a little straighter, his head lifted, his green eyes blazing. "I am the oldest of my family. It is my responsibility to keep *them* safe. Not the other way around."

I don't know what possessed me, but I reached out and laid my hand on top of his. Giving him a squeeze, I glanced up at him and Amadeo held my gaze. My heart squeezed and I could see the man beneath the monster. All of the pain, uncertainty, and stress were right on the surface.

No wonder he's such an asshole.

"Tell me about your family," I said, pushing the rest of the conversation aside for now. "I want to hear about them."

Amadeo grinned. "They're all dicks."

"Sounds like it runs in the family," I muttered.

"You ready to eat those words when we get home?" he asked.

I licked my lips. "Absolutely, Daddy."

Chapter Fourteen

Six

"Yeah, I'm okay." I smiled as I talked to Ty and Amadeo hovered nearby. "No, you don't need to send the FBI after me." I laughed nervously.

"Are you sure? Why did you stop answering my calls for so long?" Ty asked. "I mean what the fuck? I thought your dumbass had died!"

"Language, Ty," Clay growled in the background.

"Sorry, Daddy." He sighed and talked to me again. "I'm glad you're okay. When can we meet up?"

I groaned. "Hold on, let me see what I have to do." I put the phone on mute and held it against my chest. "Ty wants to hang out. When can I go?"

Amadeo's eyes searched my face before he said, "This weekend. Maybe Saturday."

Nodding, I unmuted the phone. "Saturday?"

"Yeah, I could do Saturday. Want to come over?"

I didn't think that was a good idea. Amadeo was having a hard enough time letting me meet up with him; if I said I was going to a guy's house, he would probably flip his lid.

"How about we grab lunch in the city? You've got to be tired of country life by now."

Ty laughed. "You'd think so, but I'm not. Lunch in the city sounds good though. I'm sure Clay will want to come."

"Hold on." I stabbed the mute button again. "His boyfriend wants to come too."

"Absolutely not," Amadeo snapped. "You just need to surround yourself with men?"

I growled. "Don't make it sound like I'm a slut."

Amadeo glowered, but he waved a hand. "I'm not saying that, but the answer's still no."

"Ama..."

"Don't call me that."

I groaned. "Daddy, please?" I knew he liked it when I went all soft for him. "Just this one time?"

"The answer is no. If you keep asking, I'll take the phone and you won't be going anywhere," he growled.

"Fine," I huffed.

I was sitting on the floor in front of him while he was on the couch. He leaned over, grabbed my shoulder, and squeezed firmly. "Lose the attitude."

"Yes, Daddy," I muttered. When he released me, I tilted my head back and looked up at him. "I'll see if it can just be the two of us."

"Fine."

I hit unmute. "Sorry about that."

"Why do you keep disappearing? What's going on?"

"Nothing, nothing," I said quickly. "Can it just be the two of us this Saturday? I want to catch up with you alone."

"Alright, I'm sure Clay won't mind. Send me an address when you pick a place and we'll go."

"Sounds great. Bye, Ty."

"Later."

I hung up and put the phone beside my leg. Amadeo tapped my shoulder and the motion became more persistent as I ignored him. I snatched the phone up and shoved it at him.

"Damn, prisoner bullshit," I muttered.

"Keep it up," Amadeo said. "I have no problem upgrading from my hand to a paddle on your ass."

I swallowed hard. "Sorry, Daddy."

"Good boy." He played with my hair. "Why don't you run upstairs and get ready?"

"Okay."

I hopped to my feet and jogged upstairs. We were going to an underground fighting match and I was excited. *Maybe Calix will be there.* It might not be his fight, but sometimes he stalked around and watched the other fighters, studying them. He was a good friend and I hadn't been able to see him either for a while.

But I hadn't told Amadeo I might know someone. What was the point of him locking me up in the house if Calix wasn't even there? He could be insanely jealous for some reason and I wanted to be able to go out. If I saw Calix, I could deal with it later.

Amadeo hadn't demanded I wear a tie, so instead I went with a button-up blue shirt, jeans, and sneakers. I grabbed a jacket just in case I got cold and froze. Slowly, I raised it to my nose and took in a breath. Once more, it smelled like Amadeo. All of my clothes did.

What is he doing? Rolling around in them every night when I'm asleep?

I was going to have to ask him that next time I remembered. Amadeo called me and I fixed my hair before I left my room. He was in the hallway, a black button-up strained against his chest, the sleeves were rolled up the way I liked, and he was wearing black jeans and loafers. I took in the sight of him from head to toe and sucked in a sharp breath.

"Damn."

Amadeo grinned. "Like what you see?"

I swallowed hard. "Nope."

He yanked me forward by my shirt and kissed me so hard my legs buckled. Amadeo held onto me, shoved me against the wall, and pinned my body there as his tongue slipped into my mouth. His hand pushed underneath my shirt and he scraped his nails over my sensitive flesh. I moaned, my cock hardening as he panted against my mouth and looked at me.

"Get in the fucking car before we don't go anywhere."

"Yes, Daddy."

I moved fast before he stayed true to his word and made me stay in bed again. He would do it in a heartbeat and I needed to get out of the house and do something fun. Anything. Amadeo's footsteps fell right after me and I jogged down the stairs faster until I reached the front door. He pushed me aside and opened it for me.

I stared up at him. "You don't have to-"

"Move your ass."

I laughed and kept walking. If Amadeo wanted to open my door, who was I to stop him? He did the same when we reached the car. Angelo was already waiting and along with him was the man Amadeo had clearly punched. C was all I'd heard anyone refer to him as, but he'd been silent ever since he returned to the house.

"How far is it?" I asked Amadeo.

"Not far at all," he said as he patted my leg. "Calm down."

"That's impossible," I muttered. "I'm so ready to do something fun."

"Are you saying I'm not fun?" Amadeo asked, raising his brow.

I rolled my eyes. "The only thing we do is fight and fuck," I blurted out. "Which yeah can be fun, but not as fun as going out sometimes."

Amadeo nodded. "I'll remember that," he said as he gazed out the window.

I leaned over, searching his face. "Are you upset?"

He turned to me, his face confused. "No, not at all. Does that worry you, me being upset?"

I had no answer to that. Shrugging, I quickly turned back toward the window and felt my entire body heat up. When I glanced back, Amadeo was smiling to himself and my heart skipped a beat.

He makes me crazy.

We didn't have to push through the throng of people like others had to do. Instead, we were greeted at the door and taken personally to front row seats next to the ring. The man that led us there shook Amadeo's hand and spoke rapidly before he walked away.

"Do you think he could have actually reached your asshole if he puckered up anymore?" I asked.

Amadeo burst out laughing. "Do you have a problem with that?"

I shook my head. "No. It's just crazy watching them trip over themselves like that."

"You would too if you had any common sense at all, boy. But you don't."

I shrugged. "My mom used to say I was dropped on my head as a baby. Repeatedly."

"That's probably true."

I smacked his arm. "Watch it or I won't suck your dick tonight."

"As if you have a choice?" He leaned over and whispered against my ear. "We both know if you don't, I'll force you to your knees and make you suck it."

Holy hell. I instantly shut up, only nodding as he straightened up with a smug grin on his lips. I couldn't even say anything or defend against it, because he was right. If he really wanted me tonight he would take me and I would enjoy every minute of it.

Glancing up at the ring, I forced myself to pay attention to anything but Amadeo. He laid a hand on my leg and I stiffened under his grasp. When I looked over at him, he was staring straight ahead.

Do not fall for this. This man could kill me anytime he wants.

He could, but I couldn't ignore the little voice in my head that said I was safe with him. If Amadeo wanted to kill me by now, he would have done it ten times over. But I was still alive.

"Six? Six!" I tore my gaze from Amadeo and found Calix's smiling face staring back at me from the other side of the ring. He stood up and started making his way toward me.

Amadeo's grip tightened. "Who the fuck is that?"

"That's my friend, Calix. He's a fight— Ow!"

"You knew he would be here?" Amadeo's green eyes looked so cold when he trained them on me. "What? Were you hoping he would be here? Is that why you were so excited to come?"

I squirmed in my seat, feeling as if I had done something wrong. Normally, I would have told Amadeo to go fuck himself, but the look in his eyes made me keep my mouth shut. When he squeezed harder, I let out a grunt and winced before Calix was standing in front of us.

"Yo, Six! I haven't seen you in months. Where you been?"

"Around," I said, giving him a tight smile. "Are you fighting tonight?"

He nodded. "Yep. I just got in. I still need to get ready, but I'll be center stage in a little bit." His long hair was still down, brushing over one shoulder. But as he talked, he rolled a ponytail holder off his wrist and fixed his hair up into a bun. "Who's this guy?"

Amadeo gripped me so hard I knew I would have bruises that looked like his fingertips. I glanced at him and his face was blank, mouth in a straight line as he stared Calix down.

"This is my..." I didn't know what to say. What was Amadeo to me?

"I'm his boyfriend," Amadeo spoke up. "Amadeo Bianchi."

Calix's eyes widened and he looked from Amadeo to me. "No, shit? That's new." Concern knitted his brows. "Hey uh I better go get ready for the fight. You still got the same number."

"No, not anymore. Give me your number and I'll text you."

"Yeah." Calix dug in his pocket and pulled out a pen. He grabbed my wrist and was about to write his number down when Amadeo gripped his hand and squeezed. "What the shit?"

"Back off," Amadeo growled. "If you have something to tell him it can go through me. But for now, he's busy. Go fight before I break your hand and make sure you can't."

"Amadeo!"

"I said what I said," he snarled at me before he shoved Calix away. "Get out of here."

"Sorry," I muttered to Calix.

Calix scoffed and turned on his heels. "Douchebag," he muttered under his breath before he crashed into Gabriele's chest. "You wanna watch it?"

"I do not," Gabriele said raising a brow, his hands on Calix's arms to steady him. "Maybe you should pay attention to where you're going."

My friend scoffed and shoved past Gabriele. I sank into my chair and wiped a hand down my face. *That was embarrassing as hell.*

"You didn't have to do all of that," I muttered. "Calix is my friend."

"I don't give a fuck. No one has permission to touch you. Ever." He grabbed my arm and pulled me toward him. "Do you understand me?"

I glared at him. "You act like a bastard."

"And? So what if I do? Did you forget you still owe me?" He grabbed my inner thigh and pressed on a nerve that made electricity shoot up my cock and balls. "Your body is mine. Everything you are is *mine.* And I will not share you with a single soul."

"I didn't even do anything," I said, my voice softer than I wanted it to be.

"You smiled at him." He lifted my chin. "That belongs to me too."

I pulled out of his grasp. "Let me go." I shot up out of my seat. "I need some air."

"You don't go anywhere without me."

"Is it illegal to take a piss now?" I hissed.

Amadeo stood up and snapped his fingers. "Angelo, Luka, you two go with him."

"Yes, Boss."

I stared at him and scoffed. Turning on my heels, I walked away before I said anything that would land me back in my own personal cell. I found the bathroom and slammed the door hard. Gripping the sink, I stared at my reflection and contemplated just what the hell I was doing. Amadeo proved time and time again that he was in fact the monster I thought he was and that I was nothing but his personal whore.

That feeling came back once more, the despair at knowing I meant nothing to him closing my throat. *It doesn't matter. He doesn't mean anything to me either. A few more months and this is over.*

I splashed water on my face and looked around. There was a window that I could just reach if I drug over the metal trash can. It would be easy to escape.

He would hunt me down.

My heart raced at the thought. No, I couldn't do that. But I could ditch my guards and get a few minutes of alone time by myself. Maybe I could even find Calix and explain what was going on. I turned on the water and pushed the can over before I climbed on top of it. Pushing the window outward, there was enough space for me to squeeze through. I hoisted myself up and slid off, falling to the ground before I groaned.

"Damn it." I dusted myself off and looked around. When I saw no one, I rounded the building and walked back inside, showing the stamp that had been pressed onto my skin when we entered. "Where are the fighters? I know Calix."

"Take a left and down a hall. A few rooms are on the right. I don't know if you'll be able to get in though. If his coach says no, it's a no."

"Got it. Thanks."

I walked into the building and turned down the hall. Amadeo was going to get pissed when I didn't return right away, but I wasn't planning to hang out all night. The fight was going to start soon and I would be back in my seat.

"Amadeo doesn't know what the fuck is going on. He's chasing his tail and we've been feeding him dead-end leads for weeks. We're this close to burying that fucker."

I frowned. That sounded like Luka, the guy Amadeo had busted up a few days ago. I pressed myself against the wall and made my way closer to the voice. When I peeked around, I saw Luka on the phone. He paced back and forth.

"We can't do anything stupid, but he's distracted. If we move soon he won't know what hit him. He's way too invested in that boy pussy he's got stashed at his house." He pinched the bridge of his nose. "I'll see what I can do about the next hit location. There's not enough of us to go head to head so we gotta do this quiet. Shit, I better get back. I'm supposed to be guarding the little house bitch."

I turned on my heels and walked back the way I came, trying not to run and draw attention to myself. The bathroom was in sight and I was full steam ahead until I crashed into someone. When I looked up Angelo was staring at me, his hands on my arms.

His eyes widened. "You're supposed to be in the bathroom."

"I uh..."

"You know what?" He held up a hand. "I don't want to know. You're here, you're in one piece, I'm calling that a win. Move. Get back to Amadeo before I rat you out and he kicks your ass."

I blew out a breath. "Thank you," I muttered.

Angelo nodded once and looked around. When he gazed back at me, he tilted his head in the direction of the seats and I followed him back to Amadeo. As soon as I sat down the man was on me.

"What took you so long?"

"I had to take a minute." I looked at him, frowning.

"What's the matter?" The blank look on his face dropped and he reached out, touching my chin. "Tell me."

I bit my lip. "I don't know if I should."

"Six..."

I closed my eyes and sucked in a breath. When I told him, he would kick that guy's ass, I knew he would. And that blood would be on me. His grip tightened on my chin and I opened my eyes again, taking in the concern on his face.

"What's going on, baby?"

Baby? When had he ever called me that? I don't have time to analyze that right now.

The fight started and I glanced over at the ring. Calix was already in motion. He ducked a punch, grabbed the other guy, and was immediately slammed onto the floor of the ring. I saw that determined look on his face and he was back on his feet in an instant.

"Six," Amadeo snapped.

"Fuck," I groaned. I didn't want to answer. I wanted to watch the MMA fight and forget that any of my problems existed. "I heard Luka saying that they were feeding you fake leads and making you chase your tail. That they want to...take you down or something I don't know. But they said I was your distraction and they would move soon."

Amadeo blinked at me. "Are you sure it was Luka?"

I nodded. "I saw him on his phone."

Amadeo released me and turned to Gabriele. I couldn't hear what they were saying and instead focused on the fight. Calix was faster than I remembered. He had the guy on the ground, his fist colliding with his face and then the back of his head as the guy curled up.

"Six, we're going."

I looked up at Amadeo. "Where?"

"Don't ask questions right now. Get up."

He wasn't playing around. I stood and kept my mouth shut as I followed him out of the building. There were a thousand questions running through my head, but from the way his jaw was clenched, a muscle twitching, it was a bad time to start getting nosey.

We pulled away from the building and I looked around as we rode in silence. There wasn't too much of a trip. Twenty minutes later we were pulling up to a warehouse. Angelo was still in the front seat, but Luka wasn't. As we sat there another car pulled up, the trunk was popped open, and Luka was dragged out.

"Angelo, you're with me. Once things are secure, you come back out and guard Six. No one knows we're here, but can't be too careful." He turned to me. "You're coming with me. I would send you home, but what you just figured out makes me reluctant to trust anyone with you, but me."

I stared into his eyes and nodded. "Okay."

He caressed my cheek. "Follow me."

We climbed out of the car and when I looked at Amadeo next, he was a completely different person. A mask of coldness had settled over his features and it made me shiver. Whatever I had thought about Amadeo and his cruelness, I had never seen him like this before. This was something entirely new for me.

I followed him closely into the warehouse and he led me up a set of rickety, metal stairs to an office on the second floor. He unlocked the door and let me in before he pointed to a chair.

"Sit here and wait for me."

"Yes, Daddy," I said on autopilot. "I'll wait."

"Good boy." He pulled me into a kiss before he backed up. "Be back in a bit."

I nodded and watched him leave. Glancing around the office, I sat down and examined it, but it was pretty empty. There was a computer that looked like it hadn't been used since 2002, a bunch of file cabinets, and a desk, but other than that the room was bare. I moved back and forth in the chair, staring at the ceiling, the floor, my hands until I got too bored and stood up.

What's going on down there?

Anxiety sat in my stomach like a weighted ball. It sat there in a ball, tightening as I thought about what was going on. Slowly, I walked over to the door and opened it. I expected Angelo to tell me to get my butt back in the room, but I was left unguarded. Which made sense. They had locked the place up tight. I couldn't stand not knowing what was going on.

I made my way down as quietly as possible, my heart pounding in my chest. *Just stay out of sight, that's it.* One look and I would return to my room and wait for Amadeo.

Chapter Fifteen

Amadeo

Drool slipped over the corner of Luka's mouth and dripped to the floor. My fist ached, a throbbing pain that sank deep into my flesh and traveled all over my arm. His blood stained my knuckles and I shook them off as if it would get rid of his disgusting fluids on my skin. Sneering, I grabbed a fistful of his hair and yanked his head back.

"What have you been doing, Luka?"

"N-nothing," he choked and tried to shake his head, but I tightened my grip. "I haven't done nothing, boss!"

I yanked his head down and drove my knee into his nose. The crack of cartilage echoed in my ears as he let out a sob. Every man was big and bad until you broke some bones. The tears rained down along with blood. My jaw ticked. Rat. A man like this was nothing. He had put my family, my organization and Six in danger. This was the least of what he deserved.

Tugging his hair back, I watched the blood drip down his face. A mess of snot and tears clouded his face as he babbled and begged. Every word fell on deaf ears.

"Luka? Luka, pay attention to me." I snapped my fingers in front of his face until he looked at me. "Who are you working with? You were on the phone with someone and I want to know who."

He shook his head. "No one."

"What do I look like to you? Do I look like a moron?"

"No, no that's not-"

I punched him in the throat and he choked on his words, gasping for air as I took his breath away. Pulling back, I let him gather himself. Six wouldn't lie to me. If he said Luka was on the phone with someone, he was. But knowing that there was dissension in my own group? That was a slap in the face.

"I'm going to give you one more chance, Luka. Either you tell me what's going on or I'll kill you, track down your family and kill them, and it'll keep going like that until I'm satisfied. And I'm a hard man to please, you know that."

He coughed and blood spluttered from his lips, sprinkling my suit. I wiped the droplets down, but they only stained more. Sighing, I crooked my fingers at Angelo.

"Go get my tools from the car."

"No!" Luka yelled, his head shooting up as he shook it hard. "D-don't."

"Get 'em," I said to Angelo when he hesitated.

"I-I'll tell you," Luka said as his wild eyes went from me to Angelo and back again. "I don't want to die."

Too late.

Did he think he was going to live past tonight? No. If a rattlesnake slithered into a house and threatened to attack the people living there, it would lose its head. Luka was going to meet that same fate after I got the information I was looking for.

Angelo turned to get the tools and I held up a hand. "Wait." I turned back to Luka. "Talk."

Luka coughed and shook his head. "I don't know who's running it," he said, a slight wheeze behind his words as he looked up at me. "I get orders, I know a few people who are working together, but that's it."

"Not good enough." I stood up and cracked my knuckles. "Let's try again."

"W-wait. I only know two other names, but that's how this is set up. The leader doesn't want us to know too much so we're only in contact with people when we need to be. I've never met the main guy or woman or whoever it is."

"Gonna need more than that," I said as I pushed my sleeves up more. "You've given me nothing and expect to live?" I clicked my tongue. "Not a fair trade."

"Please, boss," he panted. "I'm telling the truth."

I crossed my arms over my chest. "And?"

The man whimpered like a sick dog. "Please... I-I just.. I fucked up but I can fix it. Let me fix it, boss!"

His desperate pleading fell on deaf ears. I ignored him as I pulled out my gun and knife, setting them on the table beside me. His eyes landed on them and widened. Once more, he started jerking around and trying to get free of the metal cuffs that bound his hands behind the chair. It creaked and almost fell over but Luka wasn't getting away from me.

"I think this is a good place to start carving," I said as I dug the tip of the knife into his thigh. "What do you think?"

Luka's words went from desperate to incoherent as panic set in. I stared at him, but I felt nothing. I hardly ever did anymore. The only person that made me *feel* was Six. He pissed me off, drove me crazy, filled me with so much warmth it was as if the darkness of my world had never tainted my heart. And sometimes he even made me smile. Everything else was just a nuisance, something that needed to be dealt with before I could retreat to Six and find comfort in him.

And this asshole is interrupting my date.

It hadn't been going too smoothly beforehand, but it was easy to make Six calm down and control himself. We could have been back at the fight watching the entertainment and wrapped up in each other. Instead, he was upstairs and I was working.

This guy is really pissing me the fuck off.

Anger coursed through me and I wanted to rip Luka's head off with my bare hands. He had gotten in the way of me and Six. That was a killable offense on its own but add to it that he was plotting against me and he deserved to die even more.

"Boss, I don't think we're going to get anything else out of him," Angelo said as he stood beside me. "He's just babbling at this point."

I shook my head. "There's always more I can get out of him. Move." I ran the cool steel of my knife against Luka's cheek. "Stop fucking crying and look at me."

The tip of the knife dug into his chin. Blood dripped to the floor, but I kept my eyes trained on his. Luka swallowed hard, his adam's apple dancing in his throat as he trembled before me.

"Tell me everything or I'm going to start slicing off pieces. I'll start with your balls and go from there."

Panic flooded his face and sweat rolled down his skin. Even in the coolness of the warehouse, he was a hot mess. I grabbed his cheeks to hold him still and slipped the knife in a bit more slicing into his chin. The bleeding picked up and he gasped, his eyes round as saucers as he tried to hold his breath to keep from moving.

"Come on. I know there's more. You need to talk."

"I-I don't know anything else," he whispered. "Please believe me. If I knew I would tell you. Don't you think that I would? You're threatening to cut my balls off. Trust me if I had answers you would be getting them. I don't know shit!"

Standing up, I nodded at Luka. He said he didn't know anything, but I felt his lie deep in my bones. The man was full of shit. But he wasn't about to spill anything more. Or at least not without a hell of a lot more work and even then he was a tight-lipped bastard.

Luka had reached the end of his usefulness to me.

"I guess you don't need to live anymore then."

His eyes widened. "But I gave you the information!"

"And? I never said you were going to live." I gripped the knife harder, the handle digging in against my skin. "Once you betray me, you're done."

His pleas echoed around the warehouse but it was nothing more than white noise as I walked around. as I walked around the chair and pressed the knife against his throat. Luka would be an example for whoever else was causing problems for me and my family. If they saw his end, it would be enough to deter them from going on with their bullshit.

Quick movement caught my attention and I glanced up. Six's eyes met mine. The fear on his face shot pain right to my core. He turned and ran.

I must look like a monster to him.

I was standing there covered in blood, a knife to Luka's throat. He saw me like that about to kill. Something odd twisted in my stomach and I swallowed thickly.

"Shit. Finish this," I told Angelo as I shoved the knife into his hand and ran after Six. "Wait!"

I caught up with him, yanking on a door, and grabbed his wrists. Six struggled against me, his breathing coming so fast I was sure he would pass out on the spot. I dragged him against my body, but he shoved me away.

"Don't touch me!" he snapped. "Just stay back."

I frowned. "Six, this has to be done."

"Does it?" he asked, sliding away from me along the wall.

"Yes. Luka is like an infection. If I let him live, he will infect everything until it's festering." I sighed and ran a hand down my face, feeling the half-dried droplets of blood smearing over my skin. "You should have stayed upstairs."

"I want to go," Six said shakily. "Now."

Glancing around, I nodded. Angelo could take care of the clean-up. I reached out for him and laid a hand on his back. Six shivered, but he didn't run away again. That was probably as good as it was going to get. I let us out into the night air and sucked in a deep breath. The coppery tang of blood still filled my nose and I knew Six could smell it too.

"We're going home," I said softly helping him into the passenger seat. "Okay?"

Six nodded, but his lips were set in a straight line. He looked out through the windshield, but his eyes refused to meet mine. That same strange twisting in my stomach grew until I wanted to scream.

Why won't you look at me?

I closed his door and walked to the driver's side before I paused. Reflected back at me was an image of myself covered in blood. The look on my face was hard, twisted.

The face of a monster.

Chapter Sixteen

Six

I COULDN'T GET THAT IMAGE OUT OF MY HEAD. AMADEO STANDING behind Luka, the knife cutting into his throat, the way he was about to kill him without hesitation. And then there was the look on Amadeo's face. So calm and dead as if he wasn't doing anything at all.

How could he be so okay with it?

I tugged the blanket over my head and made myself even smaller. Sure, I'd seen people get beat up but I had never seen anyone be almost killed right in front of me.

I should have stayed upstairs.

Closing my eyes and trying to sleep didn't help. I saw Amadeo covered in blood with a knife in his hand and remembered my situation and where I was. This was Amadeo's house and I was his prisoner. If he really wanted to, he could kill me without a second thought. And I had been playing games with him, sleeping with him, even enjoying his company.

A shiver wracked my body and I gripped my pillow more tightly. *I have to get out of here.*

Knock. Knock.

I sat up and stared at the door warily. "Yeah?"

"Can I come in?"

Angelo's voice was comforting. I hadn't seen Amadeo since the night before, but I knew he'd come to my room eventually. He always did.

"Yeah come in."

He let himself inside and a woman bustled past him, plopping a tray on my bed. She smiled at me and sat beside the tray.

"You must be Six," she said as she pushed the food toward me. "Ama said you had to be hungry by now so I'm bringing you dinner."

"Um, who are you?" I asked.

"Oh yeah, sorry I got ahead of myself." She held a hand out decorated in gold jewelry. "I'm Rayna. Ama's sister."

I stared at her. When I looked closer, I could see the family resemblance. Rayna had the same dark hair and olive skin. She looked expensive as if everything she wore was way out of everyone else's league. Her smile was soft, but there was something in her eyes that screamed not to underestimate her.

"Six," I said, finally taking her hand and shaking it lightly. "Did Amadeo send you in?"

She shook her head. "No, no nothing like that. He's having a meeting in his office and I was bored five minutes in so I came to see the new guest Gabriele has been telling me about." She pushed my food closer. "But do eat. No need to have an empty stomach because I'm here."

How could I explain to her that I didn't even have an appetite? That had disappeared when I watched Amadeo getting ready to kill without flinching. I tugged the tray closer and picked up a slice of pizza. Amadeo always pulled faces when I ordered it, but he had clearly had it made for me.

I took a bite and it tasted like sawdust in my mouth. Every time I thought about Amadeo, the same knot formed in my stomach and tightened. I sat the pizza down and grabbed the water bottle sipping from it while I tried to figure out why Amadeo's sister was here.

"I heard the two of you had a rough go of it the other night," she started slowly. "These things can be difficult. Our lives."

I stared at her. "Murdering people seems really difficult, yeah," I said scoffing before I sat the water bottle down a little too hard, water sloshing onto the tray. I angrily screwed the top back on. "So, Luka's dead?"

"He crossed Amadeo."

"So he just dies?"

Rayna tilted her head. "What would you have him do? Give Luka a slap on the wrist and leave him to destroy our family?"

I pressed my lips together and sat back because I didn't have any solutions. Maybe Amadeo could have locked him up or hurt him or something! But it would be better than killing him.

But he couldn't do that to each and every person that ever messed with him. Where would he have the space? And people would think he was weak. Why am I even thinking about this stuff?

I pressed two fingers against my temple and massaged away the headache that was starting to form. My life was so much simpler a few months ago. Work at my job, come home, party, go to bed. Start it all over again the next day. Now I was trying to see things from the perspective of a mafia boss.

"Look this shit's tough, but it's what we have to deal with." She stood up and wiped imaginary lint from her black dress. "It was nice to meet you. Try not to freak out over this too much. Shit happens."

Shit. Happens.

That was how they viewed this. Were all of them so numb that they didn't care that they were ending lives?

Probably.

Rayna's phone rang and she glanced at it before her eyes went to me. She quieted it and shoved it back into her purse.

"Gotta go hon. I'm sure we'll see each other again soon."

I nodded, but I had no intentions of sticking around. As soon as I could get away from Amadeo and the insanity that was his family I would. No more sticking around and waiting it out. I needed to leave before I ended up tied to a chair with a knife to my throat.

Once Rayna was gone, I picked up the tray and carried it to the door. I sat it on the ground after looking up and down the hall, but Amadeo was nowhere in sight. Angelo had been stationed right outside of my door and he looked at me and only nodded before he went back to standing guard.

I'll have to find a way past him when it's time to go.

The night before had made Amadeo even more paranoid about everything, but especially me. As he drove us back to the house, I heard him on the phone making sure things were secure and the house was safe for me. Angelo was no longer allowed to leave my side even for a minute. It hadn't even been twenty-four hours and I already felt suffocated.

I slipped back into my room and decided to take a shower. Maybe the hot water would clear my head. I turned on the shower and yanked off my clothes, tossing them into the hamper before I leaned against the wall waiting for it to heat up.

Amadeo popped right back into my mind and I frowned. I had been letting myself get close to a blood-thirsty psychopath. Or was it sociopath? Either way, it needed to stop. Amadeo was my captor, my prison guard that had locked me away and kept me from leaving or talking to anyone except for him. He'd given me the false sense that I had freedom; taking me out, letting me call Ty. But I was still a prisoner.

I stepped into the shower and tried to stop thinking about the night before. But no matter how hard I tried, it stuck with me. I cut my shower short and stepped out, wrapping a towel around my waist before I froze in the doorway.

Amadeo sat on my bed, his phone in his hand. He looked like he always did; impeccable and intimidating. One leg draped over the other, his suit jacket gone, and his dark shirt opened at the first two buttons. If he was anyone else I would say he was my type. My type couldn't be killers.

He glanced up at me. "You're finally done with your shower." He frowned, his eyes running over me. "I saw your tray outside. You didn't eat."

"Wasn't hungry," I said shortly as I walked over to the dresser.

"That can't be true. You haven't eaten since yesterday and I know how your appetite is."

Right, because Amadeo Bianchi knew everything.

I pushed through the clothes in the dresser and picked out something to wear. A pair of shorts and a shirt was more than enough for me. All I wanted to do was crawl back into the bed and stay there for the rest of the night. I wasn't up to sleeping with Amadeo.

"Six."

Should I go into the bathroom? I need to get dressed, but I don't want him staring at me. I weighed my options as I stared at the clothes in my hands.

"Six."

"What?" I answered, exasperated that he wasn't taking the hint already and leaving.

"Look at me."

"I'm trying to get dressed."

Amadeo's warm hand wrapped around my wrist and sent shivers down my spine. He turned me around. "Look at me!"

I flinched in fear and threw my hands up as I tried to pull away from him. My eyes screwed shut waiting for him to hit me. When the blow didn't come, I slowly opened my eyes.

Amadeo stared at me, his eyes filled with concern and...what was that? I couldn't decipher his emotions as they flashed over his face and disappeared as quickly as they came. He let me go and took a step back.

My throat squeezed as he turned on his heels and left the room. I stood there, frozen, waiting for him to come back or say something. He didn't return.

Why do I want him to come back?

I laid a hand on my stomach and a knot twisted. The look on Amadeo's face was pain. Had I hurt him? How could anyone hurt the head of the Bianchi family?

A stupid part of me begged to go after him, to tell him it was okay. That I was okay. It was a lie, I was still a mess, but I felt the urge to comfort him. I took a step toward the door and stopped myself.

I should leave him alone.

Instead of going after Amadeo, I tugged on my clothes and sat on the bed. But I couldn't tear my eyes away from the door as I waited.

Everything in my life had gone from making sense to complicated. And I was stuck worrying about a man that could kill me. The only thing that looped through my head was if he was okay. The hurt that had sparked in his green eyes had been because of me.

This is my fault.

Chapter Seventeen

Amadeo

I STARED AT MY PHONE. SIX HAD OPENED MY TEXT LETTING HIM know that I would return shortly. That was a few weeks ago. I hadn't said anything since, but Six continued to text me.

Six: Where are you?

Six: Why aren't you answering?

Six: Are you dead or something? If you're dead do I get to go home?

Six: Amadeo what the fuck is this!

Six: ......

He hadn't sent me a message the past few days. I moved away from the texts and pulled up the camera instead. Six was in the back garden with Angelo watching over him. The boy was pacing back and forth endlessly. He pulled out his phone and my stomach clenched in anticipation. After a minute, he shoved it back into his pocket and started pacing once more.

I touched the screen as if I could reach through and feel him underneath my fingertips. My heart squeezed and I quickly exited the program so I wouldn't keep staring at Six. Gabriele was right about my obsessions and how quickly they broke me.

My phone rang and I picked it up. "Yeah?"

"Hey, boss, doing a check-in. Six went back up to his room to sleep."

"How is he?"

"Alright, I guess. Either pissed off or quiet." Angelo went silent for a moment. "Can I ask you something?"

"If you have to," I said, picking up my tablet to scroll through my leads. Someone had to know something about who was on my ass.

"Have you ever considered this could be coming from someone...close to you?"

I froze. "What do you mean?"

Angelo sighed. "Nothing, I shouldn't have said anything."

"Tell me," I growled, my patience wearing thinner by the second.

He blew out a heavy breath. "It's just that...whoever's doing this shit has to be close to you. They're getting to your guards, they're in your house, they're sitting in on your meetings or at least most of them. What if it's one of your brothers? Or Rayna?"

I bristled. "Are you insane?"

"It's not the first time it's happened," Angelo pointed out. "Your uncle did the same thing to your father with your aunt's help. They tried to take him down."

BREAK ME DADDY

Rubbing my temple I tried not to yell at Angelo, because he was right. But he was bringing up a very dark and twisted era of my childhood that I didn't want to remember. I'd been close to my father's brother and sister at one point. Baseball games, trips to Italy, family dinners. The day I put a bullet through my Uncle's head was permanently seared into my brain.

"Boss?"

"I heard you. Keep a close eye on Six and make sure no one has access to him but you. Understood?"

"Yes. I'm on it."

"Angelo?"

"Yes?"

I frowned. "What made you think that it could be someone close to me in the first place?"

"Something Luka said the night you ran after Six. He was mumbling something about the danger being closer than you think."

I paused. "Why didn't you tell me this before?"

"It's been hard to talk to you over the past month. You've been busy tracking down leads and I've been keeping up with Six. I wanted to tell you sooner, but I honestly thought it was bullshit and Luka was trying to save his skin."

"Next time tell me right away," I said through gritted teeth.

"Yes, Boss."

I hung up and sat the phone on the coffee table. Someone close to me. I closed my eyes, trying to picture who that could be but nobody came to mind. My brothers and my cousins were loyal to me, always had been. And Rayna could be wild, but she would never betray me.

That's what Dad thought too.

Shit. I unbuttoned my shirt trying to dispel the suffocating feeling that was creeping up on me, but it did nothing. I leaned back in my seat and my fingers itched to pick up my phone and stare at Six some more. *I just want to know he's okay.*

Muffled sounds floated to my ears and I groaned. Right, I had to focus on work right now. I put Six out of my mind and the world immediately dulled once more. Tucking all of my emotions neatly back into the void they'd come from, I stood up and walked over to the man lying on a blue tarp. He was hogtied and lying on his stomach, but rocking back and forth to no doubt try to get into a more comfortable position.

Crouching down, I ripped the duct tape from his lips and he bellowed out a yell. When he looked up at me, his eyes were dark and there was fire behind them. Good. I liked someone with a bit of fight in them.

I grabbed his cheeks, my nails digging into his flesh as his jaw ticked. "You want to talk now?"

He growled. "I didn't do shit!"

"That's funny because I have video surveillance of you sneaking around the last warehouse that was broken into. So, want to try again?"

"Fuck you," he spat.

I grinned. "You remind me of someone."

BREAK ME DADDY

Dropping his face, I stood and rolled up my sleeves. I needed to find out how deep this betrayal ran. Who was slandering my name within my own organization? And where was the information they were gathering going? Luka was in no way a mastermind and I doubted this guy was either. Somewhere, someone was calling the shots.

Angelo's words came back to me and I frowned. Thinking about it being someone in my family made my stomach squeeze with nervousness. I was closest to them and to Six. I didn't want to believe that the few people I had allowed to get close to me would want to destroy me.

But that was my life. No matter how much you thought you could trust someone, it was a reality that anyone could betray you at any time. I had to look at it from all sides, consider every motive. And once I found the cancer that had dug its way into my organization's veins, I was going to cut it out with a dull knife.

I laid my tools out on the coffee table and glanced around the loft. A month of living on my own had turned me right back into the man I was supposed to be. Six was a distraction. If I went back to him, he would soften parts of me that needed to stay concrete in order for me and everyone under me to survive.

But I couldn't stop thinking about him. Even now I could see him sitting at the table or lounging on the couch. I could still smell him in my bed when he was wrapped up in the blankets sound asleep.

"Let me go!" the man on the floor shouted, breaking my happy memories.

Ice spread through my veins as I turned to look at him. The fight in his eyes flickered and whatever he saw when he looked at me made him swear under his breath before he shrunk in on himself. I picked up a small dagger and walked over to him.

"You wanted my attention. I'm here now." I crouched and ran the knife over the bare skin of his back. "Don't worry, you'll have all of my attentiveness until they're carrying you out of here in multiple garbage bags."

A shiver raced over his body. "I-"

"Shhhh," I interrupted him and the blade sliced through his back drawing a scream from his throat. "I'm in a horrible mood today and this thing, these lies, and bullshit are only making it worse. So, let's skip all the fuckery and get right to the point. Who are you working with?"

Panting, he shook his head. "No way! I'll be dead."

"Die by my hand or die by theirs, I really don't give a damn." I slipped my gloved fingers through his blood and paused. "Either way, I'm going to get the information I need. You're in the way of me being somewhere more important."

I had to make my way back to Six. No matter how much I knew I needed to put distance between us, I couldn't. Four weeks had passed like four years and I was already craving my boy.

Once I find the problem, I'm going to fix it and go back home to him. And I'll make him see this isn't all I am.

I'm not just a monster.

"I don't know shit!"

I stabbed the knife into the man's thigh. "I was thinking about something. Shut up unless it's a name. And stop screaming!"

He tried to muffle himself, but I was already thinking about Six again. I wasn't a saint. This was part of who I was too. How did I find balance? I never wanted to scare Six, not like that. Not now that we'd spent time together.

I had to fix things between us.

Chapter Eighteen

Amadeo

My body ached after spending hours with my guest the night before and I still didn't have enough information. Conor Kelley's name had come up and I knew it was beyond time to talk to him. We'd always had a tentative peace with each other, but if that was broken, I needed to know. It would start a war but some things couldn't be helped.

I grabbed a cup of coffee and let myself be distracted just long enough to stare at Six through the screen. He was in a bad mood and had been since yesterday. Refusing to come out, to eat, or to talk to anyone. I knew I had to go back home eventually. No one knew how to deal with Six the way I did.

And I miss him.

I sat my cup down and massaged my temple. No, I wasn't supposed to be thinking about him no matter how badly I wanted to. The sooner I was able to figure out what was going on the sooner I would be able to protect Six. Whoever had it out for me knew about him and that meant he was in just as much danger as I was.

Exiting out of the camera, I pulled out the slip of paper with Conor's phone number on it. Darla had tracked it down for me and I needed to get this over with. I typed in his digits and pressed the phone against my ear.

"Hello?"

"Conor."

A deep chuckle echoed in my ear. "Amadeo. I would know that annoying voice anywhere."

I rolled my eyes. "Do you really want to start shit the moment I call you?"

"Absolutely." He paused. "What's up? You're not your usual chipper self."

"When have I ever been chipper?"

"Once upon a time," Conor said. "Seriously, I've heard about your problems lately. I hope you don't think that has anything to do with me."

I carried my coffee over to the dining room table and sat down. "Are you sure about that? The gentleman that was here last night seemed to think it was your guys breaking into my warehouses, harassing my workers, and generally fucking things up for me."

He sighed. "If I wanted to fuck things up for you, Amadeo, I would do a hell of a lot more than break into some of your warehouses and torch your crap. You know that. Last I checked, you have your territory and I have mine. I haven't changed my mind about our truce. The way we were fighting back then was dangerous and stupid. I don't have time to deal with the police or the fucking feds and neither do you. Our lives are dangerous enough without going at each other."

I frowned and ran my fingers over the prickly stubble on my chin. Conor was right about that. We'd seen the destruction and danger that landed on our doorsteps when we danced on each other's toes. Neither of us wanted that. But if it wasn't Conor then who was stupid enough to stir things up?

"Maybe you're right," I muttered. "But I want to impress upon you the fact that if this is you and I find out, I won't hesitate to slit your throat."

Conor laughed. "Aye, I know how you are," he said, his rich Irish accent popping up. "Trust me, I don't have any plans to go head to head with you anytime soon. And if I did you would never even see me coming, Amadeo."

"Is that what you think?"

"That's what I know," he said pointedly, the humor fading from his voice. "Just my advice, but you should focus your attention elsewhere. As far as you and I are concerned there's no drama."

"And you swear that? On your mother?"

"On my dear Mother," he said solemnly. "Tell you what if I hear anything, I'll let you know."

"You don't have to go out of your way," I said as I picked up my mug and sipped my coffee.

"No, no. Consider it a gesture of goodwill. When I bring you the guy's head who's doing this, you can shove it up your ass for thinking I'm lying to you. I gotta go."

I grinned. "Yeah, we'll see. Alright, thank you."

"You got it."

Once we hung up, I stared at the phone and shook my head. Conor was as rash and crazy as always. I didn't know whether or not I believed him, but all I could do was wait.

Sitting the phone down I grabbed a cigarette and lit it. Smoke curled into the air as I contemplated what to do next. So far, I was still at a dead end. There were only so many leads I could track down before I became stomped once again. Heat crawled up my spine as the frustration of my situation set in.

All I wanted to do was go home and be with my boy.

I held in the smoke until my lungs screamed for relief and I finally blew it out. Angelo was working his own angles for me, but there was only so much he could do while he watched over Six. But I didn't trust anyone else to protect the boy. There could be countless other spies in my household and I wasn't going to let anything happen to Six.

My phone buzzed on the table shaking me out of my thoughts. *It never ends.* I snatched it up and saw it was Gabriele calling me.

"I'm in the middle of something," I said as soon as we were connected.

"Six is gone."

Ice shot through my veins. I couldn't make my mouth form words as I stared straight ahead and wondered if I had just heard my brother correctly. No, he hadn't just said that Six was gone. My stomach clenched and I growled low in my throat.

I sat up straighter. "What the fuck are you talking about?"

Gabriele sounded out of breath. "I mean he's gone. He was on the balcony all morning and then he locked the bedroom door after I left. I thought he wanted to be alone, but when he wouldn't talk to me a little while ago, I knew I had to check on him. Angelo got me in the door and he's gone. I don't know where the hell he went."

I shot up out of my chair and it slammed against the floor. "What does the room look like? Could someone have gotten in there?"

"No, it doesn't look like he's been taken. The shower is still wet, the drawers are half-opened, and his shoes are gone. If anything I'm pretty sure he took off on his own."

I gripped the phone hard. Six had run off? That was unacceptable. I tossed the cigarette into my cup of coffee and ran upstairs to grab a shirt and some shoes. *I was going to do more than spank his tight ass when I got my hands on him.*

"What do you want me to do here?" Gabriele asked.

"I need to check something. Hold on."

I scrolled through the apps and pulled up the tracker I had on Six's phone. The small red dot was blinking right where he was supposed to be, my house. *He left the damn phone. I'm going to kill him.*

"Get some guys and start looking. How long has he been missing?"

"He can't have been gone for more than an hour."

I nodded and snatched my car keys off the dresser. "He has no car or money so I doubt he could have gotten too far. Get moving. I want him found now!"

"Yeah, I'm on it."

"When you guys find him, just keep eyes on him and tell me the location. I don't want anyone touching him."

"Yep."

Gabriele hung up and I stopped to take a deep breath before I snapped. Shit. *I never should have left him alone.* I stormed out of the door and slammed it behind me as I waited impatiently for the elevator.

What the fuck is he thinking?

Six couldn't escape me. He had to know that by now. No matter where he ran or how far he got I would always be right there to drag him back to me. Six was my boy, my property, my everything. I couldn't lose the one thing in my life that held any meaning.

"Fuck!"

My fist crashed into the steel elevator doors and pain shot up my wrist. The elevator dinged and the doors opened before I stepped inside and shook out my hand.

Breathe. I'm going to get him back even if I have to drag him kicking and screaming. Even if I have to lock him up and keep him from the world altogether. I will not lose my boy.

I stepped off of the elevator focused. Six was the only man I wanted and I would be damned if I let him get away from me. I couldn't.

Not when I was pretty damn sure I was falling in love with him.

Chapter Nineteen

Six

Every pair of eyes that stared at me felt like they would report back to Amadeo. The feeling of dread that had followed me for months when I was running from him in the first place returned and my stomach turned. Amadeo could be anywhere, around any corner. He or his goons would snatch me up, toss me into a car, and I would wake up in the same dirty cell as before.

Once more his prisoner.

I couldn't do it anymore. Couldn't take living in a cage. I thought I was miserable when he was there demanding me to pay him back with my body, but the truth was that when he was gone it was more unbearable somehow. There was no one to distract me from the constant nothing that was my days and nights, no one to spite and direct my anger at. For a solid month, I had been left alone with my thoughts except for the times that Rayna or Gabriele visited me. And even that hadn't been enough to keep me from losing it.

No, I had to get and stay the hell away from that house.

I tugged my jacket around me tighter and caught a slight whiff of Amadeo's scent. Tugging it away from my skin, I shivered. Glancing around, I couldn't stop myself as I shoved it against my nose and inhaled him. My eyes closed and I stopped walking. It was like he was right there, dragging me into his arms.

Ever since he'd left, his scent had been fleeting. I caught it here and there, but it was no longer clinging to all of my clothes, my sheets, my skin. And I hated it.

Seriously I need to get it together. It's not like we were dating. Captive. Prisoner. That's all it is.

I let the jacket fall from my fingers and opened my eyes. Right, I was on a mission. I needed somewhere to go and the only person I could think to ask was Tyler. The guy I'd hitchhiked into the city with had let me use his phone and I was able to set up a meeting with Ty. Once I saw him I was going to come clean about everything and maybe he could let me lie low in his place out in the country. Amadeo wouldn't find me there.

Or at least I hoped he wouldn't. I couldn't put Ty and his Daddy in danger because of my own stupid choices.

I found the coffee shop and stepped inside. The smell of coffee and sweets made my stomach growl and I laid a hand on it. I had barely been eating the past few days. Every time I sat at that big table, I was reminded I was completely alone. And even eating in the room, I was surrounded by the fact that this was not my home, not my place.

"Six!"

I glanced up at Ty. He was in line and waved me over, a concerned look on his face. I made my way over to him and his frown deepened.

"You look like hell."

"Thanks," I said, pushing my fingers through my hair self-consciously. It had grown out and I was desperate for a haircut, but I refused to ask Amadeo for anything. "Can I get a cup of coffee? And a muffin? I would pay for it but..." I shrugged, unable to admit that I was flat broke and practically begging.

"Don't worry about it, I've got you." We reached the counter and Ty ordered our drinks and food. We carried them back to a corner of the shop away from the windows and sat down. "Okay, now what the fuck is going on? You've got me worried, man."

I held up a finger and downed coffee like it was going to solve all my problems and make me feel like I wasn't half dead. Hot as hell, it burned going down but some part of me relished that feeling. It was better than feeling so fucking numb I no longer had any idea who I was.

"Six."

I sat the coffee cup down and cleared my throat as I picked at my strawberry cheesecake muffin. "The guy I stole all that money from? He caught me."

"Shit." Ty's brows furrowed. "Are you okay?"

How was I supposed to answer that without sounding absolutely batshit insane? No, I wasn't okay because he was gone and leaving me the hell alone? Yeah, no one was going to understand that I was in a game of tug of war with my own mind.

I hate Amadeo.

I want Amadeo.

I hate him.

I want him.

My brain was on a rollercoaster and I had no idea when I was going to be able to get the hell off. Glancing up at Ty, I realized he was still staring at me waiting for some answer. So I gave the easiest one I could.

"Yeah, I'm fine. But he's making me pay it off."

"How?"

I choked on my muffin and cleared my throat. "Um well with uh..."

Ty's eyes widened. "Is he fucking you for the money? What the hell? Are you okay with that?"

I shrugged again. "It's not like I could afford to pay him back any other way and he wants me. Six months. That's all I have to put in before he'll let me go. Until then I'm supposed to be staying in his house and working it off."

He frowned. "He let you out today?"

"Nah, I ran."

Ty groaned. "Six, you fucking moron."

"I know. I know. But he's been gone for a month and I needed to get out of that house for a little while."

"Are you going back?"

I chugged more of my coffee. "I don't know," I said when I put it down. "I haven't made my mind up yet."

"If he found you once, he can find you again you know," Ty said as he leaned closer to me. "This is dangerous."

. . .

"Trust me, I know." I sighed and bit my lip. "I didn't think before I did it. One minute I was standing in the room and the next I was climbing over the balcony railing and shimmying down the damn drain pipe. I never said I was the smartest guy that ever existed."

Ty scoffed. "Tell me about it."

I glared at him. "Thanks a lot!"

"Well, it's true! I thought I was impulsive but you're on a whole different level." He shook his head. "What are you going to do now?"

I toyed with the empty muffin paper, twisting it back and forth. Now that I had some food on my stomach I felt a little better, but that feeling of dread hadn't disappeared.

"Could I possibly stay with you and Clay?"

Ty frowned. "Shit. I would have to ask him. I mean we do have some extra room and I'm sure he wouldn't mind, but this whole thing," he said gesturing around us, "I don't want it hurting Clay. You're involved with a dangerous fucking guy, Six."

"I know," I muttered, closing my eyes and rubbing them. "Trust me, I know."

He tapped my arm and I looked at him. "I'll ask him right now. Just let me talk to him."

"Okay."

Ty smiled at me. "You know I'd do anything for you."

"Yeah, I know," I said quietly. "But I don't want you to if it's going to cause a problem."

"Shut up. I'll be right back."

I smiled until Ty was out of the coffee shop and I was left on my own. *I'm an asshole.* Putting this burden on Ty felt shitty. He hadn't stolen that money, I had. I frowned. *I can't go back to Amadeo.*

"Get up and follow me quietly."

The whisper against my ear shot a shiver right down my spine. I stared straight ahead, my heart racing as I instantly recognized his voice. Slowly, I turned around. Amadeo stared down at me, his face calm, but his eyes blazing.

Shit. I'm dead.

"Amadeo, I was-"

"Up. Now."

I swallowed thickly and stood up. Amadeo grabbed my arm, his fingers digging into my skin through my jacket as he dragged me out of the coffee shop. Eyes followed our movements, but no one interfered and it wouldn't matter even if they did. Amadeo was on a mission.

"Hey, what's going on?" Ty called as we walked past him. "Six?"

Amadeo stopped and turned back to look at him. "And you are?"

"Who the fuck are you?" Ty asked right back, scowling.

"Amadeo Bianchi."

Ty's eyes widened. "Shit. Wait."

"It's okay," I said quickly as Ty started walking toward us. I wasn't going to let him get hurt because of me. "I'll just call you later."

"Six..."

"I have to go." I shook my head at him once Amadeo began pulling me along once again.

"You won't be calling anyone anytime soon," Amadeo informed me as he opened a car door and pushed me inside. A guard sat up front, but he didn't even look in my direction. "You're lucky you were spotted this quickly. You," he said to the guard. "Have my car picked up and returned to the house."

"Yes, Boss."

Amadeo handed the keys over before he slammed the car door. I moved as far away as I could, pressing myself up against the door as if I could get away from him. I grabbed the handle and tugged, but the door was locked.

"Try that shit again," Amadeo growled.

I swallowed thickly. "I'm sorry," I managed to get out, my throat tightening. "But you were gone. I figured if you didn't need me to be around anymore, I could leave."

Amadeo glared at me. "Is that what you thought?"

I stared up at him and anger took over every emotion. How was he sitting there angry at me? It was true, he hadn't been around and my only purpose was to fuck him for six months. If that's not what we were doing then I should be free to go.

"Yes," I snapped. "If you don't want me, just fucking say so and I'll go back to living my life! It's one thing if you're making me work this stupid debt off, but if you're just going to-"

My eyes widened as his lips crashed against mine. His tongue slipped into my mouth, claiming every inch of it as his hand wrapped around my throat. Fingers tangled into my hair and he dragged me closer, holding me in place as he kissed me so hard my pulse tripled and I forgot how to breathe.

"You are mine," he growled against my lips when he came up for air. "Until I say you can leave, you belong to me."

I shook my head. "No, I'm not your property," I panted.

"Yes, you are." He bit my lip and I cried out. "And you will never be anyone else's."

Amadeo's hands tore at my clothes. My head went foggy as he undid my jeans and shoved them down my hips. I tried to push him away, but he knocked my hands to the side and kept going until he freed my cock. His lips wrapped around it and I let out a moan.

No, don't like this. I shouldn't want it. I shouldn't want him.

"We're...in the car," I panted. "With..." I looked into the front seat. With an audience.

"I don't give a fuck," Amadeo growled.

My head tilted back and I thrust my hips forward. Shit. Once more I was on display, but Amadeo didn't give a damn and I was close to not caring either. Amadeo moaned around my cock and I forgot how to breathe right. My fingers shoved into his dark locks and I gripped them tightly as his head bobbed up and down. Nothing compared to the fire that was Amadeo. Even if he was a bastard.

He reached up and shoved two fingers into my mouth. Without thinking, I sucked them in. I worked my tongue around them, lathering them with saliva, sucking and licking them as if it was his cock in my mouth. I closed my eyes and imagined that's exactly what was happening. My mouth was wrapped around his dick, tasting him and taking in the heady scent of him.

Amadeo pulled his fingers free and I let out a pathetic whimper. My eyes fluttered open and I took in his heated face, his flushed cheeks. Amadeo pulled free of my cock and licked his lips making them glisten. I wanted to kiss him all over again.

"You missed me," he said matter-of-factly as he tugged my clothes all the way off and pressed a finger against my hole.

"No," I said, shaking my head, but the word held no conviction.

"Yes, you did." He pushed his finger inside and I sucked in a breath as he pushed in deeper and pressed against my prostate. "Don't lie to me, boy."

My hips jerked and I craved more. I needed his mouth wrapped around my cock again, I needed more stimulation. Fuck, I just wanted him to *touch me!*

"You're an asshole," I muttered. "Daddy."

Amadeo grinned and my heart fluttered. "Say it again."

"You're an asshole, Daddy," I panted as he worked another finger inside of me, opening me up.

"And you missed me."

I closed my mouth. Now that I wasn't willing to admit to. Not yet. Amadeo chuckled and the sound was like music to my ears. The world had been too quiet without his voice, his chuckles, his growls, his moans.

I'm stuck on this insane man.

"That's fine," Amadeo said, his eyes dragging over every inch of me and making me shudder. "Before the day is over I'll make you say it again and again and again." He captured my lips, his body pressing against mine. "And you will beg me to never leave your side again."

I shook my head, but the truth was that I was terrified that he would do just that. Reaching out, I clung to him and for the first time, I realized he wasn't dressed in his usual button-up and slacks. He was in a pair of sweats and a t-shirt. Amadeo's gaze followed mine and he looked back up at me.

"When I heard you were missing I ran out the door as quickly as I could."

I rolled my hips and he pressed against my prostate more firmly. "Mmm you were...worried about me? Or angry?"

"Both," he growled. "Don't ever do that shit again. Do you understand me?"

"Then don't disappear for a month," I snapped.

"Fine."

I blinked at him. He was agreeing just like that? Before I could ask him anything, he moved back down and took my cock into his heated mouth once more. All of my thoughts were wiped away and I gave in.

Amadeo was on a mission. The more he sucked and licked and kissed along my cock, the more I wanted to cum. But each and every time I reached the top, he stopped. I growled in frustration before his head came up.

"Tell me you missed me, baby."

I shook my head. "No, I didn't."

He grinned. "Are you sure?"

I sucked in a breath and pressed my lips together. Amadeo's eyes darkened and he went back to toying with me. I writhed on the backseat, my cock twitching and my balls drawing up desperate to cum. My eyes trailed to the movement of his free hand as he shoved his sweats down and spit into his palm. He gripped his cock and stroked himself, his eyes trained on me as he got off.

"Fuck," I groaned. "That's...not fair."

"What? Me touching myself?" he asked, his voice so deep and rich my toes practically curled. "Do you want to be the one touching me?"

"No!"

"Liar," Amadeo said. He groaned and slipped my cock inside of his mouth as he hummed.

I shook my head. I wasn't a liar. Touching him, feeling how hard he was in my hand, how hot he was against my skin was the last thing on my mind!

Ugh, I'm such a liar.

Amadeo's hand sped up on his length. I watched every moment of his movements, my body dying to touch him just a little, to watch him moan and writhe for me. He panted, his stomach tightened and I watched as cum decorated his hand and belly. Releasing his cock, he reached up and pushed his cum covered fingers into my mouth.

My eyes closed and I lapped at his fingers. This taste...had I gotten addicted to it? I cleaned him up, moaning at the taste of him as he brought me to the brink once more.

And he stopped.

"No, no," I panted, shaking my head as my eyes flew open and I gazed down at him. "Daddy, please. Please let me cum. Please."

I never expected this to be the outcome of running away from him. Honestly, I was sure he would hurt me, lock me up, or at the very least I would be put over his knee and spanked until I couldn't take it anymore, but no, Amadeo was giving me every bit of attention that I hadn't received over the last month.

Why is he being so nice to me?

The last thing I'd done to him, that look of pain in his eyes. It still hadn't left my mind. So, why was he being so good to me now?

Amadeo took my mind off of everything but him as he fondled my balls and sucked my cock like he couldn't get enough of it. Every single thought flew out of my brain and I gave into his mouth and fingers. As I approached the edge, I expected him to stop, but he sped up, his moans echoing around me until I cried out.

"Daddy, yes!"

I gripped his hair as I came in his mouth, my hips jerking and thrusting on their own as I rode the wave of my orgasm. Panting, I fell back, my body weak and shivering as I panted. Amadeo sat up, showed me my cum in his mouth, and swallowed.

"Shit," I mumbled.

That was too hot.

Reaching out, he pushed his fingers into my hair. "Do not ever run away from me again. Do you understand me, Six? This time, I'll forgive it. Next time, I won't be so kind."

I shivered. "Yes, Daddy."

He brushed his lips against mine. "I missed you."

My heart sped up all over again. He had missed *me*? As we kissed, I held onto him tightly and tried to keep the flood of emotions back that threatened to spill.

Amadeo was changing me in ways I never expected.

Chapter Twenty

Amadeo

The sun rose to find me already awake. My mind was still on everything that was going on, everything I had to do and figure out. Every time I tried to close my eyes my thoughts raced and I couldn't settle.

Six shifted beside me and my thoughts drifted to him. He was naked underneath the heavy blanket that I had draped over us the night before. I ran my fingers over his back, up and down, tracing his skin. I knew I'd worn him out, but being with Six was the only thing that calmed my mind. I could have punished him the night before, but I couldn't bring myself to do it. I just wanted to hold him close.

It had been ages since I had allowed anyone to sleep in my bed, but Six felt like he belonged with me. I buried my nose into the soft silken locks of his hair and inhaled his scent. When it was surrounding me, I felt more like myself. More alive, more awake. More everything. Six was magic in a way that made no sense to me, but I didn't want to be away from him. *Ever.*

Slowly, I shifted out of the bed when my bladder refused to wait. I glanced down at him admiring the planes of his face and the way his lips pursed when he blew out a breath. For all of his fighting, mischievousness, and insanity, he was soft around the edges. In the places that no one could see, he was someone who needed a man like me. A Daddy to love and protect and cherish him for the jewel that he was.

When I couldn't put it off anymore, I shuffled to the bathroom and relieved myself. Once my hands were washed, I walked back out to my bedroom and picked up the hoodie that he had been wearing the night before from the floor. Picking it up, I gave it a sniff and realized how little my scent clung to it. I grabbed my bottle of cologne and sprayed it lightly, just enough so that he would smell me and know that I was right there with him even if I was somewhere else.

I draped the hoodie over the back of a chair and walked back over to the bed, climbing in beside him before I nuzzled my face into the back of his neck. Six moaned, wiggled his ass against my cock, and sighed softly.

"Do you have to be hard this early in the morning?" he mumbled.

"It's almost noon and it's not my fault. This is natural."

"Natural for a pervert maybe." He rolled over, his bleary eyes gazing up at me. "Hi."

"Hi."

For a moment, I didn't know what to say to him. Instead, I stared at him, taking in every inch of his face before I reached out to draw my fingers over his skin. He was warm beneath my fingertips and I wanted to touch him just like this for the rest of the day.

Fuck moving, fuck work, fuck the drama that was going on within my organization, I just wanted to enjoy *him* for a while.

"I almost thought...." I trailed off, pushing the thought down and swallowing thickly. "Nevermind."

"Tell me," Six said.

"I almost thought I would wake up and somehow you would be gone again."

Six frowned. "I told you I wouldn't go anywhere last night. There's still a debt to pay and I know you'd just track me down if I tried to get out of it." He shook his head. "Besides, it's not like I could have left anyway. You had me locked against your body the entire night."

That much was true. I gripped him against me so tightly, worried that he would disappear out of my arms while I was asleep.

"Yes well, you did run away."

"And you disappeared for a month," he snipped. "So how about neither one of us brings up the past?"

I knew I should be irritated, but I grinned. "I didn't think me going away would affect you so much. You always pretend as if you hate me."

"Sometimes I do," he whispered. "Sometimes," he glanced away. "Sometimes, I don't."

My heart squeezed. Six was usually so closed off that hearing him say he didn't hate me all the time felt as if he was saying he loved me. And maybe he did. His bright eyes looked into mine and I saw something there I hadn't seen before.

I traced my fingers down his cheeks, over his jaw, and laid my palm on his chest. Six didn't pull away. Instead, he pressed forward like he wanted to be even closer to me.

"What do we do now?" he asked. "I know you're pissed I left."

"Yes," I said slowly, gauging my words. "But when it comes to you I can have moments of forgiveness.

A grin spread on Six's face. "What? You? What alien abducted and replaced you?"

I shoved a pillow into his face and growled at him. Leave it up to Six to make me feel self-conscious about what I was saying. *I sound like a teenage girl. Shit.* The boy was really affecting me in ways I had never expected.

"Are you going to tell me why you left?" Six asked after he'd stopped laughing and he scooted closer to me. Whether he did it on purpose or instinct, I had no idea. But I liked it.

"It was a mix of things," I admitted. "You acted like I was going to hurt you. I mean really hurt you."

He frowned. "I know. I'm sorry. But I didn't do it on purpose; it was just instinct."

"I know," I sighed. "But... it's still a shitty feeling to know that your first instinct with me is to cower. I may spank you, but I would never, ever, abuse you. That's not who I am as a person. I might be a killer, but I'm not a dick."

Six raised a brow. "Are you sure about that?"

I shoved the pillow into his face again. "I'm trying to have a mature conversation!"

BREAK ME DADDY

Laughing, Six yanked the pillow away and pounced on me. I fell back against the bed and he laid his head on my chest, his fingers tracing over my bare skin. The feeling was soothing, lulling me into a state of comfort and security. I could almost fall back asleep.

"I'm sorry, about that night," Six said slowly. "Just seeing you like that shook me. I knew what you did for a living, but seeing it was a completely different thing. Scared the shit right out of me."

I frowned. "So you're afraid of me now?"

Six lifted his head and glanced down at me. "Don't you want me to be? Big, bad Mafia boss? I thought you would want to scare people."

I reached out and cradled his cheek. "The world views me like that, but I don't want that to be all you see in me. I want you to see...something more."

He tilted his head and I watched as his eyes searched my face. *What was he looking for?* I didn't move, didn't speak. I just let him take his time after dumping my emotions all over the quiet moment we were having.

"I do see something more," he finally said, his voice feather-light. "But it's still hard to see someone covered in blood and about to kill a guy. I mean that's someone's father, brother, or friend. What gives anyone the right to decide who lives or dies?"

My fingers danced over his back as I digested his words. He was right. Who made the rules, who decided what was right, wrong, or something in between? It was the role that I had to take on, but that didn't mean I was any more qualified to make those decisions than any other man.

"All I can do is the best for my family and the ones I love," I said finally. "No, I probably don't make fair or right decisions, but if someone is threatening my life, my family's life, then I have to take action. Maybe it's not right, but it's what I can do. Do you understand?"

Six nodded a little. "I guess I do."

"Being around me you might not always be so innocent," I pointed out. "There might come a time when you have to kill to stay alive."

Six shivered. "I hope not."

"I hope not either," I said softly.

The possibility of Six having to become anything like me made my stomach turn. He was a mess, but he wasn't a killer. The world needed more people who could survive and thrive in a bubble. People who were safe and sweet and didn't have to know the ugliness of everything around them. Six had seen some of the bad in the world, but not the worst.

"Why else did you leave?" he prodded, changing the subject quickly.

I sighed softly. "Come take a shower with me and I'll tell you all about it."

Standing up, I took his hand and led Six into the bathroom. I turned on the water and made sure it was warm enough before I led Six inside. Grabbing a loofah, I poured body wash on it before I began to wash him.

"I can clean myself up you know," he pointed out.

"No, I'm going to do it for you and that's the end of that."

Six didn't challenge me. Instead, he turned around, placed his hands on the tiled wall of the shower, and stuck his ass out. I stared at the curve of his body, wanting to fill him like I had the night before, but I forced myself to focus.

"Daddy, tell me," he said as he glanced over his shoulder. "What's going on?"

I sighed. "You already heard some of it. Someone is trying to take my organization apart from the inside and I have to figure out who it is. I've made some calls, investigated, but I still don't have any leads." I shook my head. "Angelo thinks it might be someone in my family."

"Shit," Six mumbled under his breath. "What do you think?"

I shrugged. "Right now? I don't know. As much as I want to believe it's all coincidence and has nothing to do with my family, I can't discount anything. Family betraying each other in this line of work isn't anything new. I have to be careful and figure out what's going on."

Six turned around and laid his hand on my arm. "I'm sorry," he said softly. "This must be a lot for you to deal with."

I stared at Six, unable to take in his kindness. That didn't exist in my world, but he was showing it to me. Instead of speaking, I raised his leg and rested it on one of the shelves of the shower, washing him up intently. My mouth didn't know how to form the right words to express that I was grateful to him.

"I hope you figure it out," Six said quietly. "So you can have some peace."

My heart ached all over again. Bratty, defiant Six was the sweetest man that I had ever met. He never asked anything of me, never pushed me in the wrong ways. Instead, it seemed as though he wanted to relieve the tension in me.

"Let's get dressed and grab food," I said, changing the subject again because I didn't want to think about the myriad of issues heaped onto my shoulders. "We can talk more later."

Six nodded. "Okay, Daddy."

Two simple words and my heart tried leaping from my chest. I didn't have to poke or prod Six for them, he said it naturally and I smiled at him. I always wanted him to feel as if I was not only his Daddy but the perfect Daddy.

The words *I love you* danced on my tongue, but I swallowed them thickly. Not yet. This was not the time to say that to Six. But I would one day soon.

I just prayed he loved me too.

Chapter Twenty-One

Six

I LOOKED IN THE MIRROR AND DECIDED TO DITCH WHAT I WAS wearing. Looking around at the piles of clothes on the bed and chair, I knew I had gone through just about everything I owned, but nothing felt right. I wanted something casual, that didn't look like I was trying too hard. But something that wasn't plain, boring, or *too* laidback. Frowning, I stared at the clothes and pushed through the piles before I picked up a long-sleeved baby blue button-up and dragged it up my arms again.

Never had I gone through so many clothing options for a dinner. Usually, I threw on the first thing I had and did what I had to do. But now that Amadeo was waiting for me, I couldn't decide what would look best.

Finally, I settled on a pair of jeans and the button-up shirt and decided that was going to have to be good enough. I pushed my fingers through my hair, smoothing back my wild locks. My face was starting to get stubbled again, but I hadn't shaved. Part of me was waiting for Amadeo to grab me, sit me down, and do it for me so I could look up and admire the serious intensity on his face as he cleaned me up.

A knock on the door brought me back to reality and I realized I'd been staring into the mirror for a while. I pushed my fingers through my hair, sucking in a deep breath as I steeled myself to open the door and let Amadeo in. As soon as my hand curled around the knob my heart raced, but I forced myself to breathe and yank open the door.

Standing on the other side was Angelo. I blew out a breath, the disappointment clear on my face as I stepped back a bit. My stomach twisted.

Was he going to say that Amadeo had left again? Was I on my own?

I was too afraid to ask.

"Amadeo is waiting for you out in the garden. He says you can meet him there for dinner."

I smiled at Angelo and nodded. "Thanks." I paused. "Does it ever bother you? Having to look after me and being the one who runs all his errands like this?"

He raised a brow. "Why would I mind? This is my job, I'm paid to do it. It would be no different if I was out in the real world doing menial tasks for my boss. Right?"

Well, he was right about that. Everyone knew how it was to have a job and listen to their boss. I did it plenty of times at the casino, doing my best to smile and be cordial to the people I knew made sure my paycheck was a reality each week.

"Right," I said finally, smoothing down the front of my shirt. "You're right. Um, I can go down myself."

Angelo smiled at me. "Alright. You better hurry. He's not that patient tonight."

BREAK ME DADDY

Neither am I.

Something had me on edge as I nodded and took every single step as if lead was in my shoes. Why was my heart in my throat? It squeezed and I gripped at my flesh, holding onto my neck as if that would make the lump disappear but of course, it didn't.

I walked past the dining room where we usually ate together and out the back door. Following Angelo, I tried to make my brain slow down as countless thoughts filled my brain and made my stomach flutter.

Why am I so anxious? It's just Amadeo.

I tried to remind myself of that, but all I could see was Amadeo fucking me in his car. Him kissing me like he was starving. The way his fingers pushed into my hair when he climbed on top of me in bed. How gentle he was as he washed me up and made sure that I wasn't too sore from the night before.

There was so much more to him than the monster he wore on the surface. I was starting to realize that and now that I had, I wanted more. I wanted to consume every moment of Amadeo's time and know that I was at the center of all his attention. Being obsessed over by him? It was a dangerous drug, but I was already addicted.

All of my thoughts came to a screeching halt when I saw Amadeo. He sat at a small, round table with a white tablecloth. There were candles flickering on the table and flowers, so many flowers. He stood up and adjusted his jacket before he smiled at me and I thought I was going to pass out as warmth flooded me.

Who the fuck is this man?

Who knew Amadeo had a side... like this?

"I-" I shook my head as words failed me. "What is all this?"

He cleared his throat and waved a hand. "Dinner. Sit down."

I did as he said and he laid a napkin over my lap gently. "I can see it's dinner but uh...why is it like...this?" I asked, waving a hand around at the romantic display around us.

"Because I wanted it to be," he said gruffly. I saw the slight tinge of pink on his cheeks.

Is he embarrassed?

"Thank you," I said, instead of teasing him. "It's really nice. No one's ever done anything like this for me before."

Amadeo sat down and glanced at me warily. "I don't know whether to say I'm glad I get to be the first and only one or if I should be pissed off that no one has taken the time out of their lives to do something like this for you."

"Both." I smiled at him. "You can be both. I'm used to you being insane."

The smile returned to Amadeo's lips. "Yeah? That's slightly comforting," he said as he chuckled and picked up his wine glass once it was filled by a man that was waiting on us. "Cheers."

I picked mine up. "Cheers."

Every bit of nervousness started to melt away. Being in Amadeo's presence when he was so easygoing was a completely different experience. It almost felt like I was supposed to be here with him, sitting this close and enjoying the way his cologne lingered in the air. My eyes zeroed in on his lips and I traced every centimeter of them as he drank before he stared at me. Quickly, I glanced away and sat my glass down.

"So, no one's ever done this for you?" Amadeo said, staring at me as he tilted his head. "You've never dated?"

I shook my head. "I've dated, but not like this. I mean dating for me is usually a couple of cheap drinks, a loud club, and usually some very mediocre sex to finish the night up." He growled under his breath and I chuckled. "So no, I don't usually do fancy dinners or dressing up or nice nights." I shrugged. "Then again I usually date guys my age."

"Is that what men your age are into? Pathetic."

Nodding, I toyed with my napkin. "Yeah, I never liked it that much either. It's why I mostly stopped a while ago. What was the point of dating if I was just an item to warm some asshole's bed and then was dropped when someone more...put together and not so fucked up waltzed by?"

Amadeo frowned. "You're not fucked up."

I grinned at him, my shoulders relaxing from their tensed position that I hadn't even known they were in. "I am, but you're more screwed up so you don't see it," I pointed out. Waving a hand, I shoved that part of the conversation away. "But I was also too busy trying to survive. Taking care of my family when they decide to call." I sighed and then blinked at him. "Wait? Is this a date?"

Amadeo tilted his head. "What do you think?"

I had no idea what to think because Amadeo was one giant mind fuck. We were only supposed to be having sex, settling a debt, but he went crazy when I wasn't around. And I did too I realized. *So, what are we doing?*

"Tonight, we have-"

I sighed when the waiter began to speak and sat plates in front of us. *Thank you for saving me.* I didn't know what we were and I didn't want to give the wrong answer either. Amadeo's gaze lingered on me as I stared up at the waiter pretending I was interested in his words when really I was trying to stop my heart from beating out of my chest.

Once the man disappeared, I was quick to pop food into my mouth so I wouldn't have to answer anymore questions. When I finally looked at Amadeo, because I couldn't avoid his gaze forever, he was smiling. He shook his head and began to eat as well, obviously letting me off the hook.

Thank you.

Sometimes it was like he knew me more than I knew myself. And I was glad for that small moment, the knowledge that he knew not to push me anymore, but to let me be.

"Do you want to call your family soon? They must be worried," Amadeo said.

I shrugged, my stomach tightening a bit. "Honestly, I doubt it. My mom's probably deep in a bottle somewhere and my siblings are usually busy. As for my Dad, who knows? The man just kind of does whatever he wants." I frowned. "It's less of a family and more a bunch of people who were shoved into one place who can barely even tolerate each other."

Thinking about my family always made me uneasy. While they were virtually strangers these days, I had always *craved* the kind of family you saw on TV. The ones that stuck up for each other no matter what. Who loved and cared for each other and even if they fought, they came back together by the end of the episode. But my life was nothing like that. It was pitiful and empty and way more lonelier than I ever wanted to admit out loud.

A hand rested on top of mine and I glanced up at Amadeo. He had that serious look on his face, the one that said he was contemplating dangerous things. But beneath it, there was something else.

Worry.

"I'm sorry," he said quietly. "That you've been alone for so long."

My heart squeezed and my stupid eyes burned. I wanted to pull away from Amadeo, to scream at him that I was fine and I didn't fucking need anyone or anything! But I couldn't even force the lies out of my mouth, not when his voice was so damn soft and compassionate. A tear rolled down my cheek and sucked in a trembling breath.

"Shit. What are you doing to me?"

Amadeo squeezed my hand. "I ask myself that question every single day when I think about you." He reached across the table and his calloused fingers swiped away the tear before he stood up and moved to my side. Amadeo cradled my cheeks in his large palms and pressed a kiss to my trembling lips. "My family might be insane, but you'd have one here. If you want it," he whispered against my mouth. "And I would never let you be lonely again."

What was he saying? That he wanted me to stay even after the six months? My heart pounded so hard my head swam. *How can I know if he's telling the truth? If this is something that might actually last?*

As we kissed, I let the worries ebb and then flow away. Right now, I wanted to pretend that this could be something more.

Even if it was just a dream.

Chapter Twenty-Two

Six

"Are you going to go see Amadeo?" Ty asked.

I leaned back in the car as it drove through the city and nodded, a grin on my lips. "Yep. He's at the casino today so I thought I would stop by and see what he's doing. Maybe give him a blowjob or two if he's stressed out. Gotta pay this debt off you know."

Ty's laughter over the phone made me smile. "We both know you're not doing this for the debt anymore. You like it too much."

I waved a hand. "You're insane."

"Look at you! It's been three months and he's let you keep my number in your phone, you can leave the house, you have your own driver for fuck's sake! I think it's time to stop lying to yourself man. That guy is into you and you like it!"

I caught myself grinning in the rearview mirror and immediately tried to wipe it off my face, but I couldn't. Ty wasn't wrong. When Amadeo wasn't so big and bad, he was pleasant to be around. Gentle even. Maybe the scary facade had just been temporary and this was the man he really was underneath. I wasn't sure, but life had definitely become more comfortable and if I was honest with myself, easier.

"Are you even listening to me?" Ty sighed.

Nope, not even a little.

"Yeah, I'm listening," I said as I straightened up in my seat. The casino had come into view and every inch of me felt electrified as I tapped my foot quickly. "I'm at Amadeo's job so I'll call you back later."

"No you won't," he laughed. "But that's okay. Go hang out with your boyfriend."

"He's not my-"

"Whatever you say," Ty cut me off, his laughter growing as my face heated. "Later man."

Ty hung up and I stared at the phone, shaking my head before I put it back into my pocket. He was insane, but he had a point. What was I to Amadeo? And what were we going to do three months from now?

I couldn't think about those questions without my stomach twisting into knots, so I shoved it away for now. Thinking about the future and the inevitable part where I would end up alone again made me nauseous. I couldn't go back to living life the way I had before. Back then I had convinced myself that I was fine. But it was all a lie.

Walking through the casino, I waited for Angelo to get me through the guards that blocked the way to Amadeo. Every step that brought me closer to him made my heart race.

This man has me all twisted up.

I stopped in front of his office door and that stupid grin came back that refused to go away for more than half a second. After I took in one more deep breath, I knocked on the door and grabbed the knob.

"Hey, Daddy!" I called as I walked in and immediately froze.

Sitting on a couch across from Amadeo was another man. He had red hair and a beard and the most interesting blue-gray eyes. And he looked like he was about Amadeo's age, much older and more mature than me. All at once, my stomach squeezed tightly and I frowned as I looked over at Amadeo.

"Who's this?" I asked.

Amadeo shook his head. "Wait outside for me."

I blinked at him. "Why?"

He sighed. "For once, just once, will you do what I ask and wait outside?"

My face grew hot as embarrassment crawled up my spine. *Why doesn't he want to tell me who the guy is?* It was weird. Suspicious. Were they together? Was this someone Amadeo saw when he came to work and I was sitting at his house, waiting for him to return and fuck me while he had a man that looked like this on his arm?

I turned from Amadeo to the redhead. "Who are you?"

Yeah, I should stop and walk out of the office, but I couldn't. Every fiber in my body screamed at me to keep going and figure out who the hell this man was. Why did he look so comfortable on Amadeo's couch? And why did he look so good?

I compared myself to him from head to toe and in the end, I decided I was severely lacking. That only made my temper come back full throttle. How much trouble would I be in if I hauled off and punched the guy in the face?

"Um, I'm a friend of Amadeo's," the man said, a thick Irish accent lacing his voice and turning every word into liquid sex. "And you are?"

He doesn't even know who I am.

It was like a slap in the face. How often had this stranger come around and talked to Amadeo, sat in his closed or locked office? Were they sleeping together? Was Amadeo telling him all the sweet nothings he had been telling me? My heart raced and I glared at Amadeo.

"A friend? I haven't heard about any friends."

"Six, not now," he growled. "I'm warning you."

I scoffed. "Warning me of what? That you don't want me to pop around for a visit when your boyfriend is here? Or are you warning me that you don't want him to know you fuck me?"

Amadeo stood up quickly and I stepped back on instinct alone. But even being unnerved by his tall stature and dark gaze wasn't enough to stop me and calm the storm of emotions that raged inside of me.

"Outside," he snapped. "Now!"

I turned to his friend. "Nice to meet the guy he gives a fuck about."

Amadeo grabbed my arm and escorted me out before we could exchange more words. He slammed the door to his office and his secretary scrambled away after taking one look at his face. When he turned me around, he glared.

"What is your goddamn problem?" Amadeo growled.

"You're my problem," I snapped as I ripped my arm out of his grasp. "Who the fuck is that? Why are you hiding him?"

"I'm not hiding anything, but I am busy. Go home."

I scoffed. "What the hell is your problem? Is he really your boyfriend or something? Or is that the guy you're going to make call you Daddy when I finally get away from you?"

Amadeo closed the space between us and yanked me forward by my shirt. "Six..."

"You don't get to brush me off," I said as I tried to twist out of his grasp, but he wouldn't let me go. "Get off of me!"

Amadeo's face invaded my space. "This is my business, my life that you're fucking with. Do you understand that? If I tell you to wait outside the only thing you should do is nod and step out the fucking door. Do you understand me?"

I glared up at him. "I am *not* one of your little workers that you can yell at and order around."

"No. You're the smart ass that stole from me. You're the warm body in my bed and nothing more. Don't overstep your goddamn boundaries!"

All of the anger fled my body at once. My mouth dropped open, but I no longer had any words to speak. *You're the warm body in my bed and nothing more.* It played in my head on repeat as I stared at his face laced with anger. His jaw ticked and his eyes blazed.

"What are you going to do?" I asked, my voice trembling more than I wanted it to. "Lock me up again? Put me back in your weird dungeon?"

Amadeo shoved me against the wall, his hand planting beside my head as he glared. "Is that what you need me to do? Do you want to go back there? I can have that arranged right now."

I stared at Amadeo, but I was lost for words. He really would throw me back into that dingy room? I searched his eyes trying to see if he was serious, but all I could see was the resolve there. He would and could lock me up again and there was nothing I could do about it.

"Fuck you," I spat.

I shoved my hands into his chest and stormed out of the casino as the air squeezed in my lungs. I had to get out of there and away from him or I didn't know what I would do. Swinging on a mafia boss was a pretty bad fucking idea, but if I stood in front of him for one more second that's what I was going to do.

Can't believe I was stupid enough to think that he actually wanted anything to do with me. What's wrong with me?

I heard Angelo talking to me, but his voice sounded like it was coming from underwater. Even when I glanced at him, I couldn't see him right.

"Take me back home."

"Yes, sir."

I climbed into the car and stared straight ahead. Home. When did I start seriously thinking of Amadeo's place like home? When had I started viewing him as a man that I could actually be with? When did calling him Daddy start to feel familiar? One minute I detested the man and the next?

The ache that filled my chest and made it hard to breathe let me know that I felt something deeper for him. Something I kept trying to deny. But after seeing that side of him I was no longer sure what I felt for Amadeo Bianchi.

I need to get away from him.

This was a reality check. Amadeo was a monster and even though he tried to convince me otherwise, I could see who he was and what he was about. I wasn't going to stick around trying to see the good in him when all that existed there was bad.

Three months. That's all I owe him. If I run he'll just track me down. Might as well serve my sentence and then he'll be out of my life.

In the beginning, I thought six months with Amadeo would be better than six months in jail, but I was seriously starting to question that now. He was in my head, worming his way into my heart in the worst ways and I wanted to be free of him.

Now.

Chapter Twenty-Three

Amadeo

I STARED AFTER SIX, BUT I DIDN'T MOVE TO GO AFTER HIM. THE look on his face stopped me. I knew I had just hurt him and running after him right now would just end up with him being defensive and us getting into a big fight.

Or a bigger fight at this point.

Leaning against the wall, I pinched the bridge of my nose and blew out a deep breath. *He's going to be the death of me one day.* When I opened my eyes again, Darla was sitting down behind the desk, her gaze on me.

"What?" I asked, the tiredness seeping into my tone.

She shrugged and typed her password in. "I caught a little of that..."

"And?" I asked, my irritation growing tenfold having to talk about it.

"Don't you think you were a little harsh?" she asked, her head tilting slightly as she gazed up at me. "Six came all the way here to visit you. And he was so happy when I saw him come in. Maybe you should talk to him."

I shook my head. "I'm in the middle of an important meeting right now. I can't."

Darla nodded and turned in her chair. She didn't say anything, but I could tell from the set of her shoulders and the way she sighed that she didn't agree with me. I pushed off of the wall.

"What?" I asked.

She shrugged. "You didn't ask for my advice, Sir."

"Well, now I'm asking," I growled. "Spit it out."

Darla turned to me and shook her head. "All I can say is if someone I cared about was upset, I would worry about them first and a meeting second."

"Yes, but this isn't about you. Last I checked, you don't have an entire organization of people, employees, and family depending on your every move. I can't run off whenever Six feels like being dramatic."

"Was he being dramatic?" she challenged. "It didn't sound that way to me." Darla turned around and resumed typing. "I won't interfere with your meeting, Sir. I'll bring coffee in soon."

I stared at Darla for another minute and wanted to tell her to fuck off, but I couldn't. She didn't understand that I had to look out for *everyone.* That I had to keep everyone safe and protect my name and their lives.

But she wasn't wrong. I care about him and I don't want to lose him.

I chewed my lip, unsure of myself for the first time in forever. I was used to making the hard decisions and doing what was best for everyone, except me. But if I lost Six...

The thought made my fists tighten. Pinpricks of pain shot up through my hands as my nails dug into my flesh. *I can't think about losing him.* Even trying to address it made me want to go feral and kill everyone in my path.

I remembered Gabriele's words, the way he told me that I would lose it if I fell for Six. He was right, of course. My obsession with the boy ran deep and even now I just wanted to grab him, hold him against me, and tell him that I was a bastard, but I was a bastard that didn't think of him as just a hole to fuck. If I wanted that, I could have it in spades. There was no shortage of men and women who threw themselves at me, but I didn't want any of them.

I wanted Six.

"Amadeo." Turning on my heels, I put away the conflicted expression I knew was on my face and donned the mask once more as I faced Conor. "Are we continuing this meeting?"

"Yes, of course. But let's make it quick, I have things I need to see to."

He grinned. "I can see that. A certain dark-haired jealous man that just ran out of here."

I groaned and strolled past him into my office. "Let's not talk about that. Why are you here, Conor? We can skip all of the formalities." I closed the door when he stepped inside and threw the lock this time since he hadn't done it before. "Have a seat."

Conor sat down again and nodded. "Just like you I've had a couple of break-ins lately at my places of business. Things have been coming up missing, fires were started, it's becoming a pain in my ass. I thought maybe it had something to do with your problem."

I frowned. "You think it's someone trying to fuck with both of us?"

"I do. And I think they're trying to make me believe it's your guys doing it. I spotted the rose and skull tattoos that your men have on the security camera. If I was my father, I would be here trying to kick your ass, but I'm not. We already talked and I'm pretty damn sure you wouldn't be lying to me and starting a war for no reason."

"Exactly." I sat across from him and laced my fingers together. "The last thing either of us wants or needs is a war. We're already on the cop's radar, we have businesses and family to protect. Trust me, I don't want to hurt any of that."

Conor searched my face, trying to see if I was telling the truth. But I had no reason to lie. Just like he felt he was beyond his father, I didn't follow everything mine did either. The time of rampant and open violence and crime was gone. Technology was more advanced, the cops were more equipped. We had to run our businesses with more smarts and less brute force. That was the only way our organizations could thrive in these conditions.

Finally, Conor nodded. "I believe you. We both have common goals, it's why we get along as well as we do." The door opened and Darla pocketed her key as she came in with coffee. She sat a cup in front of each of us before she disappeared as quickly as she had come in. Once she was gone, Conor grabbed his cup and frowned. "But that does leave the problem of someone purposely stirring up trouble between us. We can't have that either."

"No, we can't," I agreed.

BREAK ME DADDY

"Do you have any idea who it could be?"

I shook my head. Right now, I wasn't willing to tell him that there was more than dissention in my ranks. That it could be family, it could be someone close doing this to me. Telling him I had no control over my own family wasn't something a guy like me could do. We exuded control, ego, and being poised or we would end up losing the trust and faith of those around us. It was a delicate balance, one that we couldn't afford not to maintain.

The world was always ready to tear us apart.

"Amadeo," Conor said, pulling my attention back to him. "We need to figure this out as quickly as possible."

"I know," I nodded. "Trust me, I know."

But that was easier said than done. Someone was clearly working close to both of us or at least knew our men. That made it harder to weed through them and pick out who was starting shit.

I don't have time for this.

My mind immediately went back to Six. I needed to be with my boy right now, pulling my foot out of my mouth and trying to calm him down. Six was always reckless and he just might do something crazy since I had snapped at him.

Pulling my phone out I sent a message to Angelo. I needed him to post more guards on Six and make sure he didn't try to slip out of the house and do something insane. He had already escaped once. My stomach turned at the thought of him getting away from me again.

He wouldn't leave. We both know I would hunt him down and lock him away in my bedroom. I can not lose my boy.

"Amadeo," Conor sighed. "Seriously, go and grab your boyfriend and talk to him." He held up his hand when I started to object. "You're no use to me, to this organization, or to yourself when you're distracted. You know me. I want to go up against the best and kick your ass every time. I can't do that when you're daydreaming about him."

"I'm not daydreaming," I growled. "You make me sound like some schoolgirl in love."

"Aren't you?" Conor grinned. "Look at you. Usually, you're all work all the time, but I can see how distracted you are. And the fact that you keep looking at your phone just makes me think you're pining over him even more."

I flipped him off. "I'm not pining."

Even while my finger was still in the air, I was reminded of Six. *Shit! Six is turning me into him!* When was the last time I had flipped someone off? His childish antics had somehow worked their way deep into my brain and I found them charming. Six was wild, crazy, and a mess on a good day, but he was *my* boy and I didn't want to hurt him unless it was my palm against his plump ass.

"Shit," I muttered.

Conor stood up and grinned. "Why don't you call me when you find something out and I'll do the same on my end. Until then I'll see what I can find out."

I stood as well and nodded. "That's probably for the best. It's not like we're going to solve anything right now. We still need to investigate more."

"Exactly." He stuck out his hand. "We'll figure this thing out."

BREAK ME DADDY

"Do we have a choice?"

I shook his hand and Conor grinned before he turned on his heels and left. After he was gone, I pulled out my phone and stared at Six's name. I stabbed at his name and pressed the phone to my ear. Every ring made my jaw tighten and I started to pace. When it went to voicemail, I called back and waited again, but still no answer.

"Shit," I swore under my breath and shoved my phone back into my pants. "You better not be doing anything crazy."

I snatched up my jacket and keys and jogged out of my office. I only stopped when Darla looked up at me and then smiled gently. As if she knew all too well what I was doing.

"I'm only going because I'm done with my meeting," I snapped, unsure why I was even arguing with her.

"Of course, Sir," she said, her smile growing. "It was a very short meeting."

I narrowed my eyes at her. "I will fire you."

"No," she said as she turned back to her computer, "you won't."

Darla went back to typing at lightning speed and I stared at her. *That woman is evil.* She wiggled her fingers at me as I started walking for the door and I shook my head. She knew her place and had every confidence in it apparently. And I couldn't fault her for that. Darla was invaluable.

I slipped behind the wheel of my car and gripped it tightly. Six was hopefully just ignoring me and not already running for the hills.

Can't believe I said I would lock him up again.

He'd pushed me so much I lost my temper, but I couldn't keep doing that. Not if I wanted to keep him in my life. We had three more months together. That was all the time that was left for me to convince Six that he was right where he was supposed to be.

Chapter Twenty-Four

Amadeo

The river back home felt like it was taking forever. I sped up more than I knew I should, but I didn't give a damn. If I was pulled over and taken to jail, then let it happen because I wasn't going to slow down getting to Six.

As soon as I walked through the door, I jogged up the stairs and to Six's room. I stopped short and swallowed thickly. None of the guards had reported him missing and I had checked my phone on the way over and saw him pacing around the room. He was there so why was I so damn nervous.

What the fuck is this feeling?

Six was driving me insane. What was it about him that made me want to skip all my hardness and be softer? I rapped on the door, my heart in my throat as I waited for him to open up. Instead, I was met with silence.

I yanked my phone out of my pocket and checked the camera. Six sat on the bed, glaring at the door like a petulant child, his arms crossed over his chest. Every instinct in me wanted to drag him over my lap and smack his ass until he stopped trying to shut me out, but that wasn't the best solution right now.

Breathe and don't do anything crazy.

I knocked again, but when he still wouldn't move the irritation grew. Six shoved his hand up and flipped off the door. My jaw ticked.

Okay, that was the last straw.

"Six, you can open this door or I can open it for you."

He shook his head and dragged a chair over to the door. I wasn't used to Six not talking my ears off. His being silent felt wrong and my skin began to crawl as he jammed the chair under the doorknob.

"You might think you're smart, but I will break this door down. Six!"

"Fuck off!"

Nope, I was done. Turning on my heels, I walked downstairs and out to the back shed. The dark, dusty space was cluttered with tools, but what I needed sat leaning against the far wall. A sturdy ax. I picked it up and slung it over my shoulder, an eerie calm settling over me as I stepped into the house.

I returned to Six's door and tried the knob, but it was still locked. I pulled out my phone and made sure Six wasn't in danger of getting hurt. He was lying in bed, his back to the door. I shoved the phone back into my pocket, picked up the ax, and swung it.

Crack!

BREAK ME DADDY

The ax stuck in the door and I had to tug hard to dislodge it. As it pulled away, a hole appeared. I glanced through it and saw Six staring at the door, his mouth hanging open.

"What are you doing?" He yelled.

"I told you to open the door," I shrugged. "You're making me do this."

"I'm not making you do shit!"

Shrugging, I stepped back and swung again. I had warned him to open the door. As far as I was concerned that was more than fair.

The blade cut through the door, splintering pieces of wood flying through the air as I hacked through it. I could have gotten wood in my eye, but even that didn't matter to me right now. I wanted my boy and I was going to have him.

I reached in through the hole that I had created and knocked the chair away before I unlocked and opened the door. Six backed up, his face red and his fists clenched. There was a small hint of worry on his face, but he was being brave as always and trying not to show that he was scared.

"You're batshit insane," Six snapped.

I closed the door behind me and put the ax down. "Listen, let's-"

I turned around in time to see something flying toward my head. Leaning to the left I ducked out of the way and Six's phone slammed into the wall. My calmness broke.

"That's enough!" I snapped as I crossed over to Six and threw him on his bed. I climbed on top of him as he thrashed around. "Hai perso la testa, cazzo! You could have killed me with that goddamn thing!"

"Fuck you!" Six grunted. "I thought you had a meeting with your little boyfriend."

"You're acting like a jealous child. Do you need me to remind you who has my mind twenty-four hours a day? Who I am still obsessed with?"

Six shoved his knee into my stomach and I grunted, but grabbed his wrists and slammed them to the bed. "Yeah, right! And you could have killed me with that ax, yeah you really care."

"No, I watched you on the camera first. I would never put you in danger."

His eyes widened. "You told me there were no cameras in here!"

"I know." My lips curled into a smile as I lowered my head and brushed my lips against his ear. "I lied. Six, I'm always watching you."

He shivered underneath me and it felt like live wires were dancing under my skin at his reaction. The heat of his firm body pressed against mine made me want to hold him for the rest of the day and into tomorrow.

Six felt like home.

"You're a jerk," Six growled trying to squirm away from me again.

I sat up and straddled him, pinning him down. A few times he was able to gain the upper hand and I was surprised and he desperately tried to buck me off of him. Not wanting to waste any more time, I slipped off my tie and grabbed his wrists. Quickly, I tied his wrists together and pressed them against the bed before I grabbed his cheeks and looked him in the eye.

"I lost my temper with you earlier and that was shitty of me. You saying all that bullshit just pressed the wrong buttons when I was already stressed out. But you know that you're my boy, right? I would never let you go."

Six frowned. "You said some really messed up stuff."

"I know. My temper has always been crappy, but lately, it's worse. You're the only person that helps me calm down at the end of the day. That meeting was important. I've already told you about Conor, but you didn't want to believe me. You just wanted to yell at me for some reason." I frowned. "Why?"

He looked away from me. "I don't know."

"Do you not believe me when I say I want you?"

Six shrugged. Just like I hated the door being locked, I detested the way he wouldn't look at me. Any way that Six could cut me off was a hard no for me. I needed him to be open with me so I could know every little thing about him inside and out.

"Six, I want you," I pressed. "Do you understand me?"

"I don't know."

I leaned over and searched his face before he tried to hide again. The anger that had been there before was gone and now he was pouting. I ran a hand down his chest, my fingers moving between his thighs. I gave one a tight squeeze and he rolled his hips before he went still again.

"Do you want Daddy to make you feel better?"

Six shivered. "I don't-"

"You do know," I said sternly as my grip tightened and he groaned. "Either we can talk about the situation or I can show you how much I'm sorry."

He finally glanced at me, his eyes watery. "Show me," he whispered.

I leaned down and took his lips in a rough kiss. Six melted against me, his chest pressing up against my body as he moaned. I was quickly learning that Six didn't want words. Before I had assumed it was because he wanted to not think about them, but while that was still slightly the case, it was more than that. Words could be empty things, but actions? Well, seeing was believing.

Nodding, I kissed Six's neck. His breathing stuttered and he sucked in a shuddering breath. I traced his neck down to his collarbone, breathing in his scent.

"Are you still mad at Daddy?"

"Yes," he muttered. "You know what you did."

I smiled a little at him. Not because he was upset, but because he didn't say I wasn't his Daddy. He wasn't pushing me away anymore either. In fact, his legs widened and I could feel the need he had to be closer to me.

"Do you really think I would be seeing someone? When would I have the time, boy? You're always on my ass."

Six glanced up at me. "I have to be, you're a jackass."

I clicked my tongue at him. "Now, that wasn't very nice."

"*You're* not very nice," he pouted.

I chuckled and kissed down his chest before I settled between his legs. "I'm not? Let's test that."

"What are you...oh. Shit," he swore as his hips lifted from the bed.

I lapped along his length taking in the taste of him. Six sighed, his head falling back against the pillow as his bound wrists rested on his stomach. I took my time exploring him, taking in every piece of warm, hard flesh that slipped in and out of my mouth.

"Daddy," he moaned, his fingers curling into my hair. "I'm still mad at you," he said, his words barely a whisper.

"You can keep being angry," I said as I stared up at him. "But you can't stop being mine." My fingers dug into his thighs and Six gasped. "Do you understand me?"

Six gazed at me, his pupils blown before he bit his lip. "Don't fuck anyone else."

I blinked at him. "You don't want me to?"

"No," he said, his tone taking on a dangerous edge. "For as long as we're doing...whatever this is I don't want you doing this to anyone but me."

"Ask nicely," I said dragging my nails down his skin and forcing a moan from his soft lips. "Come on baby, ask Daddy nicely."

Six groaned. "Please, Daddy. Don't fuck anyone but your boy."

My cock throbbed. *Shit.* The needy look on Six's face, the desperation behind his plea, I knew he really meant it. Six wanted me to be with no one but him. I held onto my boy so tightly I was sure there would be bruises in the shape of my fingertips tomorrow, but I didn't want to let him go.

"I won't," I said. "Just you. I only want you, Six."

I moved up his body quickly and took his lips in a hard kiss. His soft moan against my mouth was music to my ears. I pushed my fingers into his hair, stroking him and tasting him. The boy I was falling in love with.

When we pulled back from each other, his eyes were glazed. I slipped back down his body and took his cock in my mouth once more. This time, however, I didn't hold back. I slid my mouth down his length and bobbed my head up and down, sucking and licking at his cock as he moaned underneath me.

Six squirmed wildly, his body tensing and relaxing and tensing again as he rode out the pleasure I gave him. His legs spread more and I ran my fingers over his balls before toying with them, squeezing them gently and making his moans grow. I was starting to know my boy's body and I loved exploiting that fact and making him lose his mind.

"Daddy, I'm right there," he sighed as he raised his hips and shoved his cock further down my throat. "Please."

I wasn't going to tease him, not after the day he'd had. So, I picked up speed and his toes curled. His hands tensed and flexed, my sapphire tie still wrapped around his wrists. I wanted to just stare at him for a while, but more than that I wanted my boy to cum.

He cried out and spilled his seed on my tongue moments later, his breathing merely pants. I came up and swallowed every drop refusing to waste any of it. Anyone would be lucky to taste my boy and I was the only one that would have that privilege from now on. Even when our time was up, I would refuse to let Six go.

"Daddy?" Six asked.

"Yes?" I climbed next to him and undid his wrists, rubbing them lightly before I kissed the inside of one.

"Would you really lock me up in that room again?"

I gazed down at him and saw the worry in his eyes. *Shit, I scared him.* I reached out and brushed bits of hair from his sweat-slicked forehead before I shook my head.

"No, I would never do that to you again. I can't."

Before, it would have been easy. There had been plenty of times when I thought about locking Six away and punishing him, but the more I was around him, the more I knew that was impossible. I cared about him too much and I wasn't going to hurt him.

"I can't promise that I won't lock you up here," I muttered. "You already ran away once."

Six let out a breath and laughed. "You're going to hang onto that forever, aren't you?"

"Yes," I said lying beside him and kissing his lip before tugging the bottom one out a bit and releasing it again. "Because the one thing I can't stand to lose is you."

He stared at me, his eyes widening before he nodded. I watched his adam's apple bob up and down before he shook his head. Whatever was on his tongue, he swallowed it, and instead, he tucked his head into my chest.

"Hold me," he muttered.

"For as long as you want," I said, kissing the top of my head.

"Wait," he said, pulling back to look up at me. "Don't you want to have sex?"

I always wanted to have sex with him. My cock was still rock hard and dying to be wrapped in the hot, silky walls of Six's ass. But he wanted me to hold him and that was more important.

"Not right now," I said, pulling him against me more tightly. "Let's just lie here for a while. Okay?"

"Okay, Daddy." He nuzzled against my chest and was quiet for a minute. "You owe me a new door by the way."

I looked over at it. "And a new phone."

"That too," he laughed and his hand tightened around my shirt tightly. "Or I can just move into your room."

I smiled so hard it hurt my damn face. "I like that option a hell of a lot more."

Chapter Twenty-Five

Amadeo

"Where's your new toy?" Gabriele asked as he strolled into my home office and sat down.

"Out with a friend." I sat my phone down and stared up at him. "And he's not my toy."

"Then what is he?"

I glared at Gabriele. "Get out."

My brother chuckled and shook his head at me. "Calm down. I'm not trying to be disrespectful, just trying to figure out what you two are now. He's always around, you hover over him, and now you're giving him the freedom to be out with his friends? Don't you think he'll run off again?"

"No."

There was no hesitation in my voice as I said the word because I didn't have to worry about that anymore. Six and I had finally come to some kind of an agreement that he didn't want to be without me and I didn't want to be without him. There was no more locking him up in basements or following him around everywhere. Sure, I kept guards posted on him because of the situation I was dealing with, but Six was practically a free man.

And he came back home to me each and every night.

"Wow," Gabriele whistled. "You trust him."

"I do," I said as I turned back to my computer and started typing. "Are you here to talk to me about my personal business or did you want something?"

"Nonna wanted to know where you were and why you haven't been coming to dinner. Everyone else has been harassed so now she's on my ass about where you are." Gabriele cleared his throat. "And you know? I haven't seen you around either. What's going on?"

"I've been working," I said, refusing to look up at him.

"Working?"

"Yes, that thing that puts money in all of our pockets."

"And that's the real reason?" Gabriele asked.

I finally glanced up at him. Gabriele looked as if he could already see right through me. He knew I was holding back and the truth was that he was right. I didn't know what was going on, who I could trust. I wanted to believe that my brothers and cousins were a safe haven, but this world was known for deception and disloyalty. I couldn't risk Six's life by being blind to what might be going on around me.

"Everything's fine," I said finally. "Maybe I'll stop by this Sunday and eat with the family. I have been missing Nonna's meals."

Gabriele's eyes searched mine before he nodded slightly. "Alright, I'll let her know." He stood up and pushed a hand into his pocket.

"In the meantime, try answering your phone sometimes. You're not the only one that's been dealing with problems."

"I know." The guilt I felt crawled up my back and I sighed. "I'll call you."

He nodded. "Thanks."

Gabriele left and I stared at the monitor for a little while longer. *Shit, this thing is getting complicated.* Whoever we were dealing with was throwing a wrench in all of my plans. When I found out who it was I was going to personally break each and every last one of their bones.

I took a deep breath and picked up my phone as it buzzed. As soon as I saw Six, I smiled.

Six: Checking in Daddy. We're still at the restaurant, but we might go walk around the park for a while since Ty's Daddy said he could. Is that okay?

My heart felt like it was going to burst right out of my chest. Six was asking for permission. *Six.* He was the most stubborn boy I'd ever met, but I was starting to understand him. He wouldn't give peace to just anyone, but with me? He was starting to. No more absurd pranks, no more fighting and ignoring me. Six was softening and he was turning me into a big softie too.

Amadeo: Yes but stay with your guards okay?

Six: Yes, Daddy!

My heart skipped a beat. Yes, Daddy. Two little words and every time they were coming from Six I forgot how to think straight. He had the potential to be a good boy, polite, obedient and sweet, but I was pretty sure he would never lose that bratty edge. And I didn't want him to.

When my phone buzzed again, I expected another text from Six. Instead, there was a number I'd never seen before and a picture message downloading. I opened it up and my eyes widened.

Six was standing outside of the restaurant with his friend, Ty. The two of them were laughing, none the wiser to the fact that someone was watching them. Under the picture, a text came in.

Unknown: I'll get him soon and you won't be able to stop me.

A shiver worked its way up my spine and I was moving before I could even think. I grabbed my gun and shoved it into its holster before I dialed Angelo's number.

"Bring Six home, now. Have someone else drive Ty back home."

"Yes, boss."

I hung up the phone and it rang a few minutes later when I walked downstairs. As soon as I pressed it against my ear, Six was cursing.

"What the fuck? You said I could go!"

"Calm down. Something came up and I need you home. Now."

He quieted. "What's wrong?"

"Nothing I want to discuss over the phone, but I do want you here with me."

"We're on our way now."

"Be safe."

"You too," Six said. "If you die I'll be pissed off."

I grinned. "I'll keep that in mind, baby."

Once we were off the phone, I dialed up Dario and gave him the number to have it tracked down. I knew the possibility of it coming back as a text app or a burner but I had to try. Someone was taunting me, threatening my reason to get out of bed every morning. And I wasn't going to stand for it.

"I'M HOME!" Six yelled as he raced through the door and right into my arms. "What happened? You sounded scared. Are you okay?"

Had I sounded scared? I hadn't even noticed. But when I thought about the way my stomach twisted and the cold sweat that dotted my forehead, I recognized the signs. I was terrified of losing my boy.

I caressed his cheek. "I'm fine, trust me." I pulled back and looked him over. "With everything that's going on I need to make sure you can defend yourself. Let's go to the gym and I can show you some moves."

He raised a brow. "I know how to fight."

"Do you?" I asked.

Six chuckled. "Oh yeah. Calix showed me how like two years ago. I got tired of getting my ass kicked over stupid shit."

"Hmm. Okay, then show me."

I took his hand and Six didn't protest. Leading him through the house, I took him to the gym and closed the door behind us. Just having him in my sights was making me feel a hell of a lot more relaxed than I was before.

I released Six's hand and nodded to the mats. "Go lay those out."

"Yes, Daddy," he said as he went to grab them.

I wonder if he even knows he does that? He says it like it's automatic now.

Six dragged the mats over and I helped him lay them out before I slipped off my jacket. I rolled my sleeves up my forearms and caught Six staring and practically drooling. Grinning, I snapped my fingers and got his attention.

"Focus, baby."

"Kind of hard," he muttered, adjusting his dick through his shorts.

I chuckled. "I'll take care of that later. For now, I need to see what you can do."

Six nodded. "Okay, but don't get mad if I hurt you."

This time a loud bark of a laugh fell from my lips. "I think I can handle you."

He shrugged. "Whatever you say."

Six tugged his shirt over his head and tossed it to the side. I raised a brow and he grinned back at me, a mischievous twinkle in his brown eyes. *What is that look about?* He moved onto the mats and raised his fists.

"Alright, I'm going to see if you can block me," I said as I raised my fists as well. "Ready?"

"I'm ready."

Six circled me and I did the same to him. He was still grinning, but this was a serious thing. I needed to make sure he was going to be safe if anything happened to me. As much as I wanted to attach Six to my hip and keep him right near me twenty-four seven, I knew that wasn't possible. Anything could happen and I had to be prepared for that and so did Six.

He moved toward me and my instincts kicked in. I punched Six in the arm and immediately stopped when he hissed.

"Shit, are you o-"

My world shifted as I was thrown to the ground and my back hit the mat. The wind rushed out of me and I stared up at Six in shock as he climbed on top of me. He pinned my wrists to the ground and grinned.

"That punch was pretty hard, but I've had worse," he chuckled as he squeezed his thighs on either side of me. "So, do you think I can look after myself now?"

"But I thought I had hurt you," I managed to get out.

Six shrugged. "Yeah, that's what I wanted you to think. It's easier to take the hit and then your opponent lets their guard down more quickly. That just makes it easier for me to attack." He leaned down and pressed his lips to mine before he sat up a little. "You should have seen the look on your face when I took you down. I mean, you had *no* idea what was happening."

He laughed and I couldn't take my eyes off of him. Six was...beautiful. The way his head tilted back and the way his hair shifted as his shoulders bounced, all of it was amazing. I sat up and pulled him into my arms, holding him tight.

Six was the reason I was able to smile. He was the one that made me feel like I was a human being. I might be obsessed with him, but it was so much more than sex. Six made me feel alive in ways that I hadn't in years. I couldn't lose him. I would burn the world down if anyone tried to take away the man I loved.

"You're kinda squeezing the air out of me," Six wheezed.

"Sorry." I pulled back and he stared at me.

"What?" Six asked. "What's that look?"

The words I love you were on my tongue, but I still couldn't say them. Not yet. Those were not things that I said lightly. In fact, I had never said them. To my family, yes. But to someone I slept with? Never. No one had ever been worth it.

Until I met Six.

"Are you okay?" he asked, tilting his head and frowning as he reached out and touched my cheek. "I didn't hurt you that bad did I?"

My heart warmed at his concern. "No, I'm fine baby."

"Good." He smiled and brushed his thumb over my skin. "I know you're old as hell, but I don't want you breaking a hip or something."

I threw him down onto the mats as he laughed. "Let me show you how much that's not a concern, boy."

He wrapped his legs around my waist. "Oh, you're going to teach me something new, old man? Bring it on." He nipped my chin and chuckled. "But don't complain when I outdo you and you're all out of breath."

"That's it."

I grabbed Six and shoved him onto his belly. The yelp he let out followed by his laughter made fire sweep over every inch of my skin. My boy. He was worth the world.

And no one was going to fucking take him away from me.

Chapter Twenty-Six

Six

The weight of the gun Amadeo had given me felt heavy against my skin. It was tucked inside of my jacket, but I felt like everyone could see it. He'd insisted that even though I knew how to defend myself after two dozen or so takedowns that I needed to carry it with me.

"Are you sure I can't leave this thing in the car?" I muttered as I squirmed around beside him in the back of the car. "I'm with you. I don't need this."

"You never know when you might need it so no, you cannot leave it in the car." He laid a hand on my leg and squeezed. "I taught you how to use it and you're not the worst shot in the world. You'll be fine."

"Easy for you to say," I muttered. "You're used to this kind of stuff."

Amadeo chuckled. "I am, but you're with me so you need to get used to it too."

"Great," I huffed.

His grip tightened. "Stop pouting."

"You like it," I mumbled, looking out the window. "Where are we going?"

"I told you, to dinner."

Turning back around I stared at him. "Is that why I had to get all dressed up?"

Amadeo had insisted that I wear a pair of dark blue slacks and what he called a pewter, whatever the hell pewter was, jacket. There was a white button-up underneath the jacket and he had given me a handkerchief for the jacket pocket and a watch for my wrist. At first I'd thought he was letting me borrow it, but when I flipped it over I realized my initials were carved into the back.

L.W.

He'd bought it for me. I still didn't know how I felt about that.

"We're almost there," he said as he took my hand in his. "I want you to be on your best behavior."

"And if I'm not?" I asked, my brow raised.

"If you're not, I'll drag you off somewhere and spank your ass raw until you're crying," he said, a growl in his voice as he grabbed my throat and squeezed. "Do you understand me, boy?"

"I can't hear a thing you're saying. All the blood went straight to my dick."

Amadeo barked out a laugh before he released my neck and kissed me. "Be good for Daddy."

"Yes, Daddy. When am I not good?"

"Often," he said as the car came to a stop. "Very, very often."

I grinned at him. "But you still keep me around."

"For some unfathomable reason," he muttered as he climbed out.

I smiled to myself as he walked around the car. For a moment I just watched him talking to Angelo and my heart sped up so quickly it was hard to breathe. Being with Amadeo was turning me into someone I hadn't been in a long time. He made me crave things I had let die a long time ago. All I did was live for my family, take care of them, give them whatever they needed. But when it came to me I neglected myself constantly, because I didn't matter.

But with Amadeo, I felt like I was his entire world. And it made me want more. Lonely drunken nights, endless loud parties, random quick fucks that meant nothing; they couldn't compare to the man that had stolen me and made me see that there was more to life.

"Are you coming?" Amadeo asked as he opened my door.

I cleared my throat. "Y-yeah I'm coming, Daddy."

"Just Amadeo here," he said, his face coloring slightly.

I blinked at him. "Are you telling me not to call you Daddy?" I asked suspiciously. "What's going on? Where are we?"

He sighed. "You'll see."

Amadeo took my hand and I didn't object, but I didn't like the way he didn't want me to call him Daddy. I'd hated it at first, but now it felt familiar. Safe. *I don't love him taking that away from me. When we're alone he's going to hear my mouth about this.*

We approached the doors of a house that was even bigger than Amadeo's. A man let us in, bowing slightly. Amadeo breezed past him and I frowned.

"I thought we were going to dinner," I whispered.

"We are. My family has dinner here every Sunday."

"Amadeo! Six!" Rayna grinned as she ran down the hall, her heels clicking on the marble floor. She threw her arms around Amadeo and he hugged her back. "I can't believe you showed up." She glanced at me. "Why's he making that face?"

My mouth still hadn't closed from Amadeo telling me that this was his family's home. *His family.* All of the saliva dried up in my mouth and suddenly it was impossible to swallow. I was about to meet Amadeo's family.

And he hadn't fucking told me.

I'm going to murder him.

"He didn't know you were coming either, did he?" Rayna asked, crossing her arms over her chest. "Ama..."

"If I said anything to anyone, it wasn't going to happen," he growled. "It was this way or I wasn't coming at all."

She shook her head. "You're batshit." She flipped her hair over her shoulder. "Well come on, everyone's in the dining room. We were in the kitchen, but Nic kept sticking his finger in the sauce and Nonna was about ready to drown him in it."

"Sounds like Nic," he sighed before he gazed down at me. "You okay?" He pressed his finger against my chin and closed my gaping mouth. "Breathe, Six."

"Your family," I wheezed out. "What the fuck!"

Amadeo shrugged. "It's only dinner."

He said it casually, but the look on his face was far from relaxed. The man looked as unsure as I was and that wasn't an expression I was used to him wearing. I squeezed his hand and he led me into the dining room while I considered running for the hills.

"Hey!" a man shouted, his grin ear to ear as he waved like a madman. "Ama's here!" He jogged over to us and whistled as he looked me up and down. "Woah, when I said you needed to get laid, I didn't think this would be the guy! He's hot."

Amadeo released me and grabbed the man, his movements nothing more than a blur. He slammed him against the table and the man in his grasp grunted, but he didn't fight back. Instead, he laughed as Amadeo growled and laid his palms flat on the table.

"Calm down, Cuzzo. I'm just fucking with you!"

"Back off, Nic," Amadeo said as he kneed him in the ass. "Or I'm going to make sure Nonna drowns you once and for all."

"Will you two calm down? Nic, sit," another man sighed and stood up. He resembled Amadeo a bit, but there was gray at his temples. When he looked at me he smiled. "Sorry, they're barbarians. I'm Dario and that's my brother, Nic." He waved around the table. "You've met Rayna and Gabriele and the big broody one is Riccardo."

Riccardo nodded at me, but he was the only quiet one. I nodded back and poked Amadeo's arm. He still hadn't let go of the man that called him cousin.

"Um, Da- Amadeo. Can we sit down?" I muttered, feeling subconscious under their curious gazes.

Amadeo finally released the man and pulled out a chair for me. "Sit."

I stared at him and raised a brow. We both knew I didn't like being treated like a dog. I crossed my arms over my chest and heard the collective gasps of his family around us when I didn't immediately do what I was told. The two of us stared at each other until Amadeo took my hand and kissed it.

"Here, sit next to me," he said a little more softly.

I immediately stopped resisting and sat down. "Thanks."

"Look at you," Rayna whispered, elbowing me lightly. "You tamed the big, bad wolf."

"Rayna, don't think I won't hit you," Amadeo sighed.

She batted her lashes at him. "You would never, big brother."

"It's true, he wouldn't," Gabriele laughed. "Rayna has slapped him more times than I can count and he refuses to touch her."

Amadeo squirmed in his seat. "Women are terrifying," he muttered. "Mom and Nonna would have kicked my ass and then had Dad follow it up with another beating if I ever tried it."

"They're the best," Rayna sighed. "May he rest in peace."

All of them as if on autopilot crossed themselves. I wanted to ask what happened to him, but I knew to stay quiet this one time. All of them looked a little sad before the conversation started up again.

Amadeo glanced at me and took my hand. "He was killed," he said quietly to me.

I blinked at him. "I'm so sorry."

"It was a few years ago. It's fine."

I squeezed his hand. "It's not fine," I said, heat spreading over my body as he tried to brush it off. "That must have been so hard for you. My dad's a dick, but he's not dead. I can't imagine going through that."

Amadeo searched my face before he cradled it and kissed me. I blinked before my eyes closed and I kissed him back. My heart ached for him. I knew Amadeo well enough to know that he had probably never dealt with it and if he had, it was all on his own. He took care of everything and everyone. But who took care of him?

I will. I'll keep him safe.

"Who is this?"

A woman chuckled as she walked into the room. She was the spitting image of Rayna but blonde. She smiled at me and I immediately felt warmth from her.

"This is my mother. Mom, this is Six," Amadeo said as he stood up and I shot up with him.

She walked around the table and gave me a hug. "Welcome, Six! You can call me Isabella." She stood back and looked me up and down. "My son has never brought anyone home before. Wow, you're a good-looking young man."

"That he is," an older woman said as she smiled at us from the doorway.

"Oh, that's my mother, Nonna Anna. Well, my late husband's mother, but I feel like she's mine as well," Isabella said as she led me over to the woman. "This is Six."

"Six?" The woman raised a thin brow. "What's your real name?"

"I uh...I don't like it so much," I said quietly. "Everyone's called me Six since I was a toddler. I was the sixth born. My mom used to yell where's number six! And the name just stuck. I'm talking a lot, shit. Sorry I didn't mean to swear. Shit. I mean."

Shoot me.

The woman chuckled and patted my hand. "No need to worry, Six. We won't bite you." She tucked a silver hair behind her ear and smoothed her black dress down. "Dinner is almost done. Why don't you come in and help me while we chat? Just the two of us? Isabella, pour some more wine."

"Of course, Mother."

I glanced over my shoulder for Amadeo's help, but he shrugged. *Who knew my Daddy is a wimp when it comes to the women in his family?* I stayed to the side as Nonna Anna moved around the kitchen as smoothy as if she were dancing. For a woman who had to at least be in her seventies or eighties, she looked no more than sixty and moved like she was thirty. I was in awe.

"Well, don't just stand there," she said as she nodded to the oven. "Take the dessert out. By the time we're done with dinner, it'll have cooled." She watched as I took it out. "Good job. So, Six," she said as she turned back to the stove stirring a huge pot of sauce, "you and my grandson are together?"

I choked on my own spit. "Um...I don't know. Ma'am," I added quickly, trying to remember my manners.

She glanced over her shoulder. "You must be if he brought you here. No one's stepped through these doors with Amadeo. Not once."

"Never?" I asked. "Not even in high school or college or something?"

The woman shook her head. "Not once. I always thought he would end up being a bachelor all his life. I mean he's thirty-seven! But now he brings a nice boy like you home." She smiled at me. "It gives me hope that he won't be alone."

My face heated. "I don't know about that," I said quietly. "He'll get sick of me soon."

"If that were true, he wouldn't have invited you."

"You think so?" I asked, hope rising in my chest. "I always feel like I get in the way."

"Poor thing." She walked over and patted my cheek. "No one's going to make you feel like that here." Nonna Anna smiled and waved a hand. "Start helping me bring in the food. Sunday is the only day I don't allow any paid help in the kitchen, but I could use a hand carrying it all out."

"Yes, Ma'am."

I followed behind her, juggling bowls in my hands and carefully sitting them on the table. When I glanced up Amadeo was staring at me so intensely making heat swept through my body. I wished I could jump into his head and know exactly what he was thinking.

How much do you care about me Amadeo Bianchi?

Chapter Twenty-Seven

Six

"Daddy, can I go? Please?"

Amadeo groaned like he was dying and rolled over in the bed. He was deep into a book with too many big words for me to even understand. Of course, he'd tried to explain it to me, but I was still lost. Although I did nod and say the right things in the right places. That made him happy.

I love his smile.

Shaking his arm, I groaned right back at him. "Please? Don't you want me to have this?"

"When I asked you what you wanted to do, I didn't think fighting was going to be the answer," he growled. "Can't you find a normal hobby?"

I huffed. He was the one who had said he noticed that I didn't do anything for myself. Sure, I liked movies and binging TV series as much as the next guy, but what I really wanted to do was fight. Calix had been training me in MMA for a while and I had only dropped it so I could focus on work. But now that I was spending time with myself I was realizing just how much I had suppressed to take care of my family.

I was ready to start being *me.*

"Fine," I said as I laid down and rolled away from him. "Forget it."

I hid my grin into my pillow as I heard him shifting in bed. The scent of his bodywash filled my nose as he wrapped an arm around me and yanked me against him. Amadeo growled, that primal sound stirring my cock awake.

"Don't turn away from me with that attitude," he snapped. "Turn around."

"No," I huffed. "Fuck you."

I braced myself and sure enough, Amadeo grabbed me and pinned me to the bed. He climbed on top of me, his book long forgotten as he straddled my body and glared down at me. I stared up at him, feigning innocence as I bit my lip. He looked wild when he was on top of me, as if he would bite and mark me all up. And I loved it.

"Daddy, please," I begged, making my voice softer since it always wore him down. "I want to train and fight. It's the only thing I'm good at and enjoy. Can't I go?"

"That guy is going to be there," he spat, looking away from me. "What's his name?"

"Calix," I said gently, squirming when his hands squeezed around my wrists. "It's not like that and you know it. He's a friend just like Ty. You like Ty," I pointed out.

He'd met Ty once and deemed him not a threat. Probably because while Ty was wild and crazy, he had a Daddy that kept him on a short leash so he stayed out of trouble. Amadeo liked that about them and it allowed me to hang out with him. But Calix? That was a different story.

"Why don't you like him?" I asked.

"He touched you," he growled. "Nobody told him to put his filthy hands on you."

I sighed. "Normal people touch other people," I said gently. "It's human."

"Guess I'm not human then because I don't want you touching anyone."

Yeah, that was my Daddy alright. I tried to wiggle free, but apparently, he was in no mood to let me go tonight. I gave up and laid against the pillow as I gazed up at him.

"I don't want to touch anyone either," I assured him. "But I have to touch people when I fight-"

"You are mine!" he growled.

Right, I kept forgetting he was insane. Sometimes, Amadeo was put together and calm and rational and I would think he was like everyone else. Until moments like now when it came back to me that he was obsessed with me and would kill someone for even looking at me the wrong way.

"I am yours," I agreed. "We both know that. I'm not saying that's not true." His face relaxed a bit and I was able to wrap my legs around him. "But I want to do something for me. It's not like I still won't be here with you in bed at night."

Amadeo looked like he was contemplating it. "This is true."

I beamed up at him. "So let me go and fight! Come on, Calix is going to be at the gym today and I can talk to him about training me again."

"How do you know he'll be there?" Amadeo demanded. "Have you been talking to him behind my back?"

"No, of course not," I said as I rolled my eyes. "But he has the same routine during the week so it's not hard to know where he'll be in a few hours. We could go and talk to him. Maybe he would coach me. I would be safe with him," I added as that hard look came over his face again, his jaw clenched so tight I thought his teeth would snap. "Calix is like a brother to me."

Amadeo sighed. "If I don't let you go, are you going to pout and throw a fit?"

"Yes," I said as I grinned up at him. "And I won't let you fuck me for a week."

He rolled his eyes. "We both know that's not going to happen." Finally, he sat up and pushed his fingers through his silky hair. "Alright, we can go and check it out but I'm not promising anything. Do you understand me?"

"Yes, Daddy," I said as I sat up and tackled him down before kissing him. "Thank you!"

Amadeo's rich laughter made me feel warm all over. We stayed together in bed a while longer before we finally climbed out and started the day. Amadeo insisted on sitting down to eat lunch, have coffee, and then we could finally leave.

"Come on, I don't want to miss him," I said as I raced for the car.

"I'm coming, I'm coming," he grumbled. "You're lucky I like seeing you happy."

"You like seeing me happy?" I asked as I climbed into the passenger seat.

Amadeo glared at me. "Be quiet or we'll stay home."

"Yes, Daddy."

He was cute when he was trying to act like he was cranky. *Did I really think he was cute? What has this man done to me?*

I could barely sit still as we drove to the gym. Every street we turned down the excitement in me grew.

"Baby, you're going to burst if you don't calm down."

I blew out a breath. "Sorry, but I can't help it. I was never allowed to fight when I was younger. My parents said it was brutal and unsophisticated." I rolled my eyes. "But I've been craving it for a while. There's nothing like the rush of a good fight."

Amadeo brushed his thumb along mine. "If you can fight so well, why didn't you fight me when I took you? You could have tried."

"Um, you were a terrifying psychopath and I was pretty sure that you would just shoot me and be done with it." I chewed my lip. "Maybe part of me, a small part, thought you were kind of hot and I couldn't stop staring at you, but you were still insane."

"Were?"

I laughed. "Are. You are insane."

Amadeo grinned. "That's more like it."

I shook my head at him but leaned against his shoulder. As crazy as he was, Amadeo was starting to feel like a safe place. He saw me as more than just "Six" but a person. And I wanted that from someone, anyone in my life.

No, I want that from him. Just him.

By the time we reached the gym, I was bursting out of the door. Amadeo called me, but I charged inside and ran right into Gabriele. He grunted and rubbed his side as he laughed at me.

"What the shit are you doing, kid?"

"Sorry," I muttered. "I'm here to see Calix."

"Me too," he said as he nodded to the ring. "He's right there."

"Six, you were supposed to wait," Amadeo growled as he reached my side and laid a hand on my shoulder. "Next time listen."

Stern voice. He's not joking around.

"I know, I got excited," I said giving him a smile so he wouldn't stay angry.

He sighed. "I understand that, but you still need to listen." Glancing up, Amadeo noticed Gabriele for what seemed like the first time. "What are you doing here?"

"Working," Gabriele said as he shoved his hands into his pockets. "Nic's in back doing his thing too. I figured I might as well stick around and make sure he stays out of trouble."

"That's a good idea," Amadeo said as I squirmed out of his hold and started walking. "Six, be careful."

"Yes, Daddy," I said, my cheeks heating as I realized how loudly I'd said that. Amadeo had clearly brainwashed me because the words came out on autopilot these days. "I'm gonna say hi to Calix."

Before he could protest I ran for the ring. Calix looked over at me and a huge grin spread across his face.

"Six, what are you doing here?" He leaned on the ropes of the ring and nodded his head toward Amadeo. "Isn't your guard dog going to lose his shit again if he sees you talking to me?"

I snickered and climbed up on the ring to talk to him. "Nah, he's cool now. But don't let him hear you calling him that." I looked at the guy Calix had been sparring with and he nodded before I returned the gesture. "So, I want to go back to training."

Calix raised a brow. "You do? Last time we started you disappeared on me."

"Yeah, I know," I muttered as I toyed with the material under my fingertips. "But this time I'm serious. I want you to train me."

He looked uncertain as his eyes searched me up and down. "For fun or for real?"

I shrugged. "I've always wanted to fight, you know that. Do I think I can actually do what you do? Not really, but I want to try."

"Let him train," Amadeo's deep voice rumbled beside my ear and I felt goosebumps covering every inch of my skin. "Here."

Amadeo shoved a wad of cash into Calix's hand. I stared at it before I looked at Amadeo. He glanced down at me for a moment before he challenged my friend with his eyes to turn the money down. But I knew he wouldn't. Calix was still working his way up with his fights and he needed the cash.

"I don't need your money," Calix said, holding it back out to Amadeo. "Six is my friend. I'm going to help him because I want to."

"Keep it," Amadeo said, refusing to take it back. "It's admirable, helping him for free, but this is your job too, right? You train? Then train him. It should be enough to cover as many lessons as he wants to take."

"Listen-"

"Come on, Calix," I said as I clasped my hands together. "Teach me!"

He blinked at me and burst out laughing. "Who told you playing cute works for you? Jesus Christ, man." He shook his head. "Fine, you can train. But I'm not going to hold back from putting you through your paces because your boyfriend paid me."

"I don't expect that," I said with a grin. "When can I get started?"

"Get some proper clothes and gear and you can start whenever. Can I give you my number this time so you'll know when I'm here?"

Calix was talking to me, but he was staring directly at Amadeo. After a moment of tension so thick I could suffocate on it Amadeo nodded and I took out my phone. Calix entered his number and passed it back to me.

"Think you can be here tomorrow?"

I nodded. "Whenever you want, coach!"

He laughed again, his long hair bouncing as he shook his head. "You're such a dork. Tomorrow. Noon. And don't be late or I'll make it hurt."

I beamed up at him. "Noon."

After we turned around, I noticed Gabriele staring up at Calix. He glanced away and our eyes met. I raised a brow and he gave me a lopsided smile before he made his face go blank again. It was creepy as hell how they could all do that.

"Playing cute does work for you," Amadeo whispered against my ear as we exited the gym. "At least on me. But don't be that cute for another man again. It took a lot not to rip his hands off."

I groaned. "Can you be normal for five seconds?"

"No," he said shortly.

I sighed. "Yes, Daddy. I'll only be cute for you."

We slipped into the car and Amadeo kissed me long and hard before we started moving. He headed for downtown and I knew we weren't going back home. Amadeo was going to buy whatever I needed and I couldn't lie. I loved it.

"COME ON, Six, pay attention! If you don't kick harder you're going to get your ass handed to you!"

Sweat poured down my face as Calix yelled at me from the sidelines. The only person I'd ever met with as bad a temper as Calix was Amadeo. Together, the two of them would be terrifying to a normal person, but for some reason, one made me hard and the other motivated me.

Calix had been training me for a month and I was still shit compared to the other guys at the gym. They were all faster, bigger, or hit harder. I knew some basic moves and could get a takedown or two here and there, but I was rusty as hell.

"Take a break!" Calix called as he walked over to me and handed over my water bottle. "Hydrate."

I grabbed it and sucked down some water before I panted. "I thought I was in good shape."

"That was before you took an extended vacation to be a whore and steal money," he said, his mouth tugging into a grin. "Keep working on it, man. You're not nearly as bad as you think you are. This stuff's hard at first."

"You can say that again," I muttered.

My body had been sore every time I came back home. Amadeo insisted on having a masseuse on call so I could get a good massage when I came back. It was over the top, but it was my Daddy. He was going to do whatever the hell he wanted to do.

I glanced over as the door opened expecting Amadeo, but Gabriele and Nic walked in. They both called out their hellos before Nic disappeared into the back and Gabriele leaned against a far wall. He glanced around the gym before his eyes flickered over to Calix.

"What are they doing here so much?" I asked Calix.

He shook his head. "I have no idea, but I know it's not good. Mafia hanging around is never a good thing."

I frowned. "They're not that bad."

Calix looked me up and down. "You say that because you're dating one of them. I hate to burst your bubble but they're all bastards, Six. Maybe yours is nice to you right now, but they don't have feelings like normal humans, man. They'll kill you as soon as look at you. Watch your back. Always."

"Amadeo isn't like that," I protested. "He's a decent guy."

"Whatever you say," he answered with a shrug. "It's not my life. I'm just telling you to be careful."

I nodded, but I didn't argue with him. Glancing over at Gabriele again, I saw the man's eyes wander to Calix before he went back to scanning the gym. A shiver worked its way up my spine. Whatever he was up to, it was probably illegal and none of my business.

"Back to work, Six," Calix called. "Let's go!"

"Coming!"

I moved back into the ring and readied myself. Focusing on the fight with Calix's voice in my ear was like heaven. The rest of the world fell away and there was just me, the ring, and the will to win. I grabbed onto my opponent and went to throw him when I noticed movement out of the corner of my eye. Amadeo walked through the door looking as put together as always and I smiled at him.

Before I was slammed against the mat.

All of the wind rushed out of me and I was dying. No matter how hard I tried to drag in a breath nothing happened as panic filled my chest.

"Breathe, Six," Calix said as he appeared beside me. "Come on, you're fine. Deep breath in, stomach out. I know it feels like shit, but the more you panic the worse it'll be."

The groan that left my lips sounded horrific, but I forced myself to breathe. As wind filled my lungs, I exhaled and shivered. Calix sat me up and I took a few more breaths as I heard the commotion around me. When I glanced over, Amadeo was being dragged out of the gym. The look on his face was a twisted mask of anger and danger. My stomach clenched.

"Let go of me, Nic! Get the fuck off of me! You, come here motherfucker!"

The guy that had slammed me down, Sam, looked like he was going to piss his pants. He stared at Amadeo until he was dragged outside.

"What the fuck?" Sam muttered.

I stood up with Calix's help. "I'll calm him down. Sorry, he's just overprotective as hell."

Sam scratched his head. "Sorry, didn't mean to throw you down like that. I thought you were paying attention."

I shook my head. "That was my fault, I got distracted. No hard feelings."

Sam shook my hand when I reached out. "Go home and put some ice on your back. It's going to be a wicked bruise."

Groaning, I nodded. "Trust me, I can already feel it. I better go."

Calix waved and I headed for the door. Forget showering or changing or any of that shit. I had to check on Amadeo first. I stepped outside and the setting sun hit me in the eyes, blinding me for a second before I looked around and saw Gabriele.

"Where's Amadeo?"

He sighed. "Nic dragged him off somewhere." Gabriele shook his head. "I haven't seen Amadeo get like that in a long time. He's always so composed and he was ready to shoot that guy in front of everyone."

My eyes widened. "He pulled out his gun?"

"Yes, but I took it away from him," he said as he wiped a hand down his face. "Amadeo has always been the more restrained of us. Even with the famous Bianchi temper, he's the one most likely to keep it together. But now?" He shook his head before he looked at me intently. "Amadeo must really love you."

I stared at him. *Amadeo loves me?*

"You're crazy," I blurted out as Gabriele raised a brow at me. "Amadeo doesn't love me."

He scoffed. "Really? Because I've only ever seen him go that feral when it was over someone in our family. No one outside of it."

Amadeo loves me?

The thought that it might be true did funny things to my stomach. What if he did? Such a dangerous, wild, crazy man loving me? It was as terrifying as it was exciting. Being loved like Amadeo, there had to be nothing like it.

"Do you think one of your brothers or cousins is the one betraying him?" I asked Gabriele, anything to get the subject off of me before my brain exploded.

Gabriele froze. "Is that what Amadeo thinks?"

I shrugged. "He doesn't know what to think."

He stood up a little taller. "None of us are stupid enough to repeat past mistakes. You tell him that." We turned as Amadeo called my name and walked back toward us. "Take him home and make sure he knows where our loyalties lie. We would never hurt Amadeo. He's taken on a burden that the rest of us would crumble under." When I started to move away, Gabriele pulled me back. "Pour him a nice glass of scotch and hand him a book. He'll be okay."

As soon as Amadeo was close, Gabriele released me. I couldn't get a word out before Amadeo wrapped me in his arms and held me tightly. I wanted to protest and tell him that I smelled like sweat but I knew he wasn't going to release me until he felt like it so I held on and let him get what he needed.

Me.

"I'll kill him," Amadeo growled. "That bastard dealt a low fucking blow. When I get done with him-"

"No," I said as I pulled back and held his hand. "Come on, Daddy. Let's go home."

"Six."

I shook my head. "He didn't mean it. I was the one that got distracted. Besides, if you're going to let me do this, you need to realize that sometimes I'm gonna get hurt. That's just the way it is, okay? Now, come on. Take me home. My back is killing me." When he hesitated, I squeezed his hand. "Please, Daddy. I could use a hot shower and an ice pack."

That did the trick. He stopped glaring into the gym and took my hand before turning on his heels. Amadeo put me into the passenger seat and reached over me, fastening my seatbelt despite my protests before he straightened up and turned to Gabriele.

"Nic should stay away from me for a few days," he said matter-of-factly. "Or I'll break his nose."

"Got it," Gabriele said. "I'll let him know. Where is he now?"

"Probably still throwing up in the alley. I decked him in the diaphragm." He closed my door. "Move."

Gabriele stepped out of the way and Amadeo rounded the car. I glanced at Gabriele and he nodded before I nodded back. For some reason, I believed him when he said it wasn't them fucking with Amadeo. It seemed like no one wanted the burden of being the boss when it came right down to it.

Then who's doing it?

I stayed quiet on the drive home, my mind racing a mile a minute. Amadeo didn't say anything either for once, but I felt his eyes boring into me every once in a while. *He's worried.*

"I'm fine," I said when we made it home and he helped me out of the car. "Probably bruises but that's it."

He frowned. "I never should have let you fight."

I took his hand. "But I like fighting. Remember? Sometimes it hurts but I'm enjoying it. I've never felt so free."

Amadeo squeezed my hand and led me inside. "I know. I'll run you a shower."

Nodding, I let him lead me upstairs. While he started the shower, I poured Amadeo a drink and he walked out of the bathroom to me handing it to him. He took a sip, his eyes on me.

"I don't think Gabriele or the rest of your family has anything to do with what's been going on."

"Hmm," he said quietly. "Why not?"

I shrugged. "It's a feeling I have. Gabriele wasn't lying," I said as I laid a hand on his chest. "I think they all know they could never do the job you do. It's hard and exhausting and none of them are up for it. Gabriele pretty much said so himself."

Amadeo searched my face. "You're trying to help me?"

I shrugged once more. "Why not? You've been helping me lately."

He stopped me from walking away and Amadeo's lips pressed against mine. The taste of scotch still lingered on his mouth and I sank against him. He held me tightly, his hand dragging me closer as if we could merge into one person. When he came up for air I couldn't take it anymore.

I had to know.

"Do you love me?"

Amadeo's eyes widened and he opened his mouth. My stomach twisted and tightened waiting for the confession. What would it be like having Amadeo's love? *Dangerous but perfect.* I held onto his shirt, waiting for his answer as my heart pounded so hard I could hear it in my ears.

"I don't know," Amadeo said.

Staring at him I felt my hope crash and burn. *He didn't know? What the fuck was that supposed to mean?* He didn't know if he loved me or not?

"Oh," I said as I stepped away from him.

"It's complicated, Six," he said as he moved toward me.

"It's not that complicated," I shot back at him before I shook my head. "Think I'll shower in my own room."

"Six."

He touched me, but I yanked my arm away. Tears filled my eyes and I touched one as it rolled down my cheek. *Shit. When did I start caring this much?* It had always been there, a whisper of my love for him and wondering if he felt the same.

"Don't touch me," I said, refusing to look at him. "I need to be alone."

I took the silence that met my words as an agreement and left. Amadeo could stay by himself. If he couldn't figure out how he felt about me then he didn't deserve me.

I wasn't going to be his plaything forever.

Chapter Twenty-Eight

Amadeo

I checked my phone but Six still hadn't texted me. Usually, if I sent him a message in the morning he at least told me that he was on his way down. But so far I had gotten nothing. I switched over to the camera app and found a black screen.

"Fuck," I muttered.

Six had found the camera in his room.

I tried to give him his space, I did. But three days of being ignored had taken its toll. I picked up my glass and drank some water before I slammed it down on the table. The glass shattered, water sloshed over the table and I growled.

"Fuck!"

I had reached the end of my rope. Gabriele, Rayna, even my mother kept telling me to give it time, but I had never been a patient man. As a man ran in to clean up the table, I walked out and headed upstairs, my heart hammering in my chest. Six hadn't been in my bed for three nights and I was going insane.

I should have said I love him.

But I couldn't. The words had stuck on my tongue like glue and I don't know stupidly tumbled out. But when it came to Six, I was lost. He wasn't like anyone I had ever met. Three days ago I almost killed someone for handling him wrong and not even Nic had been spared from my wrath. If I was like that with him now when neither of us had said those three dangerous words, what would I be like once we had? Would I lose all control? What would happen to my family, my organization, my businesses? Would they all crumble as I fed my obsession of Six?

Before I knew it I was at his door. I knocked and stood there for a moment before I knocked harder.

"Six, don't make me get the ax again!"

The door unlocked and Six stood there staring at me. "What?"

I frowned. "How long are you going to stay up here? I thought you would be going to the gym today?"

Six shrugged. "Doesn't matter."

I shoved my irritation down. "It's been days. You haven't come out with me for dinner, you won't talk to me. What the hell is going on?"

"Nothing."

"Six..."

He closed his eyes and sucked in a deep breath before he opened his eyes and stared at me. "Let's go back to the way things were before."

My heart dropped. "What the fuck does that mean?"

"We're going back to the original arrangement. You fuck me, money comes off of my debt, and when the time is up, we go our separate ways."

Pain bloomed in my chest like I'd been stabbed. I wanted to reach up and rub the spot on my skin and make the pain go away, but all I could do was stare at Six. Part of me was expecting him to break out into that mischievous grin that I had gotten used to or to laugh and say he was only torturing me. But none of that happened.

"Six, you can't think that's what I want."

His dark eyes gazed into mine. "I don't care. It's what I want. The time is almost up so we need to do what we need to do and settle this already." He gripped the hem of his shirt and dragged it up his skin. "Might as well start now."

I growled and yanked his shirt back down. Never had I felt so fucking disgusted. Did he think that's who I was? Yes, I wanted Six and I always had. But not like this.

"What's wrong with you?"

"Nothing's wrong with me," he said, frowning. "I want to get my job over with for the day so I can go back to being alone."

Fire crept up my throat and I wanted to shake Six. He turned on his heels and walked into his room, but I was right behind him. I shut the door and before he could get too far away, I grabbed his arm and turned him around.

"Stop!" I snapped. "I said something stupid the other day and you're punishing me for it, but I-I."

Fuck! Why can't I say the words? It was simple. I love you. Why can't I say it?

Fear gripped my heart and squeezed. Ice raced up my spine and I was frozen as I stared at Six. Being scared wasn't a normal occurrence for me. I could face someone with a gun or talk to the cops with a body in my trunk without breaking a sweat. But now, faced with Six and the tired expression in his eyes, I felt the fear crawl up my spine.

But I couldn't let him go either.

"Six, come here."

He turned away from me and moved over to the bed. Six sat down a serene look on his face like he was far away from me.

"Can we stop?" He sighed. "Let's have sex and get it over with for the day."

I crossed the space between us and shoved him back onto the bed. A gasp left his lips as he fell back and I pinned his wrists to the bed.

"Is this what you want?" I demanded. "You want a monster who will fuck you and leave you alone? I can fucking do that, Six!"

"Okay," he said evenly. "That's fine. I'm here to give you whatever you want."

Frustration worked its way through my body until I wanted to scream. I released Six before I ended up hurting him and backed away. If I didn't put space between us, I was going to snap. He was acting as if he was a completely different person. This man, no this shell of a man, was *not* my Six. I knew him well and this was some imposter dropped in his place.

"I'm done with this shit," I snapped.

"This shit?" Six bit right back as he shot up from the bed, his fists balled up tight. "Just say you're done with me, Amadeo. Why don't you let me pay you back the rest of your money in cash at this point and I'll leave you alone?"

"Is that what you want?" I asked.

"What I want doesn't matter and I'm sick and fucking tired of fighting already. You can either fuck me or leave me alone."

I sneered. "That's your answer to everything. When I want to talk to you and figure out what's wrong, you prefer I communicate with my dick. Don't you? Because you don't want to face reality or the ugliness of it. And you don't want to talk about what's bothering you. No, you prefer to bury your head in the fuckin' sand and act like everything's okay as long as my cock is in you!"

Six stared at me. "Get the fuck out of my face before I punch you."

"Do it," I said as I stepped up to him. "Go on, right here." I pointed to my chin. "Hit me and get over yourself!"

"Fuck you," Six spat. "Get. Away. From. Me."

"No problem!"

I stormed out of his room, slamming the door behind me so hard the sound echoed through the halls. The newly patched door made a suspicious cracking sound, but I didn't give a damn. I was supposed to call to have it replaced, but I had never focused on it once Six moved into my room. Now, I stared at the cracks where it had been fixed up and all I could see was Six slipping through my fingers.

SLEEPING in my bed alone again was the worst kind of torture.

I had forced myself to walk into my room and stay there after my encounter with Six, but trying to force myself to sleep instead of destroying everything around me was difficult. *How many drinks have I had?* The nightstand held the glass tumbler and it was nearly empty. My head throbbed and that was my answer. I checked my phone.

Damn it.

Somehow, it was ten. I had spent hours with myself, my ears filled with silence. But my brain was full of noise. I couldn't stop thinking about Six, and every time I pulled out my phone to check the camera, I was reminded that he had done something to block me out. I didn't have eyes on him, didn't know how he was. And I was getting antsy.

I need to see him.

Pushing myself out of bed I walked down the hall in my sweatpants and no shirt. I didn't give a damn how I looked. As long as I saw Six, that was all that mattered. I grabbed the doorknob to his room and frowned when it opened. I expected him to lock it after our fight.

"Six?"

I stepped into his room and felt a chill travel down my spine. *He's probably in the bathroom or the balcony.* I walked into the bathroom but it was empty. When I moved to the balcony there was more urgency in my step. I threw open the doors, but there was no Six.

He's gone.

Deep down, I'd known that from the moment I walked into the room. Six had already escaped once, why wouldn't he do it again?

Heat bubbled up from my core and exploded. I grabbed the chair from the patio and slammed it into the double doors. Glass shattered and rained down to the floor below, but it wasn't enough.

More. I need more.

Slowly, my mind went blank and I watched myself as if I was watching a movie. Everything I smashed or broke or threw only added fuel to the fire, it didn't take away from it. By the end of it, I stood in the middle of the room surrounded by mess and chaos as I panted.

"Boss?"

I glanced over my shoulder at Angelo. There was worry on his face, but I didn't need his pity or anyone else's.

"Find Six," I said as I wiped the blood off my hand onto my sweats. "Now."

"Yes, Boss."

Angelo disappeared and I walked back to my room. My phone lay in the same spot on the pillow that was Six's and I snatched it up before I dialed his number. Part of me strained to hear it ringing distantly, praying he was somewhere on the grounds. But I knew he was gone.

"Please leave a message…"

I hung up and dialed him again. And again. And again. Every time I didn't get an answer the despair grew until I yelled and threw my phone across the room. I gripped my bed and held on tight trying not to destroy my room as well.

Six is going to need someplace to sleep when he comes home and if I fuck my room up he won't have that. Keep it together.

I forced myself to calm down and sent out a message to everyone who worked for me.

Amadeo: No one sleeps until Six is returned home. Get on it now.

I ignored the pinging of the phone as they responded. The only thing I wanted to read was a message saying that someone had found him and he was coming back home safe.

"Crazy asshole," I muttered. "Don't you remember I was trying to keep you safe?"

There was still someone out there who wanted to get to my boy and I couldn't allow that to happen. I traded in my sweats for a suit and pushed my fingers through my hair. No one was going to bed tonight. Not me, not my men, no one.

Six was going to come home and when he did I would get my head out of my ass and tell him how much I loved him. Because the truth was that I couldn't live without my boy.

I needed Six.

Chapter Twenty-Nine

Six

I SHOVED THE KEY INTO THE DOORKNOB AND TURNED IT. A WAVE of stale cigarette smoke filled my nose and I coughed as I stepped into the shabby motel room. There were questionable stains on the carpet and blanket, but I wasn't going to sleep anyway.

I set the backpack I'd snagged onto the little table and sat down after checking the chair. Glancing around the depressing little room made my stomach clench. *Right back where I started, huh?*

No, it shouldn't bother me. I was used to living in places that other people might turn their noses up at. But for some reason, I was itchy as if bugs were crawling over my skin. I stood up and started pacing back and forth trying to force myself to think about anything but the home that I had left behind.

"This is fine," I muttered to myself. "I'm fine."

I glanced at the clock across the room. My phone had been left behind. I was sure by now they'd found it tossed into one of the bushes in the front of the house. There wasn't a lot I could do but wait until the buses started their next runs and try to get the hell out of Atlanta. There was one more I could catch, the 1:15. I couldn't go back to Florida, but I could survive anywhere.

Before I could think about it I pushed out of my seat and grabbed the motel phone. My fingers dialed on autopilot and I held my breath as the phone rang. There was clattering before I heard the familiar sound of my mother clearing her throat.

"Hello?"

"Hey, Mom."

She sighed. "Oh, it's Leonidas."

I groaned. God did I hate that fucking name. I know Amadeo had found out my name from the start, but he never called me by it. For so long I had been Six or Baby and now I was once again Leonidas. I shivered.

"Just Six, Mom," I reminded her for the hundredth time.

"Oh please, Leo. Don't be difficult." She sighed more deeply. "And where are you? No one's heard from you in months."

"I've been...busy," I said, leaning my hip against the derelict dresser. "Working and stuff."

"You can't remember your own family when you work?" she huffed. "I was calling you like mad a few weeks ago and your phone was shut off. If you're working so hard, where's all of your money?"

In your pocket. And Dad's. And my siblings'. Everyone gets a piece but me.

"Sorry," I muttered instead, wiping my hand down my face. I didn't feel like arguing with my mother tonight. "I was just checking on everyone."

"We're fine, of course we are," she said and I could practically see her nose pushed up in the air. "Of course, we could use a little help around here..."

Here we go.

I didn't know why I thought something would be different calling home. *I wanted comfort, to hear voices that missed me.* But that wasn't what my family was. They weren't warm, welcoming or sympathetic. No, they were cold and closed off.

"I'll see what I can do when I get settled," I said as my chest ached and I rubbed it. "Listen, I have to go but I'll call soon."

"That's what you always say, dear," my mother sighed. "Well go on, run off again."

I gripped the phone so hard my palm ached. The tone of her voice felt like I was annoying her when all I wanted was to be comforted. But all she could think about was herself. That's how all of them were. When would I learn?

"Bye, Mom," I said tightly. "I love you."

"I love you too, dear. Call more often."

"Yeah, right," I muttered when she hung up. "I'll get right on that."

I felt the old wall climbing back into place as I put the phone down and stared into the mirror. Distancing myself was easier than dealing with any of it. Than dealing with Amadeo and his uncertainty or my loneliness or the fact that I was running again and this was going to be my reality for the rest of my life.

My eyes watered and I wiped at them angrily. "Get it together, Six. What the hell?"

I scrubbed at my cheeks until they were burning and red, but at least the tears were gone. There wasn't going to be any crying over Amadeo, my family, or my pathetic situation. What we had was always supposed to be temporary and I had lost sight of that.

This pain is my fault. I shouldn't have let him in.

"What did I expect?" I mumbled. "A fucking mafia boss? Why would he be able to fall in love with anything?"

I closed my eyes and when I opened them I forced myself to get moving. The only reason I'd rented the motel room was to stay out of sight. Hanging around outside before I needed to was a sure way for Amadeo or one of his guards to see me. If they drug me back to that place, I knew I wouldn't be leaving again.

Amadeo's face flashed in my mind and it took everything not to go running back to him. I already missed the bastard. He was a son of a bitch, but the way that he took care of me, his grumpy face, his smile, the way he protected me; it was hard to let those things go. With him, I felt as if someone finally wanted me for me. Trouble and all.

I was glad I'd ditched my phone because if I hadn't I would be calling him already and telling him to pick me up. Being on my own had always been my life, but now it felt emptier. Sadder. I never noticed how lonely I was until I met Amadeo.

"Bastard," I muttered. "He really messed me up."

My entire body ached. I just wanted Amadeo to pull me into his arms and tell me he loved me. And I would punch him in the chest for making me wait. But he'd kiss me again and I would give up because all I wanted was for Amadeo Bianchi to need me as much as I had started to need him.

BREAK ME DADDY

I tossed the wallet I had pickpocketed onto the dresser and walked away from the mirror so I wouldn't have to see myself crying again. What was the point of sobbing over it? It was over and done.

But even though I told myself that the hope kept coming back that any minute Amadeo would burst through the door and yell at me. Every sound of footsteps that crossed the window or hushed voices that passed in front of the door made me hold my breath.

I'm acting like I'm insane. Stop it!

I knocked my fist against my head and went to the bathroom to splash water on my face. The coolness did nothing when it came to thoughts of the man that I had been calling Daddy for months, but I was pretty sure nothing would help with that. Instead, I paced around until the clock showed it was time to get to the bus stop. I left the wallet in the room and pocketed the rest of the cash before I snatched up my bag and peeked out of the window.

There were cars parked, but barely anyone was out. A few prostitutes on the far corner, a couple of guys that were definitely selling drugs, but no Amadeo. No Angelo.

I winced when I thought about Angelo. *Amadeo might kill him.* That thought alone made me freeze in my tracks and keep staring out into the night.

Fuck. I had completely forgotten about Angelo. He'd been looking out for me since I arrived in Amadeo's life and now I was screwing him over. My stomach twisted and I laid a hand on it. *I should go back. I can't live knowing I'm the reason he'll get killed.*

But what if I was already too late? I could go back right now and it might be all for nothing. No, I couldn't turn back. Besides, no one could stop Amadeo from doing what he wanted to do. If he wanted to kill Angelo, he would. I just hoped he wouldn't. Angelo hadn't done anything wrong. Yeah, Amadeo was a hothead, but he wasn't that cruel, was he?

Probably.

I tugged my hoodie up over my head and inhaled a cloud of Amadeo's cologne. The scent wrapped around me like a hug and I ran my hand over the hoodie slowly imagining Amadeo's palm sliding down my chest as he whispered in my ear, threatening me. My body heated and I craved him before I shook my head and started walking.

I have to leave him in the past.

I slipped out of the door and looked around one more time before I kept moving. The faster I could reach the bus stop the better. There would be somewhere I could duck out of sight hopefully and wait until they started letting us board. Once I was on it I would feel a hell of a lot better.

My heart throbbed in my throat making it impossible to swallow. Every time I tried it felt like I was being strangled. My feet were ten pounds each and my head throbbed the more I walked away from Amadeo and everything that we had.

I walked on autopilot, my mind back on the house and the man that I was leaving behind. He would be hurt. I'd seen that look on his face once and I had never wanted to be the reason he made it again.

But he doesn't even know if he loves me. If I mean so much to him, then why can't he just fucking say that?

I needed actions more than anything, but I needed the words too. Three little words would have kept me by his side annoying and supporting him until he got sick of me and was ready to move on.

BREAK ME DADDY

But he couldn't do it and I couldn't wait around on someone who didn't have the balls to be real with me.

Lights flashed up ahead and I watched as a car drove past the bus stop. Right, that's where I was supposed to be going. I picked up the pace. I had to buy my ticket and then I could ride and go to sleep.

Tires screeched and I watched the car that had just passed the bus stop whip around and drive toward me. My body trembled as fear gripped my chest. I took a step back and the car kept coming.

It's not a coincidence. Shit. He found me.

I turned on my heels and ran. Every instinct screamed not to, but I wasn't going back. I couldn't. Turning down an alley I raced around a corner and waited, panting as I listened for footsteps. My body wouldn't stop trembling as I held my breath trying not to make a single sound.

Minutes ticked by, but I refused to move. Eventually, I blew out a breath and slowly looked around the corner. An empty alley greeted me and I sighed in relief. Maybe I was wrong. Maybe no one was after me and I was being paranoid.

I held onto my backpack a little tighter and carefully made my way back to the main street. No cars, no people, nothing. *I'm going insane.* I turned toward the bus stop and grunted as I smacked into something. I stepped back and looked up into a familiar face.

"Angelo? Shit," I cursed. "You can tell Amadeo to fuck off and leave me alone. I am *not* going back to his house."

The man tilted his head at me. "You're right, you're not."

My heart sped up all over again. "Is he making me go back to that room?" I asked as I took a step backward.

Angelo followed me. "Nah, he's not doing that either. In fact, he doesn't even know I'm here," he said, grinning before he pulled out a gun. The car that had raced toward me pulled up and he gestured to it. "Get in the car, Six."

I swallowed thickly. "What's going on?"

The man's smile fell away. "Get in the fucking car you brat or I'll shoot you right here and be done with it."

I stared at Angelo in shock. What had happened to the cool, collected, nice Angelo that I had gotten to know? The one that seemed like out of everyone Amadeo worked with was actually a good guy?

"Move!" he yelled.

I jumped and raced for the car. The gun Amadeo had given me was tucked into my backpack and wrapped in a sweater. I hadn't wanted to get my bag searched and end up in jail for having a gun that didn't belong to me. Now I wished I had kept it out at least until I reached the station.

Angelo slid into the car beside me and I was stuffed in the middle between him and another man I didn't recognize. I looked into the front seat and spotted one of Amadeo's guards, but the driver was a stranger too.

"Keep your mouth shut and your hands where I can see them," Angelo said as he held out a hand. "The backpack."

I handed it to him and he tossed it into the front telling the guy to check it. The man rifled through my stuff before he held up the gun. Angelo raised a brow at me.

"I knew you'd kept that damn thing," he laughed. "Too bad it's not going to do you any good now."

"What is this?" I snapped. "I don't understand why you're-"

Angelo's hand crashed into my cheek and my ear rang as my jaw burned. I grabbed hold of my face and groaned through the pain. *Don't fight back. Four against one is a death sentence.*

"I said keep your fucking mouth shut," Angelo threatened, pushing the gun against my thigh. "This drive will go a whole lot smoother if you do what you're told. You're used to being a trained whore. Go back to that."

My stomach squeezed and I counted slowly in my head. *Don't hit him. Don't hit him.* It felt impossible to control my temper when fear and humiliation rampaged through me equally. But I closed my eyes and stared straight ahead.

Amadeo's going to kill you and this time I'll happily watch.

Chapter Thirty

Amadeo

I threw the vase across the room and watched porcelain pieces rain down on my office floor. No one could find Six. How was that possible? A broke twenty-one-year-old with no car, no resources, and no one who lived nearby couldn't be far.

"Call Calix again," I growled as I gripped the edge of my desk.

"He's not with him," Gabriele said. "Trust me, I've asked him more than once. No one's stupid enough to try to lie to us. You know that?"

"Bring him here and I'll ask him my fucking self."

"Six isn't with Calix," Gabriele said as he looked over at Dario. "What have you found out through that thing?"

Dario scrolled through his tablet, his fingers a blur as he texted and navigated a map. We'd found his phone easily with the tracker, but Six was smart enough to ditch it. *I should have sewn a damn tracker under his skin. Fuck freedom.*

The thought of Six out there alone, roaming the world desperate and alone made my skin crawl. He had been safe with me, well taken care of. And above all else, I loved the hell out of that bratty, smart-mouthed pain in my ass. I thought giving him everything would be enough to keep him by my side.

But I was wrong.

"I'm going into the city's security cameras," Dario said. "When he left the house I was able to pick him up on several cameras, but then he disappears. I'm guessing that's because he went somewhere that's not heavily surveilled." He pushed his glasses up his nose and laid his tablet down before he began typing on his phone. "Wait, I might have something but I need to get into another system."

All of it was taking too damn long. I grabbed the heavy desk and growled as I flipped it over. My computer crashed, papers went flying, and my books toppled to the floor.

"Somebody better fucking find him before I start slicing off body parts!" I yelled. "Do *something*." I snatched my jacket and tugged it on. "I can't sit here waiting for you all to come up with something. I'm going to go get him."

"I'm going with you," Nic said snatching up his keys. "I'm not that good with technology anyway. We can look around the last area Dario was searching and see what we can find."

For once, my cousin wasn't laughing and joking. It was easy to see the other side of him, the scary beast that lived just underneath the surface but was constantly hidden by his joking nature. There was a reason I kept my family the closest to me. And now that we were all in one room desperately looking for Six, I knew that none of them could have betrayed me.

"Riccardo, you see what your people can tell you," I said.

"Already did," he grunted as he stood up and showed me his phone. "Some of our girls saw him on Cherry Boulevard a while ago. They said he was walking in the direction of the bus station and he was by himself. There's a motel in the area."

"Text me the address," I said as I nodded to him. "Get everyone's asses out on the streets and looking for him. There's some asshole trying to get to him and he decides to fucking leave."

"He wouldn't have left if you'd just manned up," Rayna snapped at me.

I glared at her. "What the fuck is that supposed to mean?"

"You know what it means. Everyone can see you care about him, but I bet you said something stupid. Or you yelled at him. Or you hurt his goddamn feelings and he left. Jesus, Ama. You've been a brick wall for so many years and I keep telling you that it's not protecting you the way you think it is. If you never see him again would it have been worth it to you whatever you fucking fought about?"

I crossed over to Rayna and grabbed her by her shirt. "You don't know-"

"I know everything," she spat. "I know *you* even though you don't think I do. You think none of us do and that's wrong. Yes, you run things but none of us has ever told you to take the burden of all of this on your shoulders alone." Her eyes watered. "You're so stupid, Ama. Either let people in or keep losing them."

"Come on," Nic whispered as he laid his hand on mine. "She's right and we have to go find your boyfriend."

Rayna stared up into my eyes her glare not wavering for even a minute. Her words stung a part of me that I had closed off a long time ago and I knew she was right. I had shut out the world so I could be above it and do all of the fucked up, dangerous, important things I had to do. But I had shut everyone else out and now? It was costing me the man I loved.

I released Rayna. "Keep doing what you can to find him," I said before I opened my mouth and closed it again.

She touched my hand. "I know, Ama. And it's okay, you don't have to say sorry to us. Ever. We get it," she said as she glanced around at the rest of my family. "Now, let's find Six. We all like him."

They nodded in unison and I realized it was true. All of them liked the man that I had dragged home and now called my own. He fit in with them. The memory of him laughing at the dinner table with my mother and Nonna made my heart squeeze painfully. He was perfect.

"Address, Riccardo."

"On it," he said as he went back to typing. "Sent.

"Come on, Nic."

My cousin filed in behind me and we climbed into his car. The entire house was chaos. Guards staked out around the property, people on the phone tracking down leads, cars coming and going as they searched the grounds just in case Six came back. No one was stupid enough to let him slip away if they found him.

"Keys."

Nic tossed them to me without complaint and I climbed behind the wheel of his Venom F5. I started it up and peeled out of the driveway before shooting down the road. Nic didn't complain as our speed climbed and climbed. Once I hit one-twenty, he didn't even protest. Instead, he pulled out his gun and started checking it over.

"Think he's still in Atlanta?" he asked.

"I don't know."

"We'll find him," he said with a nod before he slammed the clip back in and glanced over at me. "I found him the first time didn't I?"

Nodding, I switched lanes. Nic had been in the car on the ride back to Atlanta when he'd snagged Six for me the first time. I hadn't trusted him to get the job done safely at first, but I knew he was fast and he was like a dog with a trail if he had an objective. I gazed over at him and saw that serious expression that had taken over and intensified. He was focused on nothing but the mission.

We pulled up to the motel and I went right to the office. The man behind the counter glanced up at me and then back down at his phone.

"ID and it's sixty for the night."

"I'm looking for him," I said as I pulled out my phone and held it up. Six was my wallpaper, grinning at me after he'd just got through torturing me with more of his horrible food choices. "Was he here?"

The guy's eyes flickered up to me. "Can't give out that kind of information."

My hand shot out and I yanked the man forward by his shirt before I slammed him down on the counter. I pulled out my gun and shoved it against his temple before I released the safety and cocked it.

"Let's try this again. Was he here?"

"Y-yeah."

"Is he still here?"

The man shook his head. "I saw him leave a little while ago with a backpack on. He went that way," he said as he pointed down the street. "He had a different ID."

I released the man and nodded to Nic. "Find out if there's a security camera and get rid of it. And keep an eye on him." I looked down at the balding man who was now cowering away from me. "Room?"

"Five."

He handed me a key and I snatched it before I walked out of the office and down the row of rooms. *Please still be here. Come on, come back. I know you did. You had to.*

If he didn't I had no answers and I was back at square one. I let myself into the room and glanced around before I stepped in fully. The scent of stale smoke and dust clogged my nose, but I walked in further anyway and saw a wallet on the dresser.

I picked it up and flipped through it. There was a picture of a guy that obviously wasn't Six, but nothing else. He'd left nothing behind. I turned on my heels ready to walk out when I noticed it. On the floor, kicked underneath the table was the watch I'd given him with his initials engraved in it.

L.W

"Six," I muttered.

I squeezed the watch in my hand ignoring the jagged pricks of pain that stabbed at my palm. Had he taken it off? Or had it fallen out of his bag or pocket? Was he intent on throwing me away?

Shoving the watch into my pocket, I stilled myself for a moment and told myself to breathe. If I went wild right now, I wouldn't be using my head and I was going to need to if I wanted to find him.

I should have just said the fucking words. I'm so damn stupid. Don't let me lose the most important person in my life. I can't live without Six.

I gave the room one more look-through and determined there was nothing else left behind that was going to help me find Six. I wasn't sure if he had enough money for the bus stop, but hopefully, he would still be there if he'd actually gone. I stepped out of the room and my phone rang.

"Yeah?" I answered.

"Dario found something," Gabriele said. "We know where Six is. Or where he was."

Was? My stomach pitched and I grabbed onto the wall of the motel to steady myself.

"And where is that?"

"Angelo has him."

I frowned. "Angelo? He hasn't called me."

"And he won't be. He kidnapped Six, Ama. The video didn't have sound but he pulled a gun on him and Six looked scared."

I stared at the phone as it chimed and stared at the still image of the video that they had taken. Six's eyes were huge and he looked pale. I ran my finger over his face on the phone and suppressed the scream that tried to work its way up my throat.

I'd trusted Angelo. I had left him with Six many times thinking he was the only person I could put my faith in. He was my right hand, the person I trusted almost as much as my family.

"I'm going to rip his eyes out of his head with my bare hands," I snarled as any semblance of calm flew out the window. "Where is he?"

"We're trying to track the car he was in now, but it's going to take some time. There are more systems to hack into. I was about to leave, but Conor showed up and I told him what was going on. He wants to meet up with you and help."

"Fuck!" I screamed before I shoved the phone back against my ear. "Give him this address and then send me every scrap of information as Dario gets it. I mean it, everything. I don't care if it's right, wrong, or you're unsure. I want him found. Now!"

"I'm on it," Gabriele said. "Conor will be there shortly."

He hung up and I walked toward the office with renewed fire in every step. When I flung open the door, Nic trained his gun on me before he lowered it once more.

"We got anything?"

"No, but Kelley is coming."

"Shit," Nic cursed. "That Irish bastard is helping?" I nodded. "Should we leave?"

"Did you take care of the camera?" I asked.

"Done, no problem. And our friend here is going to be real quiet about this little encounter. Ain't that right, Roz?"

BREAK ME DADDY

The man nodded so hard I thought he'd give himself an aneurysm. Nic had clearly done a little threatening of his own. We left the motel office together and climbed into his car.

"We'll find him," Nic said, squeezing my shoulder. "You know that."

"I don't know what I'll do if he..."

"Don't even think like that," Nic growled. "We'll find him and he'll be fine. Six knows how to survive."

"Angelo has him."

Nic's eyes widened. "What the fuck?"

"Yeah. Text Dario and tell him to dig into Angelo. I know everyone was vetted, but things change. I want to know what he's been up to in the past few years."

"On it."

I watched as he took out his phone before I stared through the windshield out into the dark night. Angelo had always been loyal so why would he suddenly betray me?

The reason doesn't matter. What does is that I find him and make him pay very, very slowly. Hold on, Six. Daddy's coming.

Chapter Thirty-One

Six

A DULL ACHE WORKED ITS WAY UP MY SPINE. I BENT MY BACK away from the chair trying to relieve it, but that only made the ropes digging into my wrists hurt more. I tried to twist them to get the ropes to loosen up a little, but they weren't going anywhere. Finally, I stopped when my skin started to burn.

I looked around. *Where are we?* Angelo had made me put my head down after we drove for a few minutes and I had no clue where I was. The room I was in held nothing but the chair I was in and a boarded-up window.

How long have I been here?

Every second that ticked by felt like forever. I was tired of being tied down and it was harder and harder to convince myself to calm down. I wriggled around trying to push the cloth in my mouth against the duct tape, but I couldn't get it out of my mouth.

A frustrated sound crawled up my throat and vibrated against the gag. *Stupid. I am so fucking stupid.*

I never should have left Amadeo's side. He was the only person I'd met who made me feel completely safe and I had left him for what? Because he didn't say he loved me when I wanted him to? The realization hit me how incredibly stupid I was. Once again, I'd let my temper and short-sightedness get the better of me and I was paying for it.

My breathing picked up and my head spun as I tried to draw in a breath. The more I tried, the harder it was to breathe. As I rocked the chair trying to get myself free the door opened and Angelo walked through. He stopped and stared at me before he walked over and stood there, watching as he shoved his hands into his pockets.

"You're going to pass out if you keep that up."

No shit!

"Don't glare at me like that. This isn't personal, Six." He reached out and ripped off the tape making me yelp. "I need Amadeo here away from all the security and guns and support that he has."

I spat out the cloth that had been shoved into my mouth and glared up at him. "What the fuck? Did he do something to you?"

Angelo looked me up and down. "He did a hell of a lot to me. And then the first day you move in, he's smashing my goddamn hand. Bastard," he spat. "I'm going to make him hurt."

I stared at him. "So, what? You're going all super villain because Amadeo hurt your feelings or something? That's fucking dumb!"

The back of Angelo's hand connected to my face and I felt my lip split. Blood dripped from it and I licked the wound as I turned back to look at him.

"Amadeo's going to kill you when he sees that."

He laughed. "Amadeo isn't going to have the chance. I'm going to kill you in front of him the way he killed the man I loved right in front of me."

I blinked at him. "Amadeo wouldn't do that."

"He would," he snarled, his face right in mine as he spoke. "I watched him take that goddamn gun and put it right up to Matty's temple before he blew his fucking brains out. He didn't hesitate, wasn't even bothered by it. And Matty was here a hell of a lot longer than I was. Amadeo Bianchi doesn't give a damn about anyone or anything but himself and his money." He straightened up. "Until you came along. Finally, the man has a weakness that can be exploited. I would be a moron not to help take him down."

I shook my head. "Why did he kill him?"

Angelo sneered. "Are you listening, kid? The man is a grade-A fucking psychopath. Do you think he loves you? One day he's going to put a gun to *your* head and you won't see it coming."

No, I didn't believe that for a second. Maybe before I would have doubted Amadeo's sanity when it came to my life, but not after everything I'd seen him do for me. How soft he was when he was around me and even his family. Amadeo had a dark side, but he wasn't a monster and I knew he wouldn't kill me.

"He had to have a good reason," I said. "Amadeo wouldn't just go around killing people for fun. What did Matty do?"

Angelo's meaty fist collided with my face and the chair tipped back. I slammed into the floor and my head spun. The sound of Angelo's feet coming toward me sent a cold shiver down my spine, but I refused to show him that I was afraid.

Any minute Amadeo is going to come through that door and kick his ass.

I had faith in my Daddy. He wasn't the most sensitive man and he could be crazy, but deep down I knew that he loved me. I could feel it in the way he held me, the way he touched me, the way he fussed over me to make sure that I was okay. Amadeo felt more like home than anywhere I had ever been before.

Angelo righted the chair and leaned in close to my face. It took every ounce of restraint that I had not to spit in his face as I stared at him. Slowly, I twisted my wrist and I felt the rope give a little. I couldn't look back and try to see what had happened, but I had a little bit of slack.

I was going to kick his ass my damn self.

Amadeo had trusted him and asked him to look over me. I knew he never would have done that unless he trusted Angelo deeply. He'd betrayed my Daddy. Fire filled my chest and I thought of every horrible thing I could think of happening to Angelo. He deserved every horrid fantasy of his death and worse.

"Aww, what?" he asked, mocking me. "Are you mad? You should put away that temper of yours and realize you're about to die. Nothing's going to stop that," he said as he turned on his heels.

"Amadeo will," I said, my voice wavering as I clenched my fists behind my back. "He would never let anything happen to me."

"It's not like he has a choice, kid," he laughed as he walked through the door. "Go back to shutting the fuck up or I'll stuff that gag right back in your mouth."

I clamped my lips shut. If I was gagged again, I wouldn't be able to breathe. I had to do everything I could to make sure I could get out. Amadeo needed to be warned before he walked in and saw...

Closing my eyes, I sucked in a deep breath. I didn't want to think about Amadeo being hurt like that. Of course, I didn't want to die either, but I would be gone and he would be miserable for the rest of his life. Amadeo didn't deserve that.

I stared at the door until I was sure Angelo wasn't going to return. Twisting my wrists, I ignored the scraping, burning pain of the ropes biting into my flesh. *I'm getting back to Amadeo. Almost there. I'm not going to give up on us.*

The rope gave a little more and a little more. I stopped when footsteps passed by. A head poked into the room, one of the men I didn't know. He stared at me and I stared right back refusing to look as if he intimidated me. Really, I just didn't want him coming anywhere near me. I was so close to having my wrist free.

"Don't try to do anything stupid."

I shrugged. "I don't have to try."

His eyes darkened. "You're lucky Angelo said I can't stomp your ass before Amadeo gets here, but your time is coming," he said with a grin.

What the hell did I do to that guy? I was an asshole, but it's not like I'd ever even seen him. Apparently, he just wanted to hurt me. I shivered and he laughed as if it was the funniest thing he'd ever seen before he disappeared and slammed the door shut behind him.

"Asshole," I muttered.

I slipped my wrist free and stared at my red, raw skin. When I looked around, I knew I couldn't do anything yet. There was no way to hide and the windows looked like they were boarded up good. I would be heard if I tried to get out.

"One option left."

I shoved my wrist back into the rope and tightened it with my other hand as much as I could. For now, I had to wait and pray there would be some kind of distraction that would let me slip out. Escaping and running away was what I did best. And I was going to do it one more time to get back to Amadeo.

I STAYED awake by thinking about all the things I wanted to get back to. Amadeo, MMA, pizza, my friends, Ama's family, his bed. Even as my body started to get exhausted from sitting in one place and staring at nothing, I forced myself to stay awake. I had to be ready to move when the time came if I wanted to stay alive.

And if I wanted to save my Daddy too.

My eyes flew wide as I heard the sound of gunshots. There were only a few at first, but then they were coming nonstop. *Amadeo.* It had to be. I yanked my wrist free and tore at the ropes until both hands were out. I raced for the door and turned the knob, but it stayed in place.

"Fuck, shit, damn it," I muttered as I stared at the doorknob. There was nothing to pick, but something much better. A tiny hole.

I looked around frantically before I spotted a nail lying underneath the window that had been boarded up. I ran over and snatched it up before I jogged back and stuffed the nail into the lock. After poking and jiggling it a bit I felt it give and heard the distinct click of a lock disengaging.

I ripped the door open and stepped into the hallway just as a man ran into me. Pulling back my foot I didn't think, I just kicked. *Calix would be proud of me.* I followed up the kick with a right hook before I grappled the man to the ground. I kept him in a chokehold as he flailed and slapped at me before he slowed down and then stopped, passed out.

"Thought you were going to stomp me out, asshole?" I muttered as I stood up and stepped over him. "Guess not."

I moved down the hall toward the gunshots. When I looked around the corner my heart sped up so fast I thought I'd pass out.

Amadeo.

He stood in the middle of the room with his gun out and Conor beside him. A shot fired from Amadeo's gun and someone on the other end of the hall cried out before there was a heavy thud. He turned around and our eyes locked. I raced for him and Amadeo dragged me into his arms.

"Six," he said, his voice a sigh. "You're okay."

I nodded hard, my voice suddenly caught in my throat. "I'm okay now that you're here," I said, my voice cracking as I held onto him. "I want to go home."

"I know, baby." He pulled back and cradled my cheek. "We're leaving right now."

"No, you're not," Angelo's voice filled my ear and I felt the heat of the recently fired muzzle of his gun as it pressed against my back. I gritted my teeth even though it burned like hell. "Drop the gun, Amadeo."

I shook my head at Amadeo, but he crouched down and sat his gun on the floor. Conor did the same. I could still hear gunshots outside, but inside of what I could see was a little house, it was eerily quiet.

"Why, Angelo?" Amadeo asked. "We've had our issues, but why are you going this far?"

Angelo's hand wrapped around my upper arm and he shoved the gun into my spine harder. "Matty. You killed him for no goddamn reason."

Amadeo's face scrunched in thought. "Matty? What does he have to do with you?"

"He was my goddamn man," Angelo growled. "But you wouldn't know that because you're too goddamn self-absorbed to see anything that goes on around you if it has nothing to do with benefiting you. That's why it was so damn easy to stay close to you for two goddamn years while I plotted how I would destroy you."

"Over Matty?" Amadeo scoffed. "He was a goddamn traitor and a thief."

Angelo cocked the gun and pointed it at Amadeo. "You're a fucking liar!"

Amadeo stared at him. "When have I ever lied? I'm a lot of things, Angelo, but you know I don't lie. I never have and I never will. I don't have any reason to lie about the things I've done." He shook his head. "Matty was caught stealing more than once. I gave him one chance to make it right and he did it again before he started selling information to other organizations."

"You have no idea what you're talking about." Angelo's voice cracked as he cocked the gun.

"Matty had a serious drug problem. If you were with him then you know that, right? I reasoned with Matty way too many times before I had to put an end to him. It was him or everyone else who relies on me and there was no room to negotiate." His gaze flickered to me. "Give me Six and walk away, Angelo."

"No," he laughed, his voice sounding unhinged. "I'm going to put a bullet in his head while you watch."

Amadeo looked at me. "Did he do that?" he asked, running his finger over his cheek and lip. When I nodded, his head bobbed up and down and he looked at Angelo with a look I had only seen once in the warehouse. "You know I'm going to kill you, right? I don't care what you do to me, but him?" He shook his head. "Six is a different story."

I watched the darkness fill his eyes and I knew Amadeo was about to go off the deep end. That cool, collected calm that I admired was breaking. Because of me.

I'm not going to let Amadeo get hurt.

Angelo wasn't jabbing the gun into my back as much as he was before, too busy focusing on Amadeo to even think about me. I shifted back quickly and grabbed Angelo before I slammed him to the ground. I wrapped my hand around his wrist and slammed his hand on the floor.

"Let it go," I growled trying to dislodge the gun from his grasp. "Let it go!"

"You little bitch!"

His fist collided with my face, but I returned the favor. Blood slipped from his lip as he grunted and went after me again, but I wouldn't let him go. Angelo tried to lift his hand that held the gun as he shoved me away. I stumbled and heard the sound of the gun as it went off.

My ears rang and I wanted to cover them, but I jumped on him instead. Angelo had pissed me off past the point of no return.

"Move, Six."

I scrambled out of the way as Conor stepped on Angelo's wrist and twisted his foot. Angelo howled, dropped the gun, and I grabbed it before I moved back again. When I looked up my stomach dropped. Blood ran down Amadeo's arm as he walked toward Angelo.

"You're not smart enough to pull this off by yourself. Who's really running things?"

Angelo spat at him. "Fuck you."

"Look away, Six," Amadeo said as he raised his gun. "Cover your ears."

I didn't fight with him. Even though I knew he was doing what he had to do, I knew he was protecting me by telling me to look away. I covered my ears, closed my eyes, and waited, every muscle tensing in my body. A bang rang out and I shuddered. When I opened my eyes Angelo was staring at the ceiling, a bleeding hole in his head.

"Come on," Amadeo said softly. "Come here."

I jumped up and ran into his arms. He wrapped me up and held me close before I remembered the blood and shot back. When I moved his shirt, I saw the bullet hole in his arm.

"Fuck," I whispered.

"It's fine," he said softly. "I'm okay. Are you?"

"You're hurt," I snapped, suddenly angry at him. "Why are you worried about me when you're the one that was shot! I never should have jumped him. It's my fault. I should have-"

Amadeo captured my lips and kissed me long and hard. My eyelids fluttered closed and I leaned into him sinking even more deeply into his embrace. I didn't know it before, but a kiss from Amadeo was exactly what I needed right now.

"I love you, Six," Amadeo whispered against my lips. "Stay with me, forever."

I pulled back and stared up at him. "You mean it?" I asked, my voice barely audible over the ringing in my own ears. "Are you sure?"

Amadeo smiled. "Of course I'm sure, smart ass. You're mine," he said as he grabbed my chin and tilted my head up. "I love you."

"I love you too," I said as I held onto him. "I've loved you for a while."

"I know," he said as he stroked my swelling cheek. "Now, let's get the fuck out of this shit hole." He took my hand. "Nic?"

"Right here," he said as he charged into the room and grinned at me. "There he is! I was really hoping you weren't dead. That would have been a pain in the ass."

"Nic," Amadeo growled.

He threw up his hands. "Sorry, sorry. Well everyone out there is taken care of. There were ten of them from what I counted out there and five or more in here."

"All my men?" Ama asked.

Nic shook his head. "Nope. Some had ink I haven't seen before. I already sent pictures to Dario."

"Good. Call the doctor and have her meet us at the house. I'm losing blood and I'm pretty sure I'm going to pass out if I don't get this taken care of."

I bristled. "Why are you saying that so calmly? What the fuck is wrong with you!" I yanked off my shirt and tied it around his arm tightly to stop the blood flow. "You are the goddamn worst."

Amadeo chuckled. "Remind me to punish you later for showing your body off like this so freely." He gazed at Conor as we left the house. "I owe you."

Conor grinned. "Oh trust me, I know." He winked at me. "Good luck, Six. You're going to need it with him."

I watched as he strolled away, stepping over bodies like they were nothing. *Was this my life now?* I shook my head. Yep, and I wouldn't change it for the world.

I glanced around when we stepped outside and realized the house we were in was out in the middle of nowhere. Even if I had managed to escape, there was nothing but woods that probably went on for miles. If Amadeo hadn't come for me, I would have died.

"Thank you for coming for me," I said after Nic and I helped Amadeo into the backseat. I sat on the floor refusing to be away from him. "I knew you would."

Amadeo hummed softly. "It's not like I had a choice. What would I do without you?"

My heart raced and I rested my head on his shoulder. "You need me?"

"You have no idea how much I need you. Look at me, Six." When I lifted my head, he reached out and cradled my cheek. "You are the only person that has made me come alive since I was young."

My stupid eyes started watering and I couldn't figure out how to make my mouth work. Instead of trying to figure it out, I just kissed him. My mouth on his seemed to be enough as he relaxed and moaned against my lips.

I would show Amadeo that I belonged by his side. No matter what I had to do to keep that position.

"I love you," I whispered. "Now that I've finally said it I can't stop," I laughed.

"Don't," Amadeo growled. "Say it to me every day, every hour, every minute. I want to hear you say you love me until you're sick of saying it and then say it some more."

I smiled at him. "Yes, Daddy. I love you. I love you. I love you." I brushed my lips over his. "No matter how batshit crazy you are."

We both laughed and I held onto his hand as we flew through the city. I realized we were in the car I had come in and raised a brow.

"Why are we in here? Angelo took me in this one."

Nic groaned. "I left my baby back there so we could transport Amadeo." He rubbed his chest. "She's the only girl I care about and I had to abandon her. You better pay me a lot, Amadeo, and Six, you owe me whatever I want. Someone could steal her before I get back!"

Amadeo rolled his eyes. "Good to have you back, Nic. Now drive the fucking car and shut up."

As Nic grumbled I chuckled. "Hey, Daddy?"

"Yes?" he asked, his eyes looking like they wanted to close, but I knew I couldn't allow that.

"Was Matty really guilty of those things?"

Amadeo sighed. "Yes. I don't go around killing people for no reason, especially not the people who work for me. Hurt them so they learn? Yes. Kill them, no." He rubbed his temple. "Matty wouldn't leave the drugs alone and I couldn't have him destroying everything and making it crumble. I know it seems harsh, but the Bianchi's are part of the scheme of things in Atlanta. If we were to fall, more trouble would follow while someone tried to take our place. Keeping everything in balance is hard, but I want to do it just like my father and everyone before him."

I squeezed his hand. "I understand. I just wanted to know."

He nodded. "I wish Angelo would have been as accepting as you." I watched his face fill with emotions. "I didn't want to kill him."

"I know," I whispered, leaning my head against his arm as I held him tightly. "I know you didn't."

Amadeo leaned over and grunted before he pressed his lips to my ear. "I have never shown anyone this side of me. But I trust you, baby. Keep this side of me safe."

My heart squeezed and I felt the tears falling before I could stop them. I couldn't do anything but nod, but I did it almost feverishly.

I would protect Amadeo every single day of my life.

Chapter Thirty-Two

Six

Nic helped me get Amadeo inside. A tall, brown skinned woman with braids down her back stood beside the bed as she opened her bag and glanced inside.

"Looks like you're going to need to get that bullet out, Mr. Bianchi. And some stitches too." She looked at me. "Oh, you're new."

"Yeah, I'm Six."

"Vanessa." She smiled at me and I felt comforted by her presence. "Could you do me a favor? This will go a lot more smoothly if I have a second pair of hands."

My stomach clenched. "I don't know what I'm doing."

"I'll help you," she said as Amadeo grunted. "For now I just need you to follow directions, okay?"

I didn't argue. Whatever she needed help with, I would give it to her to make sure that Amadeo was okay. As she pulled out tools, she handed me a bottle of pills.

"Give him two of those."

"And get the whiskey," Amadeo said.

Vanessa shook her head. "No, you can't drink on those."

"Vanessa, you're a great doctor but if you don't let me have that drink I'm going to shoot you myself," Amadeo growled.

She rolled her eyes. "Cranky as always. Fine, get him the drink. All he's going to do is pass out sooner than later."

I moved off of the bed and into his study. My hands shook as I picked up the glass decanter and poured him a drink. Drops splattered onto the counter and I wiped them off quickly before I put the decanter to my lips and chugged a bit. I coughed hard and went back to the bedroom.

"You have some?" Amadeo asked.

I nodded. "I had to."

He chuckled. "It's okay, baby. Bring it here."

I pressed the glass to his lips and Amadeo chugged the whiskey like it was water while my chest was still burning. When I pulled it away, he gestured to bring it back and I gave him more. I shook out two of the pills and put them in his mouth before he washed them down with the drink.

"This is the only time I'm letting you do this," I told him. "You got shot for me and I feel bad about it so I'm letting you drink on the medicine but never again."

Amadeo blinked at me. "Are you telling me what to do?"

"Yes," I said sharply. "And you're going to listen to me too. I don't want you dying because you're mixing this shit."

The look of shock on his face melted into a soft expression. "Will it help you not worry?"

"Yeah," I nodded. "I don't want to have to worry more about you than I already do everyday."

Amadeo smiled. "Then I'll listen. Just this once."

"Thank you," I said as I kissed him. "Now, one more sip and then no more."

"Who's the Daddy here?" he mumbled.

"Right now? Me."

Amadeo glared at me and I grinned. I would happily pay for that later if he remembered it, but it would be worth it.

"Okay, this is going to hurt," Vanessa said as she nodded to me. "And I'm going to need you so wash your hands and I'll help you put these gloves on."

I nodded and ran to the bathroom. Getting Amadeo healthy was the first goal. Everything else could wait. By the time I came back out, he had a grumpy look on his face.

"Don't leave me alone that long again."

I smiled. "Yes, Daddy. Sorry."

Amadeo grunted and I saw the pain cross his face. After Vanessa helped me into the gloves, I touched his hand and gave it a squeeze.

"I'm right here," I said. "I won't leave your side. I promise."

"Thank you," Amadeo whispered before his eyes flickered up to Vanessa. "Let's do it."

"Keep him hydrated, fed, and give him those pain meds," Vanessa said, nodding to the bottle in my hand. "He'll be okay."

"Are you sure?" I asked as I stood at the front door, frowning. "What if-"

"No," she shook her head. "Don't start thinking about the worse case scenarios. Mr. Bianchi is looking good, he's stable, and he's awake and cranky. Trust me, those are good signs," she chuckled. "If either of you needs anything, call me." She nodded to me. "Keep massaging those wrists to get the circulation working."

"I will. Thank you."

Vanessa's smile widened. "You're very welcome. Goodnight."

I closed and locked the door behind her. Gabriele nodded at me from where he leaned on the wall and I returned the gesture. They had dismissed every guard until they could dig into their activities and backgrounds one by one. But Amadeo's family decided to all stay put in the house with us. I had to admit, I felt a hell of a lot better with them around.

"Six!"

"He's still awake?" Nic asked as he followed me up the stairs. "See if his cranky ass wants something to eat. We'll whip him up something."

"I'll ask, but I doubt it." I stopped and turned to Nic when I reached the landing. "Thanks for looking out for him tonight."

Nic waved a hand. "He's my cousin. I'd burn all of Atlanta down for him."

I smiled. "I like that. Night, Nic."

"Stay out of trouble," he said. "Don't forget to ask him about the food. We'll work on something just in case."

"I'll let him know."

I watched as he walked down the stairs and immediately slung his arm over Gabriele's shoulders. Gabriele shrugged, trying to dislodge him, but it was no use. I snickered as they argued and shook my head.

"Six!"

"I'm coming," I called as I walked down the hall and walked into the bedroom. "Why are you yelling? You're supposed to be resting."

"What took you so long?" He growled.

I rolled my eyes. "You're so dramatic. It was five minutes, tops. I let the doctor out and talked to Gabriele and Nic for two seconds. Oh, Nic wants to know if you're hungry," I said as I began massaging my sore wrists.

Amadeo reached out and dragged me to him. "What's wrong?"

"Nothing," I said, puzzled before I saw him staring at my hands. "Oh, my wrists are a little sore."

"Give it here," he said, his words slurring slightly as he took my hand into his rough but gentle fingers and rubbed my wrist. "Are you okay?"

I smiled at him. "I'm great," I said, my eyes watering as I glanced away and tried to choke down my emotions. "What the hell? You've turned me into a crybaby."

"No," he said as he shook his head, "you're just you. The only thing I've done is fall in love with you."

Amadeo said it so matter of factly that all I could do was stare at him. Hearing him say it was still unbelievable like I was locked in a dream. Amadeo Bianchi loved me? I couldn't process it, but at the same time I felt warm hearing those words and I knew I loved him too.

"Other wrist."

"You're slurring," I said as I stared at him. "You should be asleep."

"Other wrist, boy."

Shaking my head, I gave it to him and let him rub that one too. "You're so bossy. Have you ever thought about being a little nicer?"

Amadeo glanced up at me. "Is that what you want? For me to be nicer?"

I thought about it. "I want you to be yourself around me, that's all. I like every side that I've seen of you, even the ones that unnerve me."

"Promise?" he asked. "You won't go running for the hills one day?"

"No way in hell," I said as I leaned down and kissed him. "Besides, it's not like you would let me get far."

Amadeo grinned. "At least you understand that." He held my hand. "I'll never let you go, Six. Ever. Now, get in the bed and go to sleep with me."

"Yes, Daddy."

I stripped out of my clothes down to my boxers and climbed in next to him. A shower would have to wait until tomorrow because

I wasn't going to leave my Daddy alone for even a minute. He needed me beside him the way that I needed to be close to him right now.

"You never answered me about food," I said suddenly as I sat up.

"Not hungry," he muttered, yawning long and hard before he sighed. "In the morning. You can bring me one of those disgusting things you call meals."

I chuckled and nuzzled against his side. "I love you."

"I love you too."

The sound of his breathing evened out and I knew he'd fallen asleep. I snuggled up to him more closely and buried my face against his warm skin. Tomorrow I could yell at him about taking his antibiotics, eating, and hydrating. But for tonight I only wanted to hold the man I loved.

Epilogue

Amadeo

Three Months Later

I leaned against the table in the dining room. My brothers, cousin, and I had commandeered it. Rayna sat in the corner, listening in as well as she typed away on her phone. As usual, I had no idea what she was up to but she looked up and grinned at me, making me shake my head.

You have a lot of secrets.

One day, I would ask her about them, but I doubted Rayna would ever tell me anything. She was a Bianchi after all. We were good at keeping our mouths shut.

I rubbed the soreness away in my upper arm. Later, I would need a bath and some pain meds, but Six would help me with both and yell at me if I tried to do anything on my own. The smile that crept across my face was quickly hidden. I liked when Six went all soft and took care of me.

"So you think this was bigger than Angelo?" Gabriele asked.

I shook myself back to reality and stopped thinking of Six. He was hanging out with my mother and Nonna in the kitchen where they had dragged him off to show him another old family recipe that they insisted would be easy to make. He'd mouthed *help* but I let them drag him off while he glared daggers at me.

He'll be a major brat about that later.

"Ama, pay attention," Gabriele groaned. "I'm trying to get caught up here and you're daydreaming about your boyfriend."

I cleared my throat. "Right, yes I think this was bigger than Angelo. Conor was able to do a little digging and it seems like the same people were tampering with our warehouses. The men at the house and one he captured a few days ago all had these tattoos."

I showed them the paper I'd had printed out that bore a skull and crossbones. A snake broke through the top of the skull's head, its mouth open and tongue out as if it was hissing.

"That looks familiar," Dario frowned. "But I can't place it. Let me see if I can find something online."

His fingers flew over the screen and I nodded. If anyone could dig something up, it was him. Just like Dario, I felt as if I had seen that tattoo before, but I kept drawing a blank whenever I tried to place it. But I trusted Dario to do what he could to find out who we were dealing with.

"Business as usual besides checking this out," I said as I laid the photo down. "Riccardo make sure our sex trade is locked down tight and every worker is safe. We get a percentage because we protect them. If we can't do that we lose them."

He nodded. "On it."

"Rayna, what are you going to be doing?"

She grinned. "Causing havoc, looking for opportunities. You know, what I always do, big brother." She stood up and winked at me. "I'll let you know if I find anything for you."

"Stay out of trouble."

"No," she called as she walked out the door.

I shook my head as my brothers chuckled. Rayna was always going to be Rayna. Wild and free. She did come up with interesting information though and new streams of income so I let her go as crazy as she wanted to.

"Aren't you going to go and save your boyfriend?" Nic asked with a grin. "I can hear Nonna bossing him around from here."

I shook my head. "No way in hell. I'll get dragged into wedding talks and someone will bring up grandkids. I thought when I came home with a boyfriend instead of a girlfriend I would be spared from those chats."

"Good luck," Dario chuckled. "I'm forty-two and Nonna still asks when I'm having kids. The answer is never, but she's persistent." He put his tablet away. "Are we eating or what?"

"You go in there and ask," Gabriele told him. "Because I'm not doing it."

"You're all a bunch of babies. Six!" I called. "Come here."

Nic snickered. "You didn't go in there either."

"Shut up."

Six walked in and glared at me. "What?"

I raised a brow. "Try again," I growled.

He batted his eyes. "Yes, Daddy?"

The collective snickers of my family made me narrow my eyes at my boy. He grinned at me, not even a hint of fear on his face. I grabbed his arm.

"Excuse us."

"Where are we going?" Six laughed as I tugged him along.

"You'll see."

"Home? Not before dinner though, right? Because your Nonna makes a mean meal and I've been craving it all week. And if we leave now she's going to be super pissed off and I will fully support her kicking your ass."

"Stop talking."

Six laughed louder. "We both know that's not going to happen."

Not yet, but I had ways of making Six be quiet. I took him up the stairs to a room down at the end of the hall. Once I stepped inside, I threw the lock and shoved Six up against it. He grunted and opened his mouth to speak before I crashed my lips against his, my tongue exploring his mouth as he held onto me.

My fingers ran over his body as I tugged at his clothes desperately. Six had been teasing me all day and I needed my boy wrapped around my cock and moaning my name. He'd been taking care of me the past few months and while I loved him riding me, sucking my cock, and stroking me as he laid on my chest at night, I was ready to be back on top.

"Daddy," he moaned when I came up for air, his eyes already half-closed. "What are you doing?"

"You know what I'm doing," I answered as I unbuttoned my shirt and turned toward the bed. "Get in."

"Whose room are we in?" Six asked as he did as he was told and climbed up onto the bed.

"This is my old room."

Six's eyes widened as he looked around. "From when you were a kid?"

I nodded as I kicked off my shoes and tugged my slacks down. "Yes. I stayed here for a long time before I finally moved and got my own place. But I don't want to talk about that right now," I said as I crossed over to him and brushed my lips against his. "Maybe later I'll show you my old high school photos."

His eyes lit up. "Fuck, that's almost good enough to say let's skip the sex and do that instead." Six reached out and stroked his hand along my cock. "Almost."

I laughed as I kissed him. When I pushed him onto his back, he went down with no resistance but shoved his arms between his thighs and pressed them together.

"What are you doing?" I asked.

"No, Daddy," he whispered. "You can't make me."

A growl echoed from my throat. "Baby, you are barking up the wrong tree."

He grinned. "Am I? You're not all that scary anymore you know."

My boy was really trying me. It was to be expected after weeks of softness and sweet behavior. He was itching to get in trouble and I was as bad as he was. I grabbed his arm and shoved him over onto his stomach. My hand came down on his firm ass, my palm growing hot as Six moaned. He shoved his ass up in the air and I smacked it again.

"You missed Daddy spanking you that badly, baby?" I ran my hand over his warm skin and struck him again. "Don't worry. I'll make up for every missed opportunity."

Six glanced over his shoulder, his eyes glazed. "Yes, Daddy."

He took his spanking happily, his moans only muffled by the bed as he buried his face to keep himself quiet. But I didn't care who heard him. Six was mine and I would let the entire world know that he belonged to me.

I pushed Six onto his back and he watched as I dug out a tube of lube from the pocket of my pants. Because of him, I had to keep them stashed everywhere these days. There was never any warning before he'd jump me or vice versa. I lubed up and shoved his legs open before I laid between them.

"Don't tell Daddy no," I whispered against his ear. "Or I'll have to keep punishing you."

Six groaned. "What if I still say no?"

I bit his neck and he shivered under me. His legs fell apart and I pushed my cock inside of him letting out a groan at how tightly his hole squeezed my length. One roll of my hips and Six dug his nails into my back and gasped.

"I thought you were going to say no," I teased as I sat up and gazed down at him. "Where's your fight?"

He groaned. "Please, just fuck me. Please, Daddy."

I grinned. "Such a well-behaved boy," I said as I slammed into him and his head fell back. "Daddy's going to give you every bit of attention you need, baby. Hold on tight."

Six did just that. His long legs wrapped around my waist and I buried my face into the crook of his neck to inhale his scent. I gazed at his face to take in how amazing he looked; I licked and nipped every inch of him that I could reach. Six was perfect in every way and I couldn't get enough of him.

His soft moans set my body aflame, but they weren't enough. I picked up speed, lifting his legs up and pushing them back so he was completely opened up to me.

"Daddy," he hissed. "What the fuck?"

I chuckled. "You were too quiet for me. Let's see how you do in this position."

"We both know I- Fuck! Oh, God fuck!"

"That's more like it, baby," I moaned as I rocked into him roughly. "Stroke your cock for me. I can't wait to taste you."

"Shit, you don't have to say it like that," he groaned as his legs trembled.

"We both know I do."

Our bodies moved together as Six stroked his cock. The quiet moans turned into loud ones and I grinned. *That's much better.*

"Cum for me, baby," I told him. "Cum for Daddy."

Six didn't need anymore encouragement. He cried out as cum shot from his cock and painted his belly. I let his legs down and thrust into him as I slid a finger through his seed and lapped at it hungrily. Six moaned, the look on his face desperate and needy.

"I love you, Amadeo," he whispered. "Fuck I love you so much."

My heart sped up and I crashed my lips against his. "I love you too," I whispered when I pulled back a bit. "You will always be mine."

Six's arms wrapped around my neck. "Yeah, I know. Yours," he smiled. "Always yours."

I came so hard I saw stars. Someone had fallen in love with me for who I was and he didn't try to change me? That was some kind of magic I was sure I would never experience and here Six was giving me everything I could ever need.

There was no one on Earth like him.

"Um do we have to go back downstairs?" Six asked, his face turning red. "I-I don't think I can look anyone in the face."

I laughed. "I'll be right there with you."

"No," he groaned. "Let's sneak out the back and go home. Please," he stressed.

"We'll miss the orecchiette," I pointed out.

Six's mouth dropped open. "Nope, I can suffer through the shame for a while for that."

"There's my boy," I said, leaning down and taking his lips in a long, slow kiss. "Let's go eat, baby."

Six gazed up at me and I could see the love in his eyes. "Yes, Daddy."

Thank you for reading Break me Daddy. Amadeo and Six are a match made in hell. I had so much fun digging into my darker side with this story. Amadeo is a daddy that I've been wanting to write for a long time and Six is his perfect match. I do hope you enjoyed their story as much as I loved writing it.

I hope you're looking forward to Fight me Daddy, Gabriel and Calix's story. It's going to be rough, wild, and so much fun.

If you wouldn't mind leaving a review informing other readers your thoughts on Break me Daddy, it would be greatly appreciated.

Skyler Snow

MAFIA DADDIES SERIES
(Contemporary Daddy Romance)
Break me Daddy
Fight me Daddy

About the Author

Skyler Snow is the author of kinky, steamy MM books. Whether contemporary or paranormal you'll always find angst, kink and a love that conquers all.

Skyler started off writing from a young age. When faced with the choice chef or author, author won hands down. They're big into musicals, true crime shows, reality TV madness and good books whether light and fluffy or dark and twisted. When they're not writing you can find them playing roleplaying games and hanging out with their kids.

— Skyler Snow

Printed in Great Britain
by Amazon